# Paradise Lost and Found

By

K. Aten

FLASHPOINT
PUBLICATIONS

Paperback ISBN: 978-1-61929-550-6

Hardback ISBN: 978-1-61929-549-0

Flashpoint Publications First Edition: July 2024
Printed in the United States of America.

Cover design by Kelly Aten-Keilen

www.flashpointpublications.com

## Dedication


For Lyss.


Your friendship, support, and insight
are worth the world but all I've got are words.

# Chapter One

"Lyss, vanilla frappe, two shots!"

Jess started upon hearing the similar name, but it wasn't hers or her order so she settled back at her table against the wall in the Bean Bag. She'd had no choice but to stop on the way to work after her coffee machine had gasped its last breath just that morning. Jess glanced at her watch and sighed. She had fifteen minutes to make a ten-minute drive and the baristas were taking their sweet time.

"Jaye, Chai Tea Latte with whip," called out a tall man who was sporting a beard and a ponytail.

Jess drummed her fingers on the table as she waited. A young woman with a backpack approached and Jess reluctantly met her gaze. "Can I help you?"

"Uh, yeah. The B-Bag is pretty busy today and you look like you're just waiting. Can I have this table?"

"If you're so hot for the table, you should have gotten here earlier. I'll leave when I get my drink." Jess was tired, her knees ached, and she didn't feel like standing to wait for what was, apparently, going to be an eternity, in the coffee shop.

"Dude, you don't have to be such a bitch. And you wouldn't be in such a hurry either if *you* had gotten here earlier. Jesus." The woman moved over to lean against a wall before Jess could respond.

"Anne, plain black coffee."

Jess raised her hands like she was praying to a higher power. "Oh, my freaking God, are you kidding me?"

A female barista behind the counter nearest to Jess gave her a strained smile. "Sorry, ma'am. We're short-staffed today and the drive-through orders are increasing wait times. Thank you for your patience."

Drive through. She should have just done that because, clearly, they were given priority over the walk-ins.

"Coffee black, skim, two sugars—" Jess leaned forward to stand until the barista added, "Luce." She collapsed back into her seat.

She saw a tall, broad-shouldered woman striding away. "Fuck's sake," she muttered beneath her breath, then glowered toward the counter.

"Peggy, caramel mocha latte."

Jess glanced down at her watch again. It was seven fifty. She was about to walk out without her precious bean juice when the hipster dude called her order.

"Jess, coffee black, skim, two sugars."

"Ugh, it's about damned time." She grabbed her paper cup and strode out of the busy coffee shop. It would take a miracle or a lead foot for Jess to arrive at work on time but, come hell or high water, she'd do her best to make it.

****

Jess didn't make it and her day hadn't gotten any better by nine. A traffic backup meant that she was five minutes late and she got a stern word from her senior manager about setting a good example. It wasn't her fault. No amount of running yellow lights could compensate for idiot drivers.

Now she had to deal with this. Jess sighed and addressed the thirty-something man in front of her. "Listen, this isn't rocket science. You're not on the vacation calendar and I need you here. If you don't come in to work, you'll be disciplined and most likely fired as a no-show." The firing part was a bluff but he didn't need to know that.

The man shifted nervously with his hands clenched into fists. "But you told me a few months ago I'd probably be fine to take these two weeks off so Sue and I could bond before the baby comes in September."

"I also told you to fill out a formal request a month in advance, exactly as policy states. And while two months ago may have looked good at the time, things change. New contracts come in every week. You're behind on your project and I need that finished by the deadline. A fact you've already been warned about twice."

"Jess, I've worked for this company six years and that's totally unfair. I don't ask for much here. I just wanted this one thing before life gets crazy. I'm sorry I forgot to fill out the form—"

"There's a saying around here, Jon. Your lack of planning is not my emergency. We have rules for a reason. The calendar has already been filled for those two weeks so your request is denied. Check the schedule for June or July vacation availability. You'll still have plenty of time to bond or whatever then."

Jon threw his hands in the air. "I can't believe you. It would serve you right if I walked out and never came back!"

She smirked at him. "With a baby on the way? You may lack good planning skills, but you're not stupid. My decision is final, and I'd like to remind you, yet again, about the project you're behind on."

Rather than answer, he spun on his heel and stalked out of her office. Lucky for her, the door featured a soft-close device and couldn't be slammed if you tried. And he tried. When she was sure Jon was gone, she retrieved a bottle of ibuprofen from her desk drawer, washing three down with the sad remains of her cold coffee. Then she tossed the cup in the trash can.

A quick wiggle of her mouse brought the computer out of hibernation. She stared at the company's vacation calendar on the screen. The two weeks he wanted were already blocked off—by her. The two weeks immediately after were open but Jon already said his wife couldn't take those dates off. Company policy said none of the engineers could be off at the same time as their manager in order to guarantee there was always a contact available for the client. They weren't Jess's rules, but it was her job to enforce them. It wasn't her fault that he never submitted the forms and she forgot about the throwaway request from months before. "You snooze, you lose, Jonny-boy."

A knock rattled the door and a five-foot, curvy, redhead pushed inside before she could close out the vacation calendar. Jess looked up to see Fabrimation's HR manager, who also happened to be her best friend. Shell was frowning and Jess rolled her eyes. "Miss Stevens...of course you'd show up. I suppose you were his next stop?"

"You're not making many friends today."

Jess leaned back in her chair. "My job here isn't to make friends. It's to manage a bunch of millennials and gen z's—whoever came up with those stupid fu—" A raised eyebrow made Jess amend her words. "Flipping names anyway? My point is, they all want exceptions made because everyone is so special."

"That's a little harsh, don't you think?"

"We-have-rules-for-a-reason." Jess emphasized each word with a knock on her desk.

Shell sighed and turned to make sure the door was shut tight, something that Jess dreaded because it usually meant her friend was going to get serious and personal. She took a seat across from Jess's desk. "I've gotten a handful of official complaints for your attitude during the past few years."

"And? I make sure the job is done and my team runs on time. My department has one of the best records in the company for quality and job closure."

"As much as I don't want to be the one to tell you this, frankly hon, you've turned into a..."

Shell trailed off and Jess laughed bitterly. "A bitch? It's not the first time I've heard it today and it probably won't be the last."

"That's your word, not mine. I was going to say grump. Have you considered taking some time away?"

Her suggestion put a ball of fear in the pit of Jess's stomach. Jess needed this job. She was good at it but more importantly, she had a significant retirement setback thanks to bad trust choices and worse people. "Like a leave of absence? Are you reprimanding me for something?"

Shell held up her hands. "God no! But I looked before coming in here and you haven't taken a real vacation in more than five years. You're just nickel and diming it to give yourself long weekends and you're not using your days fast enough. They'll only carry over so long before you lose them."

The memory of her previous vacation made Jess suck in a pained breath. She'd become adept at tucking feelings into little boxes and making herself forget about the before times. "I'm pretty sure you're talking about my last trip with Beth, before she left me for her university professor and took my savings and house in the divorce." Jess laughed bitterly. "I'm glad she went back to school those last few years so that I could pay for her education and get screwed when she proved to have no income."

"She was a witch, plain and simple. Tam and I never liked her."

"Yeah, well, I sure don't like her anymore either. I've only just got my checking and savings built back up by living frugally and saving as much as possible."

"I'll admit, I didn't see that drama with her coming. You both seemed to fit, you know?"

Jess shrugged. "You're kinda right, I guess. I suppose there were little signs that we'd just...grown apart. You remember that was about the time I started menopause."

Shell shook her head. "You were so early."

"Eh, my mom hit menopause when she was thirty-eight. Unfortunately for me, my libido dropped and I'm sure that played a part in our decline."

"Jess—"

"True or not, it's a thought I've lived with for years. It doesn't matter now. In the end I learned that puzzle pieces may look like they fit, but really don't. And both will be damaged if you try to force them. You want to know the last time I remember having fun as a couple?"

"When?"

She thought back nearly five years. "It was that surprise birthday party that Brandi threw for Sal. You remember?"

Shell gave an undignified snort. "That party, ugh! You two may have had fun but we were dealing with drama."

"Say what?"

"That was right around the time Kelsey and Jamie got together. A misunderstanding occurred in the kitchen that had them both leaving upset. I'm glad they figured their shit out quick. Seriously, those two weirdos are perfect for each other."

Jess shook her head. "I can't even argue with you there. I'd heard the stories about Jamie, just like everyone else. But even I've gotta admit they make an adorable couple."

The room got quiet as both women remembered a calmer time. Shell without a two-year-old, and Jess mostly happy in what she thought would be her first and only marriage. Shell reached across her desk and gave Jess's hand a squeeze. "Hon, I know you got the crap end of the stick. Beth took you for a ride and karma will come around for her eventually. But until then you've got to start living again. What's the point of making all the money back if you've lost your joy?"

There was no way she'd tell Shell that karma had already struck her ex-wife. Feeling petty and vengeful after the divorce, Jess sent an anonymous tip to the university about the affair. They investigated and discovered past evidence that the professor had been sleeping with their students. Jess's college buddy taught at the same school and spilled the tea that there was a disciplinary hearing and the professor was fired. From what Rob said, Beth also failed the class and the professor eventually landed a job teaching adult education—somewhere.

Jess slumped back in her chair. "I don't know. But I grew up poor with a lot of trust issues. Beth's actions took me back to a very dark place and I've just been kind of wallowing. Building up my savings to feel secure again is all I've been focused on." She considered her actions over the previous few years. "I'll admit that I've been a little more walled off than I used to be—"

Shell snorted. "Walled off? Jess, you've been frickin Fort Knox. You make ice queens seem cuddly. What you need is a getaway, or a retreat. Someplace where you can leave behind all the stress of job and a bad romance and just get in touch with yourself again."

Jess laughed. "Oh, trust me, after years of bachelordom, I've gotten very in touch with myself. It helps me get to sleep at night, not that I stay that way. Menopause sucks."

"Why do I put up with you again?"

"Because you and Tam love my rainbow Jell-O shots at your barbecues?"

"I mean, that's true but I'm being serious."

She glanced at the vacation calendar displayed on the computer screen facing away from Shell. "I know you are and, on that note, I do have a vacation coming up. It's actually the two weeks that Jon was clamoring for. I got permission to take all four from the VP himself if I wanted. Apparently, they're aware I never take time off and cleared another manager to take over my duties while I'm out."

Shell narrowed her eyes. "Did you bump him for yourself?"

Jess sat forward abruptly. "I would never! You remember the drag queen bingo event we went to a little over a month ago for Kelsey's birthday?"

"Yes. Jamie was supposed to be the DD but they all ended up piled into an Uber because the queens kept buying her shots."

"Yeah, well I bought ten tickets for the raffle that night. They called me two days later and told me I'd won an all-inclusive two-week tropical vacation at some queer resort. I only had to pay for travel. I looked up the place and it had great reviews. I submitted my vacation request right away. Samson told me he was considering me out for the entire month and I'm waffling about whether I should return to work, or just putter around at home for a few weeks once I'm back."

"Wow, that's awesome! And you should definitely take the entire four weeks if you're approved. It's rare for them to do that, but you've been here for twenty freaking years so that tracks."

"I started just out of college with a shiny bachelor's in design engineering. I never dreamed I'd stay at the same company this long."

"Lifer." Shell laughed as if she hadn't done the same thing with a slightly different degree. "But let's talk about the trip though. You sure it's legit? Sounds like a scam, even with paying for your own flight down. What's the catch?"

Jess told her what the person on the phone said. "There's a theme to the resort, like making yourself a better person. It's still a vacation with arts, activities, and excursions. But it's also a self-improvement retreat with classes, meditation, and exercises. Whatever it is, it'll be warm, sunny, and filled with tropical flavor. I was told on the phone that I could extend my stay for a reasonable extra cost if I wanted. Who knows, maybe I will."

"Honestly? That sounds like a dream. What's the place called? If you end up liking it, maybe I can talk Tam into going for my fortieth next year. I bet my mom would love to spoil Rory for a few weeks."

"It's—" Jess rubbed her lower lip in an attempt to jog her memory. "I think, uh, Paradise something."

Shell snickered. "That's a little cliché."

"Right? I'd have to check my email to confirm the name for you. All I know for sure is that two weeks from now, I'll be lounging by a pool with a drink in hand, not thinking about exes, St. Seren, Michigan, this job, or money."

Shell stood. "I think it will be great for you and I look forward to all the stories after your trip. Who knows, maybe you'll meet a sexy lady for a little vacation boom-boom."

Jess laughed at her phrasing. "What decade are you even from?"

She sniffed. "I'm at work and the head of HR. I have standards you know."

"Uh huh, I've seen your standards showing often enough on a Saturday night at Culture. You're a pool bully, and you don't like to wear a lot of clothes on the dance floor."

"And that's why I like to keep my personal and professional life separate, thank you very much."

Jess grabbed the belly fat she'd become hyper-fixated on the past few years. "Anyway, I'm unlikely to get any vacation boom-boom, as you put it, with this body. I know I should exercise more, I just…" She sighed.

"Do you still have your bike? I remember you riding it to work all the time."

"I do. It's just that some days I feel like I'm barely getting through the day. You know? Frankly, this menopause shit has hit me like a ton of bricks. I'm old now and pretty sure my libido is well and truly dead."

"Oh, come on, you're not that big or that old. Seriously, you've got to work on your self-esteem. You're one of those people who is stupidly cute, despite the age or weight you're so concerned with."

Jess looked back at Shell with wide eyes. "What?"

Shell ran a hand down her face, a familiar motion of frustration. "Do you ever look in a mirror?"

That prompted a scowl. "Unfortunately. And I see the same person as always. The same woman that couldn't keep her wife from cheating. Clearly, I wasn't any kind of attractive."

Hands went up as Shell must have sensed she was treading dangerous waters. "Babe, without getting into all that, I can attest that your sense of self is warped by your shitty divorce. The only reason you don't have ladies knocking down your door is…well, frankly, your attitude. Are you a little heavier than five years ago? Sure. We all are. But you've got the thickest eyelashes I've ever seen and fab hair that's shiny in a way I couldn't even achieve while pregnant. Tam says you have perfect lips, and you've never lost that bangin' ass. Honestly, my favorite part about you though is your smile. Which you seem to have misplaced."

Jess was nonplussed. "Tam said that about my ass?"

"Uh, no. The ass is my observation. Face it, you're adorable and I think you could find someone great with a little attitude adjustment. Try to be more open and interested."

She frowned. "Maybe I don't want to be open or interested. Have you considered that?"

Shell shook her head. "I think you do, but only you are able to make that realization so I'm going to stop trying." Jess opened her mouth to respond and Shell held up a hand. "I'll leave it alone. But I'm going to reiterate that you're not that old. You've only got five years on me and I've had a kid. I'm still trying to lose that baby weight."

"Five and a *half* years." Jess persisted with her usual complaint, happy to leave the rest of the conversation dead in the water.

Shell rolled her eyes. "What I'm saying is that I know it's rough right now, Tiger. Just take things one step at a time. I think getting away will do some good."

"Yeah, yeah." Jess waved her hand to shoo Shell out. "Now if you don't mind, I've got some projects of my own to wrap up before I can go anywhere fun."

Shell started for the door but paused with her hand on the knob. "Speaking of fun, Tam and I are having a yard party this weekend. You in?"

Jess burst out laughing at such a ridiculous idea. "It's April for fuck's sake, and the snow only just melted off last week!"

"True, but it's still gone and it's near the end of April. Besides, it's supposed to be eighty-two degrees Saturday."

Michigan was stupid in the springtime. "It was a high of thirty-six yesterday, and it's going to be forty today."

"You can't argue with what is, only plan for what will be. Saturday will be clear, sunny, and in the eighties. We'll grill brats, chicken, and something weird for Jenn. And don't wander in all gay-late because Tam already pulled out the grilling tools and left them on the counter in the kitchen. There is no way I'm keeping her from firing up that grill as early as possible Saturday."

"No Rory this weekend?"

Shell grinned. "Nope. He's going to grandma's house until Sunday. Let me tell you, when they say terrible twos, they aren't kidding."

Jess nodded but as a childless only child, she didn't have a clue about babies or two-year-olds. "Who else will be there?"

"Just the usual crew. Me and Tam, you, Jamie and Kelsey, Caleb and Richard, and Jenn. BYOB and your cornhole boards.

"What happened to Tam's Lions boards?"

Shell's eyes darted away. "Apparently, mice chewed into all the beanbags."

"You can order more."

"Erm and chewed the edges of the boards."

Jess laughed. "I smell a rat, and not the kind that chews cornhole bags. You probably did it yourself. Everyone knows how much you love the Packers and hate the Lions."

"Do you honestly think I would purposely sneak around the garage and hack away at Tam's precious game? She'd kill me."

When she put it like that... "I mean, I guess not."

"Exactly! However, if I accidentally spilled something tasty on the bags and boards after we put them in the shed last fall…and the rodents just happen to investigate, that's no fault of mine, right?"

"Jesus, you're as vindictive as Kelsey."

"Saturday at two and don't be late!"

"Yes, ma'am." Shell was out the door before Jess finished speaking.

On a whim, Jess opened her vacation form and extended her time off by two weeks. She'd already been given permission and more time away from the office certainly wouldn't hurt. Especially if it was paid. And if what Shell said was true, nobody at work would miss her.

****

Jess parked on the street near Tam and Shell's house a little after three. She was late but it wasn't a big deal. People were always late to parties. Jess had a cooler containing her Jell-O shots and drinks in one hand and her camp chair in the other. She left the cornhole boards in her Subaru knowing someone would help unload them later.

The wind whipped her long, honey-blonde hair into her eyes. "Damn it!" Jess looked at her wrist and realized she'd left her hair tie at home in her rush to get out the door. Grumbling, she picked up the cooler and camp chair and started across the street.

Her lateness became a bigger deal when she pushed through the gate into the backyard to see everyone nearly finished with their meals. "What the hell? You couldn't have waited until I got here?"

Shell was seated in a camp chair nearby with a paper plate balanced on her lap. "I told you two o'clock for a reason and texted you forty minutes ago."

Jess set the cooler on the ground near the group. "Whatever, you suck."

Tam laughed. "We love you too, J. Now have a seat and shove a wiener in your mouth."

Jess flipped her off then pulled her chair from the bag.

"I was late because I was nearly out of gelatin so the layers took longer to set." She scowled. "You're welcome."

Richard gave her a fake bow from his chair. "Thank you, Jess. I appreciate your sacrifice and hard work."

The wind blew Jess's hair into her face again and she gathered it all back, holding it behind her with one hand. "Do any of you have a hair tie?" She looked around the group of short-haired people and sighed. "Hell."

"I've got one." Kelsey pulled a tie from her wrist and held it out.

"Babe, you got your hair cut months ago. Why do you have a hair tie?" Jamie said.

Kelsey shrugged at her girlfriend. "Habit. That and I like to always have one handy in case Pierre or Newman want to play on the nights we knit."

Jamie snorted. "You are fucking weird."

Tam threw a chip at her head. "But you're living with her. What's that say about you?"

In a surprise move, Jamie caught it in her mouth. "Oh, I'm weird too," she replied, after chewing and swallowing. "The fact that Kelsey knits with her cats was one of the things that drew me to her."

Kelsey poked her side. "I'm pretty sure it was my ass, but you keep telling yourself that."

Everyone laughed at their interaction. Jess wasn't besties with either of them like Tam and Jenn were, but she'd been friends with the women long enough to know they were both oddballs and suited for one another.

Jess used the lull to pull her hair back into a ponytail. "Ah, much better. Maybe I should get a bob like Kelsey."

The voices all hit her at once.

"Hell yeah!"

"You'd look cute."

"Do it. It's only hair."

Richard clapped his hands together. "Girl, yes! What's it going to take to get you in my chair?"

She looked up through the fringe of long bangs and pursed her lips to blow it from her eyes. "You think I should?" Jess didn't look at anyone but Richard, since he was the only hairdresser in the small group.

Richard set his empty plate on the ground then came

closer. He moved around her with intent focus, turning her head one way then another and touching different areas of her hair. "Hmm, you've got this total modern Farrah Fawcett thing going on. And I'm not saying it's bad, but you could definitely use an update."

"What are you thinking? Undercut?" Jamie called out.

"Maybe. We'd have to leave a little extra length on top."

Jess tried to recall exactly what an undercut was. It sounded short. "Uh, I don't know if I want to go that short. I'm not butch."

"I agree with you. Your face shape is too delicate to be butch. It's more pixie-ish. Hold still." He pulled the phone from his shorts pocket and snapped a few quick profile pictures. She watched as he uploaded them into some app. He hit a few more buttons then turned it to show her the result. It was her face with the promised style. The hair was lighter, very short on the sides and styled up on top.

"Wow. The picture is like Pink, but older and fatter. That's really what I'll look like?"

"Ooh, let me see!" Shell jumped up and crowded next to Richard to look at his phone. He passed it around the group for the rest to see.

"It's your face, isn't it? You've got the length to do anything, and your hair is the perfect texture."

Jess swallowed. It was a huge step. She'd had the same hairstyle for at least ten years. "I don't know..."

Chanting began. "Do it, do it, do it."

Maybe it was time for a change. It had been years since she'd stepped out of her comfort zone. She threw up her hands. "Okay. I'll do it."

A cheer went around her group of friends.

Richard got his phone back and closed out the app then brought up another. "I'm bringing up the salon schedule right now and getting you on the books before you change your mind. Give me a day and time."

Jess scheduled her appointment then opened the cooler and began tossing the shots around her circle of friends. Richard caught his and held it up to the light. "So pretty!"

Jamie pointed to Richard as she caught her own shot. "What he said."

Once Jess had all but one served, she reached back into the cooler and pulled out a solid purple Jell-O shot. "Hey Jenn," She called.

"You know I don't eat those."

Jess smiled. "I made this small batch just for you. They're vegan."

"Oh really?" She made grabby hands. "Gimmee! How do they taste?"

"Like ass, but at least you can eat it. Is Malcom at his dad's?"

Jenn sucked the shot out of the little plastic cup. "He's actually spending the weekend with Mia and Ash."

Kelsey burst out laughing. "How did that come about?"

"He's fifteen this year and has been making noises about going into a career in emergency services."

Tam tossed a potato chip at Jenn. "You mean he doesn't want to be a doctor like his mama?"

Jenn shook her head. "He's smart enough to do it. But he's also smart enough to look at the years of education and student debt and consider other options. Besides, he's been hooked on that new firefighter show lately and Ash agreed to give him a tour of the station. Plus, grandmama Mary is going to teach him how to make her famous biscuits."

Kelsey sighed. "God, I love that woman. She's such a spitfire."

"Babe, your abuela is twice as bad."

Kelsey winked at her. "Good point."

"Hey Jess, Sal is putting together this year's softball team and we're short a few so she told me to ask around. You interested?"

She scowled at Tam. "Dude, it's been five years since I last played. How desperate are you?"

The short, butch woman shrugged. "I mean, I never played with you, but Shell says you've got a killer bat and right arm."

"It's true!" Shell sat forward in her chair, feet not even touching the ground. Both her and her wife were on the short side, and it made Jess snort every time she saw them sitting in their oversized camp chairs. "We played together for years. You're good. You've hit more homeruns than anyone else I know."

Played was obviously the key word in her statement. "While I used to be pretty decent—" She held up her hand to stave off Shell's protests. "That was probably five years and forty pounds ago."

"Come on, Jess. It's not like they're playing in the Olympics."

She looked at Jamie. "If you're so gung-ho about it, why don't *you* play with them?"

"Oh, I am." She pointed to Kelsey. "We both are and she doesn't know shit about softball. This should be a blast."

"Hey!" Kelsey punched her arm and Jamie leaned away, laughing. Then Kelsey tilted her head and shrugged. "Eh, but she is right. I was a soccer player in high school. James is taking me to the batting cages tomorrow to begin my training."

The group started laughing and Kelsey leaned toward Jess. "Besides, I've probably got forty pounds on you. You won't be the biggest one on the team, so hush."

Kelsey had a point, except the curvy woman was also taller, at least eight years younger, and a lot more mobile. Still, Jess thought about it. She missed playing. Truth was, she gave up a lot after her divorce. On the other hand, she didn't want to humiliate herself by trying to push her jiggly bulk around the bases. She looked back at Tam. "What fields are you playing on this year?"

"All at Riverside Park."

There were quite a few softball fields scattered around St. Seren. Some were utter trash, with hidden holes in the outfield that guaranteed at least a few people would end their seasons with a sprained ankle. Others had a short back fence but a giant outfield. They were the best ones for in-the-park homers. But all the Riverside fields had shorter outfields with tall fences. They were perfect for her deep hitting style. Most of her homeruns were slammed over those fences. Jess took a swig of her beer and sighed. "Damn it! While it sounds like fun to swing the bat again, I'm going on a much-needed month-long vacation in a few weeks. I'd miss too much of the season."

Shell grinned. "Actually, the first game doesn't start until May tenth, you'd only miss a few practices and games."

Jess knew when she was beat. "Fine. You can put me down as an alternate. Let me know what the fee is and I'll give Shell that and my shirt size at work this coming week." She pointed her finger around the group. "But it's on all of you if I have a freaking heart attack running those bases!"

Caleb held up both hands in surrender. "Hey, don't lump me in with the les-folk! I've got nothing to do with this. I just attend the games for the social."

Richard nodded. "Same. Let's not forget drinks and bar food at Cranker's after."

"It's too bad Thai Guys or Beast Burger couldn't sponsor," Shell mused.

Kelsey grinned. "Oh, hell yes! I'd totally be down for that."

"But, babe, Thai Guys doesn't have alcohol."

"Good point. Okay, I'll satisfy my noodle fix on the weekends and settle for greasy bar food after our games. And the beast is a heart attack waiting to happen anyway."

Jamie held her hand up to fake whisper to the rest of the group. "She says that like she didn't order wild style every other week before I met her."

A potato chip hit Kelsey's head.

"It's true. You'd eat anywhere as long as you don't have to cook," Tam said.

Before Kelsey could come after her, Tam stood and grabbed a handful of shots from Jess's cooler. She tossed them around the group one by one. Then she held her second rainbow-layered Jell-O shot aloft like a torch. "Here's to warm weather, big balls, pretty alcohol, and the best friends we could ask for."

"Cheers!" The group called out at once, then slurped down another shot.

Jess shook her head and winced at the strong rum. They were all going to be feeling it in the morning. Someday they'd learn, but it wasn't going to be that day.

****

Two weeks later, Jess woke to silence. No lights from the noise machine or her charging pad on the nightstand. Just the sound of the trash truck making its rounds on a Saturday morning. She picked up her cell phone and panicked. "Fuck, my flight!"

Jess scrambled out of bed, cell in hand. It was a lucky thing she'd packed and showered the night before. She'd just be able to check-in and make her plane on time if she did the bare minimum of grooming. She quickly dressed and pulled her black, Scion ballcap over her new, light blonde, haircut. She was surprisingly in love with it and hated wearing the hat, but time was of the essence.

Her doorbell rang while she was brushing her teeth. Jess pulled the toothbrush out long enough to rush through the house to answer. Toothpaste dripped onto her shirt as she yelled a query to the hapless pre-teen girl on the other side.

"Uh, hi. I'm collecting cans and bottles for my soccer team. Do you have any you can donate?"

Jess glanced to the left at her overflowing returnable bin and scowled. "Listen kid, I don't have time for this right now. Come back in a few weeks." Then she slammed the door in the girl's face and hustled back to the bathroom so she could spit and rinse. She was a big meanie, sue her.

Fifteen minutes later, Jess hit the gas pedal to rush through the yellow light at the intersection near her house. Tires screeched somewhere behind her, followed by a loud bang before a reflection in her rearview mirror briefly blinded her. Jess blinked and she blew out a sigh of relief as she safely merged onto the highway. There was no time to stop for whatever accident missed her. She hoped everyone was okay, but Mai Tais waited for no one.

# Chapter Two

Jess peered out the window as the small jet circled Paradise Island Resort. It was everything she'd hoped for, at least from the air. Spacious enough to boast an airport that could handle the smaller jets with plenty of other land to explore. There was no way she'd ride on one of those tiny prop planes. Jess verified her transportation ahead of time to prevent that horror. The Embraer 135 could seat nearly forty, but the cabin appeared to be half empty, which meant the seat next to her remained blissfully vacant on the last leg of the trip.

"Ladies and gentlemen, we have begun our descent into Paradise Island Resort. Please return your seat backs and tray tables to their full upright position. Make sure your seat belt is securely fastened and all carry-on luggage is stowed underneath the seat in front of you or in the overhead bins. Thank you."

The captain paused as the plane adjusted course, then he continued with his canned speech. "The weather on the ground is sunny and eighty-five degrees. A true paradise for those who find their way here. Flight attendants, prepare for landing please. Cabin crew, please take your seats for landing."

She'd already tucked her kindle into the small cross-shoulder bag so didn't have anything to do until they landed. Jess discreetly glanced around at her fellow travelers. It was a mix of men and women. Jess loved to people watch and the ones she'd just spent the past few hours with on the plane were ripe for observation. The man across the aisle from her during the flight was well-dressed with a fresh haircut. He'd recently gotten a manicure and wore an expensive watch. She recognized it because Beth liked the same brand. He'd been glued to his phone and tablet throughout the flight, clearly having paid for the inflight wi-fi. She glanced at the screens on her way to the bathroom and mentally tsked the gambling apps.

Jess had been assured by the agent on the phone that the resort catered primarily to people in the LGBTQIA community, a fact that made her happy. She wanted a safe place to relax and rejuvenate. The view alone outside her window went a long way toward assuring Jess she'd made the right choice.

Airport staff directed passengers to board a waiting shuttle bus while the ground crew transferred the luggage. There was nothing on the island but the resort, so everyone had the same destination.

"Can you move your bag?"

Jess looked up to see a thin, beautiful woman. She could have stepped off the pages of a magazine. Rather than answer, Jess huffed and shifted her bag from the seat into her lap. She wasn't as small as she used to be and didn't like squeezing in. "It's not like you need the room," she snarked.

The woman sat down and gave Jess major side eye. "You don't have to get huffy with me. I'm not the one who made you fat."

"Excuse me?"

The woman rolled her eyes. "Listen, we're all here to have fun and—" She made air quotes. "Work on ourselves. But it's pretty hard to do either one when people like you walk around with a stick up their ass. I'm hoping to grow my social media base by doing videos and posts around the resort. At least pretend like you're not angry and miserable ninety percent of your life. You queers are all the same."

Gambling guy looked up at that comment and spoke before Jess could. "Uh, hello? This resort caters to the queer community. Why the hell would you come here if you're such a raging 'phobe?'"

Bitchy woman grew pale, a color that looked as unnatural on her as the plumped lips. "You're lying!"

Another man in the aisle seat in front of Gambling Guy glanced back at Bitchy Woman. Jess followed his gaze as it flitted from her jewelry, to the Gucci bag in her lap. She may not like the woman next to her, but something about the shifty guy gave her pause. Jess clutched her own bag tighter in response.

"Yo, stop being such a bitch. You may think your

looks and popularity will buy your way in a lot of places, but your attitude is gonna see you kicked out of them. Shut your mouth and stop spoiling the scenery."

Jess raised an eyebrow. Shifty or no, even that guy had limits when it came to Miss Insta-famous. The woman wisely shut up after that. The shuttle slowed ten minutes later, and Bitchy Woman quickly stood and pushed her way down the aisle. Jess snorted as she got up. "Well, this trip is going to be pleasant."

"Don't act all high and mighty." Jess's mouth dropped open as she turned to look at Gambling Guy. He continued. "We're all here for a reason. Don't act like you're so much better than her."

She stood a little straighter and pulled her shoulders back. "I'll have you know that I won this trip at a birthday party."

Shifty guy tilted his head and smirked at her. "Did you though?"

"What's that supposed to mean?"

Gambling guy laughed. "Yeah, that's what I thought at first, too."

Jess scowled at them. "You're both kitty bonkers."

Shifty Guy shrugged his shoulders and made his way off the bus. She met the gaze of the gambler. He shook his head. "Suit yourself."

The view when she stepped off the shuttle made her forget about the other rude guests. Everything was green and lush. A cacophony of noise sounded from the canopy overhead and the scent of tropical blossoms drifted on the breeze. Somewhere beyond the birdsong Jess heard the ocean waves. It was all very relaxing in a way that the flight and shuttle ride weren't.

"Gather round, please. My name is Lucia Cruz and I'm the resort manager at Paradise Island. To save time, you were already checked in by the airline staff on the way here. If you'll all follow me, we'll get you settled into your assigned cabins so you can have a few hours to wind down before dinner is served."

Jess froze. The voice was low and feminine but embodied so much more. It was like dark chocolate, kittens, and pure distilled sex. The timber of it hit Jess simultaneously in the animal part of her brain and someplace much lower. She was afraid to turn toward the speaker because she'd surely never look away again.

But she did turn. The view before her perfectly matched the voice in her head. Tall, dark, and lean, Lucia Cruz was dangerous in an unattainable, hot girl, kind of way. Androgenous with dark hair and long eyelashes framing even darker eyes, Jess struggled to pin an age on her. Lucia had the full lips and high cheekbones that most women would kill for. The resort manager was everything Ruby Rose's aesthetic promised but could never deliver. Times ten.

"Fuck me," she muttered beneath her breath.

"Miss Parker, in the back. Did you have a question?"

Jess frowned and tried to control her reactions. It wouldn't do to let the woman know the effect she had on her dormant libido. Someone that good looking must have a massive ego already. "No."

The group of vacationers followed Lucia and a few other staff members along a pathway that led through the most beautiful landscaping Jess had ever seen. One by one they were given key cards and left at the doors of their homes for the next few weeks. Jess was the last one delivered to her cabin. Lucia held out the key and smiled with her stupid perfect teeth. Jess was careful not to touch the other woman's hand when she took it.

"If you need anything, Miss Parker, please don't hesitate to call."

"And how exactly will I do that?"

"The phone in your cabin, of course. You ring and I'll answer."

"It seems a little below the resort manager to sit around answering calls from the guests."

Lucia laughed. "You'd be surprised at what I do around here."

"Yes, well, good to know the staff is so helpful. Now, if you don't mind, I'm exhausted and I'd like to go inside."

"Of course. I'll leave you to it." Lucia bowed and turned to walk away, before stopping again and looking over her shoulder. "Oh, and you'll hear a chime in a little over two hours. That's the meal bell. Just follow the path back to the main building. The staff members on site can direct you to the dining room."

"And if I don't feel like socializing?" Just the thought of being around a bunch of people she didn't know, all of them probably judging her, made Jess cringe. She was okay with her small friend group but had never been good in crowds of strangers.

"Then you have the option of calling for room service. You'll find everything you need to know for your stay in the folder on the desk. Be sure to read the welcome letter carefully."

Lacking anything else to say, Jess turned abruptly and swiped the keycard to scan into the cabin. She wheeled her suitcases inside and looked around the spacious main room. There was a folder of papers on the desk, exactly as promised. Jess left her luggage by the closet and went to explore the bathroom. One of the highlighted amenities was a large soaker tub and she couldn't wait to submerge herself after losing a day in planes and airports.

With the flick of a switch, the roomy bathroom illuminated. There was a large sink with plenty of counterspace for her toiletries. A toilet and bidet were on the far end of the bathroom behind a privacy wall. The end opposite the toilet featured a massive walk-in shower with a square shower head that simulated rain. But no tub, soaker or otherwise. "Are you kidding me?"

Jess marched right back out into the main room and lifted the receiver. It said to dial zero for the operator so she did. It rang once before it was picked up. Even over the phone, Lucia's voice gave her goosebumps.

"Is something the matter with your cabin, Miss Parker?"

"I was specifically promised a soaker tub and the bathroom has no tub at all!"

"My apologies. I was just on my way back to the main building."

A knock sounded at the door so Jess hung up the phone and walked over to answer it. Lucia peered inside and nodded at Jess's luggage. "Oh good, you've not unpacked yet. Each cabin is unique in some way. If you follow me, I have just the place for you."

Jess draped her sling bag across her chest and grabbed the handles of her suitcases. The wheels clattered as they rolled over the stone tiles just outside her door.

"You have to understand that sometimes these mix-ups happen. But don't worry. I've got everything you're looking for right here." Lucia winked at Jess and gestured toward the cabin across from hers on the path.

It was identical to the one she'd just been in and Jess raised a lone eyebrow. "Uh huh."

Rather than hand over the new keycard, Lucia scanned the lock herself and led the way into the cabin, holding the door open. Jess reluctantly followed and a scent that was equal parts musk and tropical blossoms hit her nose when she moved closer to the other woman. She ignored it and looked around the new place. "This looks exactly the same."

"Yes, but in here..." Lucia opened the bathroom door and gestured toward it.

Jess left her suitcases by the bed and poked her head into the bathroom, not expecting a change there either. She was pleasantly surprised. "Oh, this is perfect."

Lucia gave her another devastating smile and Jess backed out of her personal space.

"I'm glad we could meet your needs." Lucia walked over to the open door and stood in the doorway. Jess followed her and held it open as Lucia walked out onto the path. "Don't forget, orientation starts at nine tomorrow. We hold it right after breakfast."

"So, if I want breakfast, I need to wake up early on my first day of vacation?"

"I'm afraid so, but just in this one instance. After you've completed orientation, you'll be able to set your own schedule for the remainder of your stay. Oh, and don't forget to wear your lanyard with your name badge whenever you're out and about in the resort. If there's nothing else?"

"No, this is fine. Exactly as promised. It's good to see someone can get something right. Good night, Ms. Cruz."

Lucia's eyes crinkled at the corners and her mouth turned up with a mischievous smile. "What, no thank you?"

Jess scoffed, "For doing your job? Please!" Then she shut the door and began unpacking. She felt a twinge of guilt for her bitchy attitude but her attraction to Lucia made her twitchy. Besides, Jess lived life by the philosophy that it was better to reject people than be rejected. She was definitely ordering dinner in and having a long soak.

****

Jess woke to the jangling alarm of her phone. She blindly swiped the screen then rolled over and groaned. "It's just one morning, Jess. Get your jet-lagged ass out of bed."

She was unusually relaxed after a quiet evening and time spent in the large tub. It was the first time in years Jess woke without the aches and pains she'd gotten used to with the onset of middle age. She dressed casually, applied sunscreen, then made her way out of the cabin wearing her cross-shoulder bag. She didn't know what the day would bring, other than the promised breakfast and orientation, but wanted to be prepared.

The interior of the main resort building was pleasantly decorated with quiet music filling the lobby. The space exuded everything the resort promised. It was warm, tropical, and inviting.

"I see you made it in time for breakfast despite the early hour. I can personally lead you to the dining room if you like. We've got a full buffet that our guests always seem to enjoy."

Jess saw the tall shadow approaching out of the corner of her eye and gave a mental groan. Just her voice alone caused goosebumps to race up and down Jess's arms. "Miss Cruz," Jess answered in an annoyed tone. "Good to see you maintain your continued diligence where your job is concerned."

Lucia gave her a playful smile. "Of course."

"If you'll just give me directions, I'll be fine. No point in taking you away from your post here." The truth was, Jess didn't want to follow wherever Lucia would lead her.

No, that would require entirely too much time staring at the woman's backside for her sanity. Broad shoulders, and a firm ass inside those tight black slacks… nope. She didn't have the mental fortitude to browbeat her libido this early in the morning. A libido she was certain was nonexistent until arriving on this god-forsaken island.

"Are you sure? It's no problem."

"I'm certain," she said through clenched teeth.

The unfairly attractive resort manager appeared hesitant but eventually conceded. "Okay. Keep following this hall to the end then take a right. There is a map on the wall at each juncture inside the main building so it's pretty difficult to get lost. Enjoy your meal and I'll see everyone for the orientation."

That piqued Jess's interest. "Oh? You do that yourself?"

"Of course. I believe a more… *personal* touch is enjoyable for everyone here at Paradise Island."

The phrasing and emphasis on personal caused Jess to swallow unexpectedly. Was Lucia flirting with her? Impossible. Seeing that Lucia continued to stare at her expectantly, Jess forced a smile and made her way down the hallway and away from temptation. "It's just been a long time. You're reading something into nothing. Shut it down, Parker," she muttered quietly. Her self-chastisement continued through her delicious breakfast, if only in her head.

Forty minutes later, Lucia's voice once again upset Jess's peace and bodily comfort. The woman standing a few feet away at the front of the room made her feel hot and twitchy.

"How was your breakfast?"

"It was great!" someone called out from a table behind Jess's.

A gorgeous, pleased smile met the small crowd of assembled resort attendees. "Excellent. Only the best for our guests, yeah? If you'll all give me your undivided attention for about ten minutes, I've got a few rules to go over and some amazing people to introduce you to."

Jess opened the cover of her kindle in an attempt to ignore the liquid gold caressing her ear canals. With any luck Jess could put her developing crush in a tiny box and send it off to Antarctica.

"Miss Parker?"

Immediately called out, Jess's cheeks burned with embarrassment. "Erm, yes?"

"Our orientation is for everyone's safety and enjoyment. I'd appreciate it ever so kindly if you paid close attention. Trust me when I say you'll have plenty of time to dive between the folds of your pages later."

The embarrassed flush turned to something entirely different and focused much lower at Lucia's phrasing. Seriously, she wasn't imagining it, right? With a quick flip of the cover, she closed the kindle and sat back in her chair with arms crossed. When Lucia continued to stare at her, she gave a negligent wave of one hand. "Go on then."

"Thank you, Miss Parker. I appreciate your fast compliance to instruction."

Fucking hell.

"Now, let's get started, shall we? Each one of you signed the forms online agreeing to the stipulations of Paradise Island Resort, regardless of how you came to be here. We are as much a mental health vacation as a self-help getaway. One of the non-negotiable rules stipulates that you must attend at least three session blocks per day or risk ending your trip early."

The familiar voice of Bitchy Woman yelled from the back. "That's such bullshit. I would never have agreed to that!"

"I assure you, Miss Coleman, that you did. It's all in the contract you signed before traveling here." She lowered her voice and tilted her head forward while making eye contact with the woman in the back. "Reading is fundamental, Brittany. Just ask Miss Parker here." She waved toward Jess to prove a point and Jess sank a little lower in her chair.

Lucia straightened again and gave the room an engaging smile. "Now, where was I? Ah, yes, the sessions. They are only an hour long and outside that requirement, you're free to relax and have fun at your own discretion. We have a number of excursions and activities available for signup each day. There should be a calendar of events in the welcome packets located in each of your cabins. Any questions?"

Shifty guy raised his hand. "Yeah, what's this mandatory shit like?"

Jess saw Lucia frown at the crude question, but her smile returned quick enough as she answered. "That comes to the next part of your orientation, introductions." She waved toward a group of staff standing off to the side. "These fine folks will be your guides here at our beautiful resort."

Half the assembled group lined up in a row and Lucia introduced them one by one. "Let's start with the nuts and bolts of Paradise Island. These are the people that keep everything running like a well-oiled machine." She addressed the assembled employees. "Step forward as I call your name. Amy is the resort's assistant manager. If you can't find me, you'll be able to find her. Doctor Kameel Dominion and Doctor Sue Berg are the resort counselors. You'll be split into two groups and assigned an hour with one each day. I highly encourage serious participation in your discussions. And don't worry, your counselling blocks count toward your mandatory daily sessions."

"You should sign up early to get your preferred time slot," Doctor Dominion added.

Lucia smiled and acknowledged his suggestion. "That, too. Also, I'd like to mention that there are no scheduling blocks available between the times of twelve and three. That time is reserved for self-reflection."

"And siestas!" someone said standing in the line behind Lucia. Nearly all the guests laughed at that.

"I'm not spending an hour of my vacation each day talking to a shrink!"

"Mr. Barber, I'm afraid this is another non-negotiable item that you approved before coming to the resort. You can refer to the packet in your cabin that includes the printed agreements you all signed."

Stan Barber was the name on the burly guy's lanyard badge. He didn't look familiar but then she had been in the middle of the bus and admittedly wasn't paying that much attention on the trip from the airport. Like Stan, Jess wasn't keen on counselling sessions either. They reminded her too much of her ex when they made a last-ditch effort to fix their failing relationship. She elected to remain silent so she wouldn't get singled out by Lucia again.

"Next we have Dr. K." A stooped, thin old man with a bit of a hooked nose stepped forward and Jess wondered how long ago he'd been in actual practice. "The good doctor will assist you with any minor medical issues and arrange for a transfer off the island in the event that the emergency is more serious." The old man gave a gentlemanly bow before stepping back again.

Jess tried to pay attention. She really did. But her mind started to wander after the first four introductions. An unknown amount of time later, she was brought out of her rum runner daydream when Lucia asked if there were any questions.

"Yeah, do you have any Americans working at the resort besides the old man and the one shrink?"

Jess hadn't heard all the names but the lineup at the front of the room appeared pretty diverse. She craned her head around to see what woman had said something so shitty. Someone named Paula Patch at the side of the room. "Bigot much? Jesus," Jess muttered beneath her breath.

Her heart raced when Lucia looked right at her and smirked. There was no way the woman could have heard her, and yet...

"Ms. Patch, Paradise Island Resort is an open and inclusive vacation getaway. We have people from all nations, levels, and walks of life working and visiting. I think everyone here would appreciate a little more respect going forward for the diversity that makes us unique."

The woman appeared suitably chastised, but Jess would bet her favorite tennis shoes that she wouldn't stay that way. Jess looked up in time for Lucia to give her a discrete wink and she squirmed in her seat.

"If the first group will step back, I'll introduce the rest of our staff." There was some shuffling while one line was replaced by another. The rest of the introductions didn't take much time and for that, Jess was happy. "There, that's all I have for you today. Anything else you'd like to know?"

Jess raised her hand.

"Yes, Ms. Parker?"

She grimaced at Lucia's insistence on using her last name. "Yeah, if we have to complete all these classes, where do we sign up?"

"That's a great question. If you'll turn and look toward the back of the room, you'll see the buffet was replaced with individual stations where you can learn more about everything the resort has to offer. Beyond that, it works exactly like your room service. You only need to fill out the cards in your room every night and hang them on the outside door of your cabin by midnight. The cards will be collected and your name added to the list of attendees the next day. It's that easy. Anything else?"

It was simple and Jess was conversely irritated by it. "Yeah, what if we want to sit on the beach, or by the pool? Is there something special we need to do for that?"

"You're allowed to visit any of the free spaces, including the gym, whenever you like. However, if you sign up for those non-sessions on your card, a staff member will reserve a place for you at the time required, as well as have a towel and refreshments ready at your request."

Lucia finally said something that made Jess smile. "Awesome." Normally you'd have to fight for a chair and wait forever for service at the big busy resorts. Maybe a few mandatory classes wouldn't be so bad after all if you got this kind of service.

"I'm glad you approve. After all, we wouldn't want you to miss out on reading or sun time."

Jess only smiled as Lucia continued with her orientation. "Seeing as how this is your first day at the resort, there is nothing on the schedule. Simply explore, check out all we have to offer and get a good night's sleep. Tomorrow begins a new chapter in your life."

The line was especially corny and something you'd expect from a supposed self-help resort, but Jess was happy to have the day to look around. Perhaps beach time was in her future after all.

Lucia gave them a little bow. "Welcome to Paradise Island Resort. I hope you find everything you're looking for."

Jess hoped so, too. She tucked her Kindle into her

sling bag and stood to check out the activity stations in the back of the room. Then she had plans to track down a beach towel and some frozen drinks.

# Chapter Three

Much to Jess's shock, the first full day at the resort started on a positive note. She felt significantly better when she woke just after eight-thirty the next morning. She had plenty of time to eat breakfast in her cabin and mentally prepare for her nine-thirty appointment with the resort counselor. Jess chose an early session to get it out of the way. After her meeting with Dr. Dominion, she was scheduled for an hour-long art class with Ronobe, then lunch.

Lucky enough, the resort had a mandatory three-hour break starting at noon. It was explained that many of the staff enjoyed working when it wasn't so hot, and the sun was a bit lower in the sky. That was perfect for Jess because she had plans to indulge in more pool time since the resort weather channel said it was going to be in the nineties. Jess signed up for a spa and massage session at five to finish out her day, before she'd head off to dinner at six-thirty.

Despite everyone's annoyance during the orientation meeting, the mandatory stuff was pretty tame. They were each given a recommended schedule that was tailored to them. Lucia explained that it was based on the personality test they took online before arriving at the resort. Hers looked mostly like classes she'd already be interested in, so it didn't seem that bad. But then, Jess hadn't attended anything yet. Maybe they'd try to sell her something in each one. Who knew?

Jess slid into a pair of shorts and sucked in her gut to zip. Then she pulled on a tank top rather than her usual T-shirt in deference to the predicted high temperatures. The entire resort was air conditioned, but it seemed a little warmer than comfortable when she'd been in the main building the previous morning.

She looked in the mirror and frowned at how snug the shorts had become during the past few years. Every year when Jess switched her summer and winter wardrobe, she told herself that she was just going to give up on the dream of losing her depression weight and simply buy new clothes. After all, she could afford it now. But there was something about the idea of it that meant admitting defeat. It was a vicious cycle. Jess's weight gain made her achy knees hurt even more and exacerbated her depression, which took away all motivation to return to her previous active lifestyle. Thus, she gained more weight and it made all the other things worse.

Jess sucked in her gut and let it out with a sigh. Instead of stressing about it, she grabbed an oversize short sleeved button up shirt and pulled that over the tank top, fastening the bottom three buttons. "That'll Do Pig, That'll Do." She giggled at the famous line from *Babe* and snagged her lanyard and sling bag before making her way out of the cabin.

Ten minutes later she pushed into the waiting area of the counselor's office. There were a few comfortable chairs spaced evenly around the room. A water cooler sat across from the lone door that she could only assume led into the office proper. Multi-colored abstract art hung on the walls and there was a decorative goat statue next to each door. They were waist high and fairly adorable, but then Jess had always had a soft spot for goats.

"Miss Parker, it's very nice to meet you."

Jess jumped and pressed her hand to her chest, heart racing. "Oh, Doctor Dominion! You need a bell on your shoes or something." She gingerly shook his outstretched hand.

He laughed. "Maybe I do. And please, call me Kam. I don't need such formality between us."

"Really? I thought most shrinks wanted to be called doctor this or doctor that to stroke their egos," Jess said, once she dropped his hand.

Kam gave her an indulgent smile then led the way into his office. He gestured toward the walls. "As you can see, I have plenty of degrees that assert I know what I'm doing but I don't have the ego you speak of. I'm merely a fan of knowledge of all sorts."

She made a face. She had not enjoyed attaining her own bachelor's nearly as much.

"But if it makes you feel better to be more formal, you may refer to me as Doctor Kam."

"Using doctor with your first name makes it seem like you're pandering to a child." Jess sounded the name out and frowned. "I don't know how, but that's even worse."

He gave her another enigmatic smile. "Just use whatever name makes you feel most comfortable. After all, these sessions are for your benefit, not mine."

"And if I said I was most comfortable not being in counseling?" He shook his head and she sighed. "Damn. I had to try."

She took a seat in the comfortable chair. The cushion was soft and wide without swallowing her. There was a sweating bottle of water already placed on the end table. She was less excited to see the box of tissues. There was no way in hell she would cry at some chintzy resort counseling session. No way.

"Are you comfortable?"

Jess nodded.

"Good. I see you listed your personal pronouns when you signed up, but how would you prefer I address you? Formal or informal?"

Jess considered all the times that Lucia had referred to her as Miss Parker since she'd arrived on the island and scowled. "Just Jess." She had the good grace to leave the, *and hopefully you can get it right*, in her head. Jess didn't like the idea of talking to someone she didn't know from Adam but was aware that it would be a dick move to take her irritation with Lucia out on the poor guy.

"Very well, Jess. Let's start with something easy. Why are you here?"

The laughter burst out before she could stop herself. "I'm here because of some gods bedamned document I have no recollection of signing when I won this trip. It was probably in the fine print. Nobody reads that."

Kam shook his head. "No, I mean why did you come to Paradise Island Resort?"

"Like I said, I won the trip."

"Didn't you have to pay taxes and organize your own travel arrangements?"

"Well, yes."

He gave her a kind smile. "We're highly advertised as a self-help resort. There are plenty of reasonably priced tropical destinations that you could have chosen in lieu of Paradise Island. Aruba, Barbados, Cancun, Bali…ones that didn't stipulate things like mandatory counselling sessions and other classes."

"I—" Jess didn't know how to answer that. Maybe it was because she was cheap and saving any money was better than not saving money. Or, perhaps winning the trip was the catalyst she needed to get off her ass and do something, anything, that was just for herself. She knew she still carried wounds in her heart from Beth. When Jess got the call that she'd won the trip, she thought it could be a good opportunity to get away and get her head screwed on straight. But she didn't tell Kam any of that. "I don't know. It looked like fun when I booked it."

He sighed and clicked his pen closed before setting it and the leatherbound notebook aside. "Miss Parker—Jess, you won't get anything out of these sessions if you don't put anything into them."

Something about his intense stare–or those dark, deep-set eyes–stripped Jess of her walls. She figured *what the hell* and gave him what he wanted. "I've been in a rut and unhappy since my divorce, and I don't know how to fix it. I—" She broke off the next sentence before it could escape, unsure how it bubbled to the top of her thoughts in the first place. Stupid counselors with their stupid trustworthy faces.

"You what, Jess?"

There it was again. Kam's voice had a calm surety about it. It made her loosen up and be a little braver than normal. "I don't like myself anymore. I'm not sure if I ever did."

Kam nodded with understanding. "Thank you for trusting me with your fears. Let me ask you something else."

Jess tensed, but his next question went off on another tangent.

"During the past month, how many kind things have you done? Something that wasn't expected and you did it just because you could. How many, and can you name the most recent one?"

Jess struggled with her memory of the last month. It shouldn't be that hard, should it? "One. I, uh, I made vegan Jell-O shots for one of my friends." He gave her a curious look so she tried to explain. "See, I make these rainbow rum shots for all my friends, but they have gelatin and Jenn can never eat them because she's a vegan. So, the last time Tam and Shell had a barbecue, I found some of the nasty seaweed agar stuff and made a special batch just for Jenn so she wouldn't feel left out."

"And what was your friend's response?"

Jess laughed. "She agreed they tasted terrible but thanked me for thinking of her. Even gave me a big hug after."

He clicked his pen again and made a few notes. "How did that make you feel?"

"Appreciated." Once again, she hadn't meant to let that slip but at least it was the truth.

"That's good. Now for something a little less pleasant. During the past month, how many *un*kind things have you done?"

That question sucked. Jess frowned and considered the past month again. Every interaction with Lucia, the confrontation on the bus, not stopping for the accident on the way to the airport, the little girl collecting cans, the coffee shop, snapping at her employees and friends…the list went on and on. Jess swallowed and her eyes met Kam's dark stare. "Too many. I'm an asshole, okay? A real bitter bitch."

He set the pen and notebook aside. "I prefer if you don't degrade my client that way." She was going to argue with him but could only nod in the face of such kindness and surety.

Kam continued to ask a variety of questions during the next forty-five minutes. He said it was to form a baseline for their future sessions. It irritated her to no end that more often than not her answers circled back to her marriage and the fallout after it was over.

"Have you ever broken a bone, or sprained anything?" he asked, when they were near the end of time.

"Sure. I sprained my ankle playing softball once.

Twisted my foot in a hole and had to sit out the last two games of the season, why?"

"And why did you miss the last two games?"

"Because it fucking hurt and was swollen like a sausage!"

Kam clucked his tongue and Jess knew it had to do with her language. "Did you walk normally?"

His questions were bordering on the absurd. "No."

"Did you limp or have to change your daily routine?"

She sighed at his stupid persistence. "Of course, I did. What does this have to do with literally anything else?"

He rested his hands, one on each thigh. "Jess, you suffered an injury that left you unable to carry on the way you normally would. I'd hazard a guess that it also affected your mood as well, right?"

"Yeah. It was already a tough year and to not even be able to finish the season? That hurt probably more than the sprain. I was angry, sad, and in pain for a few weeks."

"So, what you're telling me is that you suffered an injury that left you hurting, volatile, and depressed?"

"Yes, but—oh." His subtle meaning hit her all at once. "You're talking about my divorce. Beth."

That enigmatic smile returned. "Am I? It sounds like you're the one mentioning her. I'd also wager that you didn't play on your injured foot until the pain went away."

"I didn't. But that's not the same thing. The divorce sucked, sure, but it's just something you need to get over with time and all that."

He shook his head. "From where I'm sitting, having read through your personality test and brief background you provided, as well as listening to you today…it doesn't sound like you've healed from that injury. And yet, you keep putting weight on it."

"What do you mean? I don't seriously date or anything, and I'm not one to sleep around. By the time I was ready to get out there again, I didn't feel like I had anything to offer."

"I'm referring to the weight of expectation."

She'd been leaning forward in her chair, worked up at the memories and emotions invoked by Kam's questioning. But that one comment caused her to sit back abruptly.

The chair cushion let out a *whooshing* noise behind her. It made more sense than she wanted to admit. She looked up through vision gone shimmery with the sudden tears. "Does that mean you don't think I'm a bad person?"

"It's not for me to judge bad and good or right from wrong. I'm here to help you realize your fullest potential, to support you in your journey to get back on track to mental, emotional, and physical wellness. I see a lot of potential in you, but it won't do a bit of good if you can't see it in yourself."

He glanced down at his watch, then smiled. "I'm going to give you an article with a list of psychology-based exercises that will help boost your self-confidence."

"But it's not just my self-esteem that has issues. I'm bitter and angry…a lot. And I know that I've become impatient and patently unsocial."

He stood and she stood with him. When Kam held out his hand, she took it firmly in her own, grasping significantly tighter than their first handshake. As if he held out a lifeline, and perhaps he did. "I have full faith in your strength of will to improve as you wish. But let's take things one step at a time, shall we?"

Jess swallowed thickly and looked toward the far wall over Kam's shoulder, taking in the diplomas hanging there and the framed photograph of two Nubian goats. Clearly the guy loved goats. She had an old girlfriend that was the same way with otters. Pictures, statues, pillows, and more. Kind of a weirdo actually. Jess shook herself from her memories and drew in a deep breath, then let it out again as a long sigh. She met that deep stare. "Okay."

"Good. Now, let's get you that information on your way out and give five minutes of your time back. Since you're the first one to sign up for the counselling session, I'll give you first dibs on the appointments each day. Would you like to stick with this timeslot until you've completed your stay at Paradise Island?"

"Yes, that would be great. Thank you."

Kam gave her a gentle smile. "It's my pleasure to help."

****

Jess only had a few minutes to recover from the counselling session before walking to her art class. Even so, she carried much of her turmoil into the room with her because she didn't know how to dispel the angry, uncomfortable emotions that Kam had stirred up.

All that frustration boiled out as soon as she saw the easels. "No fucking way."

Brittany, aka Bitchy Woman, was also in the class, along with a few other people she didn't recognize. The instructor turned and gave her a big grin. "Ah, Miss Parker. I was expecting you. I'm Ronobe but you probably already know that. We'll cover a variety of basic art techniques in this class, including painting. Please select a workstation and I'll pass out supplies in just a minute."

"There is no way I'm going to get paint all over myself. I didn't pack clothes just to have them ruined."

"Maybe you shouldn't be such a fat slob, huh?"

Jess snapped at Brittany. "Oh, shut up. Don't you have some fake friends to impress online or whatever?"

"I'm here to paint something beautiful. So, if you could set up out of my sight it would make things a lot easier, cow."

"Ladies, please. That's quite enough negativity."

Jess took one step toward the TikTok twat but Ronobe moved between them with a gentle smile. She turned in a circle and addressed the small class. "Can anyone tell me what the greatest asset is when creating magnificent artwork?"

One man, to Jess's right side, cleared his throat and raised a hesitant hand. Unwilling to continue standing there as the center of attention, she quickly sidled up to the nearest easel that was out of Brittany's line of sight.

"Go ahead, Carl."

"Skill?"

"No, but it's a great guess. Anyone else?"

Another woman that Jess recognized from orientation held up her hand. "Superior quality materials?"

"Also, a great idea, Paula, but I'm looking for something else. No one?"

Everyone glanced around, equally at a loss as to what the answer could be. Ronobe gave in and put them out of their misery. "The correct answer is passion. Or to make it even simpler, emotion. Some of the greatest creations of all time stemmed from great emotion. Because of this, I've given you all five colors, and only five colors. Red, yellow, blue, white, and black. Each easel has a square twelve-inch by twelve-inch canvas resting on it. On the table next to the easel, you'll find a plastic pallet for mixing, a selection of brushes, and a smock to keep your clothing clean."

Ronobe glanced toward Jess whose cheeks grew warm.

"Does that address your concern, Miss Parker?"

"It's just Jess."

"As you wish. And if anyone else has a preference for how I address them, don't hesitate to let me know. Now," She looked at the watch on her wrist, identical to the one Kam wore. "You have forty-five minutes to literally paint your heart out. I'm not setting any requirements or boundaries for this one. This is your opportunity to get a feel for the materials, your emotions, and to put your soul onto that space. When the alarm goes off, I want you to stop all painting and begin cleanup. Brushes and pallets can be cleaned at the sink in the back of the room. You may begin."

Jess looked at the white square and frowned. She was clueless when it came to painting. Hadn't even touched a brush probably since grade school. She considered what Ronobe said about creating with emotion. Lucky her, Jess was left with plenty after her counseling session. She tried visualizing the blank space like those kookie painting shows on cable TV.

She jumped when Ronobe appeared at her elbow. "Is everything okay?"

"I swear, everyone here needs bells on their shoes or something."

Ronobe laughed. "You know what they say, every time a bell rings an angel gets their wings."

Jess snorted. "Not like any of us will need to worry about that."

The instructor gave her a strange smile and wandered off.

Once again left to her own devices, Jess uncapped the black and squeezed a good portion on the pallet. Then she recapped it and did the same with the red. Yeah, those were good colors for how she felt. She started with making broad black strokes, swirling around the corners, then veering off to one side. Then she dipped into the bright red with a different brush and filled in the rest of the white canvas. Some spaces mixed and formed a dark cherry mud which matched her mood every time she thought of Beth.

The red was anger and the black became hurt. Jess lost herself in the brush strokes and color. She searched for something else she could do once she had the entire canvas covered in paint. There was a fan-looking brush so she picked that up and dipped it into the black, spraying it on all the large red areas. Then she did the same with red on the black spaces.

Jess was startled by the alarm and she sucked in a surprised breath. Her hands were a mess of black, red, and brown. And the painting—the image before her was pure chaos. She had never seen anything in her life that perfectly captured how she felt the day she found out about the affair. Until now. Jess dropped her brush onto the pallet and simply stared at the thing she'd created from the worst parts of her. She hated the painting. But she also loved it with the same ferocity.

"I've never seen anything like this. Your work is very powerful."

"Shit fuck!" Jess spun around and put a hand out toward whomever had come up behind her to stand so close. Unfortunately, that hand connected with the crisp white shirt of a certain resort manager. Jess's eyes widened with mortification. "I'm so sorry."

Lucia glanced at the paint mess on her shirt and gave Jess a wry smile. "While I appreciate your use of my favorite colors, I usually tend more toward conservative patterns."

Between Lucia's voice and overall nearness, and

Jess's own embarrassment, she was left feeling off balance. That only made her angry. "I swear that everyone in this damn resort needs to wear a cowbell. You people do nothing but sneak around and scare unsuspecting guests."

That elicited a snort. "I'll keep that in mind, Miss Parker."

"Please stop with the Miss Parker business," she huffed. "Just call me Jess."

"Very well, Jess. I'll do my best to be much more...vocal the next time we meet so as not to startle you from your passionate creativity." She winked. "Now, I'll leave you to your cleanup. It really is a beautiful piece." Before Jess could say another word, Lucia spun on her heel and exited the classroom. Most likely off to change her shirt and annoy someone else.

Jess nearly facepalmed at the woman's bold innuendo but remembered the mess on her hands at the last second. If she thought her emotions were in flux after the counseling session, they'd amped up even more in Lucia's presence. Jess couldn't understand why the woman got under her skin so much.

"Don't forget to clean your workstation before you leave. I've gone ahead and labeled everyone's ventilated lockers. I'll carefully slide each of your works inside once they've had a little more drying time on the easels." Ronobe's voice startled Jess from her bubble of introspection. She shook herself and gathered up the tools she'd used to create something so ~~ugly~~ beautiful.

Another woman asked, "Will we get to work on them some more?"

"I'm afraid this exercise is finished. But we'll start something new at our next class. You're free to take your painting to keep once they're dry, if you like. If not, let me know and we'll use them for décor elsewhere in the resort."

"Oh, no. I'm definitely keeping mine! My social media fans are going to love this."

Jess sneered at Brittany but continued cleaning, scrubbing under her nails with the provided little brush. She was hungry and didn't want to miss lunch. And after that, pool time. She could hardly wait.

****

She was halfway through *Coming Up Clutch* by mid-afternoon, and on the proverbial edge of her lounge chair wanting to know what Razor was going to do next. After two decades playing, Jess was a sucker for a good softball romance. Her enjoyment ended when a shadow blocked her sun. Jess had been reading on her stomach so didn't see who walked up. But given her luck of late, she could hazard a guess.

"Good afternoon, Miss Parker. How are you enjoying the sunshine?"

Jess didn't look up. "I thought I asked you to call me Jess. Now I think you're just doing it on purpose to torment me. And my sunshine was better before it was blocked." She could hear the smile in Lucia's voice.

"Speaking of block, you should probably apply some sunscreen to your back. You don't want a sunburn to ruin the rest of your stay."

Her shoulders felt a little warm but Jess knew they weren't red yet. She closed the cover on her kindle, leaving it beneath the lounger, then turned over to look up at Lucia. Jess shaded her eyes so she could see the woman through the bright sun. Same crisp white shirt, well, probably different now, and black dress pants. Hardly matching the tropical surroundings and certainly not comfortable in the heat. She caught Lucia's quick glance down to her cleavage in the sport top and ignored her libido while so exposed.

"Why aren't you a puddle of sweat right now? It's hot as hell out here."

Lucia smirked at her. "Not quite. Just the low nineties. And I've been here long enough to get used to the climate of Paradise Island. Do I look hot to you?"

It was a loaded question and Jess squeezed her thighs together. She didn't acknowledge the double meaning. "I think the better question is, do you feel hot? I suppose that's all that matters."

That elicited low laughter and Jess was drawn to Lucia's gorgeous smile that contrasted nicely with her darker skin. "I did before this conversation. Oh, before I forget—" She reached into her back pocket and pulled out a small tube of sunscreen, then handed it to Jess.

Jess took it politely and held it in front of her, as if the tiny bottle could block all the parts of her body that she felt less than confident about. The longer Lucia stood there, the more self-conscious Jess became about her abundant belly fat and thick thighs. She did what any good Midwesterner would do and tried to leave the conversation without leaving her chair. "Whelp, thank you. If there's nothing else?"

"Thanking me for doing my job? Hardly worth a thanks." She looked down at her watch and it was the first time Jess noticed that it matched Kam and Ronobe's. Perhaps free watches were a company perk. "But I do have to run along. Enjoy your afternoon, Jess." Lucia made to turn away but looked back at Jess with another flirtatious smile. "Oh, and don't hesitate to ring me if you need anything at all. Night or day." Then she strode away leaving Jess with another wink and a perfect view of that fine ass in tight-fitting black trousers.

Jess threw herself backward on the chair, tensing as it creaked beneath her. "You've got to be fucking kidding me. She's doing this on purpose." She discreetly watched as Lucia made it across the pool deck and pushed through the gate leading outside, then blew out a long sigh. "There's no way she's serious." A small voice in her head whispered, *but what if she is?* and Jess tried her damnedest to ignore it.

She may not have any boom-boom to look forward to, as Shell called it, but at least she had the promise of an hour at the spa later. Half of that would be taken up by a full body massage. She'd confirmed earlier. It was nearly as good. Well, as good as she was going to get today. But as a precaution for the rest of her stay, Jess applied the sunscreen before lying back down.

# Chapter Four

Jess was lazy and didn't feel like trying out all the different classes the resort had to offer. She had no interest in things like stargazing or survival techniques, so elected to continue with the same counseling and art class throughout the week. In lieu of spa time, she signed up for one of the excursions on the list of resort options.

The boat was scheduled to leave at four ten that afternoon and would take the passengers to a nearby reef for snorkeling. Then they could either go buddy parasailing or take a jet ski out. Jess wasn't sure how she felt about either of the last two activities, but she said screw it and signed up anyway. After all, how else was she going to get out of her head and prove there was still adventure left in her?

The small group met at the dock at four. It was her first time seeing the water since flying in and Jess wasn't disappointed. It was a clear bluish green as far as the eye could see and there was not a cloud in the sky. The dive boat was good size, plenty of space to seat everyone. There were a few jet skis tied to a large activity platform nearby, as well as a ski boat, and an inflatable banana raft. She was even happier to notice that neither Brittany nor Paula was part of the excursion.

A trim older man exited the ship and walked down the dock toward them. He was wearing the same outdoor uniform she'd seen other staff sporting. A short-sleeved white shirt with the resort logo, and khaki shorts. On top of that, he also wore a legit captain's hat. Jess could see a few other folks still on deck and assumed they were guides for the day's trip.

His voice was a pleasing baritone and he spoke with an accent. "Good afternoon, everyone. I'm Imamiah, the captain of *Pair O Dice*. But you all can just call me Eem, or Captain Eem if you like. We're a little shorthanded today so I'm waiting on one more crew member to round out the team." He turned and gestured toward a swarthy man with curling red hair that fell to the top of his neoprene collar, and a woman with skin a few shades deeper than Lucia. Both wore shorty wetsuits. "Wave when I say your name, kids. My crew today is comprised of Zepar and Lahash. They're locals who help out on occasion here at the resort."

Jess glanced around the group of guests. She saw that the shifty guy from the bus, Stephen according to the badge hanging from his lanyard, was one of the eight. His gaze skimmed away when Jess looked at him so she didn't bother saying hi. He was as much of an asshole as the rest of them.

One guy wearing baggy shorts and a water shirt raised his hand. Eem shook his head and laughed. "Don't stand on none of that here. Just ask what you need to ask, friend."

"How long is this supposed to last? The write up indicated four hours but I'm going to get hungry if that's the case. Will they still serve dinner so late or let us order to our rooms?"

"Rest assured, Mister Cuppernell, we've planned for everything on this trip. The resort's talented and resourceful Chef Azazel has prepared a veritable feast for hungry boaters. Food will be served after the snorkeling dive and before we return to the activity platform for the rest of the experience."

Jess groaned quietly at the familiar voice behind her. She didn't want to turn around because more than anything she knew that Lucia would not be wearing her usual crisp business attire. Whatever it was would leave Jess wanting more than a refreshing dip in the ocean. Best case scenario, it would match what Captain Eem had on. Jess had already made up her mind to ignore her, but Lucia called out right away.

"Miss Parker, it's good to see you venturing away from the pool area."

"I thought I told you that it's J—" She turned to address Lucia and nearly swallowed her tongue. Sure, she was dressed appropriately as a resort employee helping out on a boating excursion. Exactly like the other two guides. None of that registered in poor Jess's lizard brain. All she saw was a shorty wetsuit filled out by muscles and curves in all the right places. The legs of the wetsuit only made it halfway down Lucia's muscular thighs. The short sleeves did nothing to hide her biceps, and…

Jess's eyes slid upward toward Lucia's chest. The suit featured a zipper that ran down the center to her abdomen, and Lucia had left it unzipped a good three inches so you could just make out the cleavage beneath. "Fuck me," Jess muttered under her breath.

Lucia didn't seem to hear. She just smiled. "You were right earlier. It's quite hot today. I'm looking forward to getting wet out there."

She was saved by Captain Eem calling out to them. "Good. Now that we're all here, come on aboard so we can cast off." He looked up as Lucia followed Jess onto the *Pair O Dice*. "Good to have you aboard, boss. I can't wait to see the sunset today. Should be a glorious one."

Jess glanced back in time to see Lucia give the captain a broad smile and clap on the shoulder. "Definitely. The only thing prettier around here is the sunrise, though most of our guests never see it."

Everyone laughed at the absurdity of getting up so early at the resort. That's what the boring nine to five was for, not vacation.

The woman, Lahash, ushered everyone into the large main cabin of the ship while Eem continued on to the wheelhouse. "Please find a seat while Zepar unties us and Captain Eem takes the boat out. Once we've cleared the dock, you're free to roam around, careful of the ship's rocking. I'm here to answer any questions while my counterpart double checks all the snorkeling gear."

"What will Miss Cruz be doing?" A tall, burly guy asked. Jess recognized Stan Barber from orientation.

Lahash glanced toward Lucia and answered. "Safety dictates we have at least three crew members to assist on any excursion. My friend Luce was kind enough to volunteer when our third mate couldn't make it."

Lucia nodded. "Believe me, it didn't take much convincing to get me out of the office and on the water." More than a few chuckles went around the cabin.

"What is there to see out here? Doesn't look like anything at all as far as I can tell," Willy Cuppernell, the man in the water shirt, asked.

"That's a great question, Mister Cuppernell."

"It's Willy or Will, please."

After a brief nod to acknowledge his request, Lahash continued. "There is a gorgeous reef southeast of this string of islands with a plethora of sea life contained in and around it. The waves are calm today and I think you'll enjoy yourselves."

"How long will it take to get to the reef?" Becky Corder asked.

"About a half hour. Once we arrive at the site, Zepar and I will instruct each of you on how to properly use your gear. Has anyone been snorkeling before?"

Three hands went up and Lahash smiled. "That's good. Less work for us, right Zepar?"

"You've just said my favorite two words." The redhead's voice was much deeper than Jess expected, and he had an unidentifiable accent. He certainly wasn't unattractive. He reminded Jess of the hot guy, Jamie, from that *Outlander* show everyone was raving about. Despite being firmly in the gay category, even she felt a little twinge when he spoke. It was disconcerting and she chalked it up to being in the middle of a long dry spell.

"Which two words, less work?" Stephen called out.

The guide grinned back at him. "That or *right Zepar* because I enjoy being right."

Lahash gave him a light punch to the arm. "You're a regular comedian, buddy."

Once they were cleared to walk around, Jess went outside on the deck to stare across the blue expanse of water. The sun was bright, but she had her sunglasses and plenty of reef friendly sunblock, thanks to the resort. She sighed, wishing she had her regular camera with her instead of the cellphone.

"Is something the matter?"

Jess grabbed her chest at the interruption of her quiet moment. Lucia had walked up behind her while she was lost in thought. "Bells, dammit. You all need bells."

Lucia snorted. "I'll take your recommendation into advisement. Care to tell me what brought on the long sigh in the face of such natural beauty?"

Her gaze was intense and, not for the first time, Jess felt uncomfortable as the recipient. "I was merely wishing for my camera instead of my cell phone."

"Oh, if that's all it is, the resort has you covered. We have cameras you can sign out on a daily basis, just ask Zepar to get you one. The only requirement is for you to return it in the same condition you took it."

"But how do I get my pictures?"

Lucia winked. "Scan your badge on the bottom of the camera and you'll be logged in. A staff member will upload any photos to your account after you check it back in. Those will be accessible once your stay is complete. The resort will send you a link for download, just like the cruise ships."

"Oh, cool. Very fancy." She knew it sounded stupid, but she literally couldn't think of anything else with the hot woman standing so close. Jess took a subtle breath through her nose and appreciated the delicate scent of Lucia. Something between heady musk and tropical blossoms. The woman was too dangerous for Jess's sanity. Lucia continued to smile at her and Jess searched for something else to say. "So, uh, will you head back to the resort once we dock again?"

"I'm actually yours for the day."

She blanched. "Erm, mine?"

The quiet laugh hit places Jess swore had dried up years before. "The excursion's, of course. I wouldn't leave you all high and dry just because one activity is complete. So, I'll need to stay and assist. For safety's sake of course."

They were interrupted when Lahash walked up to stand on the other side of Lucia and bumped against her shoulder. "Good to see you out here again, Luce. Try not to scare away all the fish like you did last time."

Lucia glanced at Jess and rolled her eyes, her perfect smile looking especially bright in the tropical sunshine. She responded to Lahash. "I'm telling you they must have sensed a predator or something. Perhaps a barracuda."

Lahash shook her head. "A barracuda, sure. She leaned forward past the railing to look at Jess. "Don't listen to her.

Water isn't Lucia's element and I think the fish sense it."

Lucia shrugged. "It's true, I do prefer dry land over salt water. But there is something about the sea..." she looked off in the distance and never finished her statement.

"It's like a siren's call. It's a song as old as time. Unlike you, I enjoy the water as much if not more than the land."

"I'm well aware. There is a reason you're so good at what you do."

Jess wasn't sure they were still discussing the excursion and part of her wondered if they even remembered that she was standing there. Another darker thought popped into her head that they had some sort of shared history, perhaps romantic. Hopefully, their past wouldn't get in the way of the day's fun.

As if to answer her silent question, Lucia looked back at her. "Don't worry, Lahash and Zepar know their stuff out here. They'll take good care of you."

Lahash gave her a kind smile. "That we will."

"I certainly hope so. After all, it's your job," Jess sniped, uncomfortable with her attraction to Lucia and their sudden scrutiny. She turned and walked away.

Despite her hasty exit from their vicinity, she overheard Lahash. "Ah. This is a tough one, Luce." She had no idea what that meant and didn't care to ask.

A few hours later the *Pair O Dice* bobbed in the water next to the dock. Jess and four other guests were seated in a speedboat heading away from the island. Captain Eem drove, while Zepar and Lucia readied the tandem parasailing gear. Lahash stayed back at the dock to oversee the remaining three people who wanted to ride the jet skis.

The first pair of guests went up, Stan and a petite older woman named Tammy. Jess didn't like Stan from the second she heard him speak. He was the one who originally complained about seeing a counselor at the orientation. His poor attitude didn't stop there. He'd been making snide comments about how weak women were and thought that his opinion was the most important the very moment the *Pair O Dice* pulled away from the dock. It was weird to see such alpha male behavior in someone who was supposedly queer, but Jess knew the community was full of all types. Toxic masculinity wasn't limited by gender, sexuality, race, or anything else. Either way, he was a big jerk.

Tammy was an entirely different story. She was mousy, quiet, and soft spoken. Nearly the opposite of Stan. Unfortunately for her, Zepar paired them up by total weight. Jess glanced at the other two who were next, Stephen and Becky. She could see how their total weight could be equal to the first couple and wondered if she herself would be paired with Zepar. Terrified, but excited to try something new, Jess watched the screaming parasailers and waited her turn.

Fifteen minutes later, Lucia spoke from just behind her right shoulder as Stephen and Becky were reeled in. "Are you ready to go up next?"

She spun around, startled by more than Lucia's voice. "Oh! So soon?"

"You're the last one in this group so it's not all that soon." Lucia paused and a look of concern washed over her face. "Are you afraid?"

"Of course not! I'm merely…concerned. Who will be my partner?" She glanced around Lucia at the other four guests who'd already gone up, then moved her gaze toward Zepar.

"Me, of course. Come on." She guided Jess toward the staging deck. "Have a seat where Zepar is pointing. I'll slip into my own harness and wait for you."

Jess tamped down her gut reaction at Lucia's words. It simply wasn't fair. She squeaked out agreement, then made her way over to the bench seat where Zepar stood balanced with the gentle rocking of the waves. The boat stopped each time they prepped the next duo.

Everyone was already wearing the slim life vests featuring the resort logo. The harness itself was simple enough with straps that went around each leg and a large padded back and mid-section. Zepar threaded the strap through her vest so it wouldn't fall as she walked across the deck. He gave the standard speech that she'd already heard two other times about how to sit, where she could hold on, and what to do when going out and coming back.

"I have it, thanks."

The boat got underway and Zepar called the two of

them up to the staging deck once the chute was in the air. He had them sit down facing forward and clipped them in. Then it was only a matter of letting out the line to fly them like kites. Jess immediately screamed and shut her eyes.

"Are you doing okay?"

She cracked a single eye open to look at Lucia. "Do I look freaking okay?"

"You look fine to me. I'd say the ocean breeze suits you."

"Haha, you're funny as shit right now." She would have kicked Lucia if she thought it wouldn't kill them both. She felt herself slip in the harness and screeched. "Oh shit, oh shit, oh shit—"

"Jess! Look at me."

Her eyes remained screwed shut as she began to breathe faster. "I can't."

A hand squeezed her thigh and it shocked her so much that Jess opened her eyes. It was the first time she'd looked closely at Lucia's face. High cheekbones, lips that were neither too full nor too thin, and eyes so dark brown they appeared nearly black. "Everything is okay."

"It's not, I'm going to fall!"

"I promise that you won't. You're secure in the harness. Zepar is keeping an eye on the chute and there isn't anything at all that can tangle our line. Look at the water and see how beautiful it is."

Inspired by the surety in Lucia's voice, Jess carefully moved her gaze away from the woman who caused a riot of emotion inside her and out toward the horizon. The sight filled her with awe. "It's so blue. And I can see all the little currents and swirls."

The boat made a broad turn, and the resort came into view, showing her the decorative gardens she'd yet to visit. "Oh, look at that." She wanted to point but her bravery would only take her so far. Removing her hand from the harness was not going to happen.

Lucia didn't follow her gaze. Instead, she continued to stare at Jess's face. "See, beautiful." Jess did her best to ignore the woman in her peripheral vision. Lucia was too distracting.

Eventually their turn was over and Zepar reeled them

back in like a giant fish. Jess was excited and pumped full of adrenaline. Not enough to do it again, but still thrilled that she'd conquered her fear.

"Well? Did you like it?"

She turned to acknowledge Lucia's question. Her natural inclination was to respond with sarcasm and blow Lucia off. Especially given how uncomfortable the resort manager's attention made her. Besides, she was still irritated by the woman's confidence and good looks. She'd always hated people who seemed so effortlessly perfect. But Kam's questions about her actions popped into her head. Jess pressed her lips together so the words wouldn't come. Instead, she took a second to reflect and gave Lucia a quiet smile. "I really did. Thank you."

"Excellent. And if you're still up for adventure. I've talked Zepar into taking the banana raft out with one of the jet skis." They both sat down as the speedboat took off again, making its way back toward the dock. "I've been told it's like riding a mechanical bull. But wetter."

"Huh?"

"You've got people seated on each side of the banana and you have only a little strap right in front of you to hold on. Meanwhile, you're bumping along the waves quickly. It's easy to get thrown off. It helps to have someone strong sitting behind you."

The activities platform came into view and Jess craned her neck to see the big, yellow, inflatable raft in question. It bobbed in the water from the waves caused by the speedboat approaching the dock. Two of the jet skis were gone and Willy was chatting with Lahash. Lucia tossed her a line and the craft was swiftly tied to the cleats.

"You want the vests back?" Becky asked.

Zepar called out to the five of them. "How many of you plan to use the jet skis or ride the banana boat?" Everyone raised their hand and he smiled at the small group. "Nope. Just keep your vests. They're good for anything here.

"Zepar, you can take a break and watch for the other two jet skiers to return. I told Willy I'd take him out on the banana boat." Lahash said. "Would anyone else like to join us?

Jess and Becky both raised their hands. The rest wanted to ride jet skis.

"Is there a minimum number of people to take us out?" Jess asked.

Lahash waved them farther down the dock toward where the day-glow raft was tied. "There is no minimum but it works better if we have an even number of people. Luce, you want to join us and balance it out?"

Of course, Lahash would ask her. Jess sighed but resigned herself to her fate. She had a sneaking suspicion that she knew which side of the banana Lucia would sit on.

"It would be my pleasure. But you have to promise not to bounce us off."

Lahash gave them a smile that was all teeth. "Where's the fun in that?" She spent a few minutes showing the four of them how to mount each side and as predicted, Lucia was the one seated right behind Jess.

"Don't worry, I won't let you fall."

"Thanks" she said wryly.

"I promise that this one is pretty fun, too. Exciting like a jet ski, but you have less control. Wilder, I suppose."

"Oh, and you like it wilder?" Jess tossed her own attempt at flirting out into the world and looked over her shoulder at Lucia.

"I happen to like a lot of things." She grinned then Jess was forced to hold on for dear life as the jet ski pulled them away from the dock.

Lahash did long lazy circles far away from everyone else. The banana would bounce and nearly throw them off each time she'd cross the jet ski's wake. But Lucia stayed true to her promise and every time Jess felt her hand start to slip, a strong arm around her middle would steady her again. Eventually they turned to see the platform in the distance.

"This wasn't bad at all," Willy called out, right as they went over a large wake. Willy and Becky flew off the boat leaving Jess and Lucia laughing.

The jet ski slowed and Lahash brought them back around but didn't pull up to the duo treading water. Jess stiffened as an arm snaked around her middle but before she could protest, Lahash took off again and dumped them into the water as well. While it wasn't cold, it definitely shocked the system and her heart raced.

"I've got you."

Jess brushed Lucia's hand away. "I can swim just fine."

Lahash's laughter cut off whatever Lucia was going to say. "Looks like I dumped you all! Are you ready for a pickup?"

Becky called out, "Yes, please! You can leave Willy to tread water if you like."

"Hey! I didn't mean to jinx us."

Jess rolled her eyes. "There's no such thing as a jinx. Just overactive imaginations assigning blame, which belongs solely to the person operating the jet ski."

"Blah, blah, blah. You're not exactly making friends with the driver."

Realizing Lahash controlled whether or not she had to swim all the way back to the dock, she smiled and played nice. "Sorry, not your fault after all. It was clearly a rogue wave."

"That's much better."

Jess heard Lucia chuckle somewhere behind her.

The big yellow raft was nearest to the other couple and they helped boost each other up onto their side. Willy shrugged and looked chagrined as they pulled away much slower. "Sorry, Becky. Apparently, I spoke too soon."

Once they were secure, Lahash slowly made her way over to Jess and Lucia. Staring up at the expanse of yellow in front of her, Jess knew she'd never be able to pull herself up to the top of the raft. "Uh, maybe you could tow me back?"

"Nonsense. I'll give you a boost."

Jess groaned internally. That was exactly what she was afraid of. Lucia's hands on her body. Knowing when she was beat, she ground out a reluctant agreement.

It took only a few seconds, one firm hand on her backside, and a lot of gay panic to get Jess back in her seat. Lucia had no problem pulling herself out of the water and back on the raft.

"Maybe take it easy returning to the dock. If you dump them in again, they may choose to do the same thing to you when we get back," Lucia called out to Lahash.

Lahash met Lucia's gaze and gave a little salute. "Sure thing, boss. I only wanted to put you in the water anyway. They were just a bonus."

Everyone laughed at her comment but it irritated Jess. Enough so that she refused Lucia's offer of help onto the wood planking once they were tied up. "I don't think so. You've done enough."

"Are you forgetting that I helped you back onto the boat? Don't I get thanks for that?"

"Apparently, you're the reason we were off the boat to begin with. So, no," she grumbled. Lucia's face fell but Zepar called her away before Jess could apologize for her hasty and stupid comment. She was trying to tame her temper but something about Lucia pushed all her buttons.

Zepar, with the help of Lucia, had arranged a meal spread for the group and Jess helped herself before heading off to ride her first jet ski. She was disappointed that Lucia stayed aboard the *Pair O Dice* to help clean up while the rest of them were playing in the water. But she was also a little relieved.

As much as Jess hated to admit it, Lucia was genuinely kind and attractive in more ways than just the obvious. And Jess hated herself for being so drawn to the unattainable woman, no matter how much Lucia flirted with her. It also annoyed her that the woman was so perfect in every way. Like, how was that even fair to the rest of them?

Jess assumed that Lucia's flirty friendliness was just one of the ways the staff made the guests feel special. A smile, a tease, perhaps a few compliments. Every bit of it went a long way toward improving a person's self-esteem. And Jess wasn't immune. But she knew she only had two weeks; a month tops if she opted to extend her stay at the resort. She wasn't sure it was a good idea starting something with a staff member, no matter what Shell said Jess should do. And frankly, all the other guests she'd met were assholes. No way was she attracted to any of them. Even that pretty social media chick. Especially her, ugh. Besides, Brittany was way too young.

But Lucia...she was stuck firmly in Jess's thoughts

and Jess had no idea how to dislodge her.

The group walked back to the cabins together once the excursion was finished and they said goodbyes to Captain Eem, Lahash, Zepar, and Lucia. She'd left the camera with Zepar, who promised to get her photos uploaded to her account in the morning.

Jess unlocked her cabin and dragged herself inside. She was tired and had sore muscles that she didn't even know existed. Seeing it was still pretty early, Jess took a quick shower to rinse off all the salt water then ran a hot bath. She sank below the water and practiced the breathing exercises she'd learned during her time at the spa.

Soon enough Jess felt a calm peace steal over her. She felt loose, liquid, and horny. It had been a long time since she'd had to take care of herself without the aid of her favorite toy but the bath made her feel warm and sensuous. Jess's left hand slid across her breasts and she arched her back at the sensitivity of her nipples. Her right hand moved a slow path toward her abdomen, just tickling the wet hair between her legs.

Without permission, the image of Lucia popped into her head. Lucia in her crisp business suit, pants tight on slim hips. Lucia wearing the shorty wet suit, with zipper pulled lower and lower. She sucked in a breath through gritted teeth when the second and third fingers of her right hand circled her clit beneath the water. She imagined it was Lucia touching her, without her usual outfit, and sans wetsuit. Just miles and miles of smooth, tan skin and long, strong fingers stroking her toward orgasm.

Jess pictured Lucia's sexy smile and swore she could even smell that tantalizing scent she'd come to associate with the magnetic woman. Imagination carried her higher than she'd gone in years. She'd didn't even penetrate herself, just circled her clit while clenching and releasing her vaginal muscles until the flesh beneath her fingers grew firm with pleasure.

Jess cried out in the privacy of her cabin as she shook with the powerful orgasm. It was explosive and her heart pounded in her chest as she came down from the blissful feeling. Jess looked over the edge of the tub and saw that water had splashed out with her actions and knew one of her two towels would be sacrificed to the cleanup. She continued twitching for the next few minutes as the strength of her release pulsed inside. Jess blew out a long languid sigh and felt as though it were the perfect way to end the day. She spoke to the empty room. "Maybe I'll ask Lucia for extra towels tomorrow."

That thought made her smile. After all, the woman did say to let her know if she needed anything at all. And she didn't have to tell her the reason.

# Chapter Five

"Shit." Brittany stopped along the path to wipe the sweat from her forehead. After a brief breather, she began walking again. The air carried a fragrant sweetness and birds sang in the thick canopy overhead, but all Brittany could focus on was the sweat running down her back and soaking her bra beneath her boobs. She'd hoped to get some good shots in to post for her followers, but she was a wreck. "I don't know how anyone can live here."

"You don't?"

Brittany jumped as someone walked around the bend ahead of her.

"Oh, Miss Cruz! Sorry, I thought I was alone on the path this morning."

The imposing resort director gave her a smile, which softened the woman's features significantly. "It's Lucia, please. And a good thing to remember in life, as well as on Paradise Island, is that you're never alone."

Brittany returned the smile, charmed more than she'd ever admit to her social circle back home. "Lucia then. And how can you all survive in this heat? It's like death is sitting on my chest all the time."

She received an enigmatic smirk for her question. "You get used to it after a few T Swift eras."

"Oh, are you a Swifty too? Don't tell anyone but I'm such a big fan," Brittany gushed.

"I'm a lot of things and there is no shame in liking something or having hobbies. It's healthy even to enjoy things that are for you and you alone."

Brittany laughed, a little uncomfortable at feeling so seen. "Good to know. Anyway, thanks." She motioned forward. "I should probably get on my way."

Maybe she could shower and do a live video from her cabin.

"We'll see you back at the resort then. I heard we're having surf and turf for dinner tonight."

Brittany nodded and continued her walk, eager to return to her air-conditioned room. She didn't like queers, but even she had to admit the manager of Paradise Island Resort was an IRL thirst trap.

****

"Help, somebody please!"

Jess felt strange and introspective after her morning counseling session with Dr. Kam. She'd spent the first few hours of her free time walking around the gardens she'd seen while parasailing on her boat excursion. It was hot work though, so she donned her swimsuit beneath her shorts and tank top and went off in search of the beach mentioned in the brochure. Unfortunately, she strayed too far off the path looking at a weird, iridescent dragonfly and her foot slid on loose gravel.

Jess winced as pain shot up her leg from what was most likely a sprained ankle. "Great, I'm probably the only person who goes to a tropical island to die after falling from a footpath." She yelped as a nearby voice startled her.

"Are you okay?"

Jess was getting sick of hearing that phrase. She looked up the embankment toward the trail she'd fallen from, only to see the resort's gorgeous manager smiling down at her.

"Fucking hell," she muttered. "Of course she's the one that found me." Jess watched as Lucia did a controlled slide down to the bottom while staying on her feet. She was like some hot, androgynous land surfer. It seemed incongruous to witness such a stunt while Lucia still wore her black slacks and crisp white shirt. How she planned to make it back up to the path in those shoes was a mystery.

"You look like you could use a hand."

The polite thing to do would be to graciously say yes. Instead, Jess reverted to her basic bitch self whenever she felt embarrassed or looked down upon. "You think? I'm not just picking up ants with my ass for the fun of it." Her ankle was already swelling.

Jess's attitude didn't seem to faze Lucia. Instead, she held out her hand in an offer of assistance. "No worries, Miss Parker—"

Jess growled at getting last-named again. How many times does she have to tell the woman? "I can't exactly stand because my ankle hurts, along with everything else," she snarked. "I probably have scrapes on top of my bruises. Some vacation."

Lucia paused and nodded. "Believe me when I say that I know how hard a big fall can be on the body. We'll get you back to the resort so Doctor K can look at that foot. I'm sure he'll have you right as rain soon enough."

"Could you be any more perfect?" Jess mumbled softly.

Lucia aimed an infuriating grin her way, obviously having heard the rhetorical question. "Oh, trust me, I used to be worse."

Jess took a few deep breaths and decided she could probably get up, at least on her one good leg. She grasped Lucia's outstretched hand. "Whatever. And can you please call me by my name? Miss Parker sounds like a damn schoolmarm."

Jess allowed Lucia to pull her to her feet and leaned against the other woman to avoid putting any weight on the swollen joint.

"I've got you, don't worry."

Lucia stood so close that Jess could smell her. In an effort to distract herself from the rising heat, she glanced toward the steep bank of loose gravel and frowned with dismay. "I don't know how we're going to get up there let alone back to the resort." Jess met Lucia's gaze. "Don't you have a radio or phone you can use to call for help?"

Lucia's low voice sent shivers through Jess's body. "No need for that. Like I said, I've got you, Jess."

The tall woman leaned closer and Jess tried to discreetly keep her personal space. She felt a little like the female cat in the Pepé Le Pew cartoons, except Lucia wasn't at all creepy.

She must have sensed Jess's discomfort. "Can I pick you up?"

Jess glanced at her own, admittedly pudgy, body. "I don't know, can you?" She cringed at the thought of the attractive woman straining beneath her weight.

"I'm much stronger than I look." Undaunted, she squatted down, then scooped Jess into her arms bridal style.

"Holy fuck!" Lucia wasn't even straining.

A dark brown eye winked at her from inches away. "I told you so." Then Lucia carefully made her way back up the eroded bank, striding forward as though it were nothing more than a concrete path.

Jess knew those muscular thighs were good for more than jumpstarting her imagination. She groaned because she was equally embarrassed by her predicament and aroused. Her body was a dirty traitor when in the proximity of such hot, hard muscles. Especially given her imaginative session in the tub the night before. Apparently, her libido wasn't as dead as she made it out to be when she spoke with Shell in her office a few weeks ago. Her tropical vacation was clearly starting off great.

Not only did Lucia carry Jess up the treacherous hill, but she took her all the way to the main path. Jess couldn't wait to return to her blissfully cool room with an icepack, ibuprofen, and some much-needed alone time. Yes, ma'am, she was way too queer for this shit.

There were golf carts randomly scattered around on chargers for the guests to use. Lucia carefully placed Jess into the passenger seat of the first one they came across and drove her to the medical clinic. The resort doctor was swinging in a hammock out front.

"Hey, Jake, Miss—" Jess sighed and Lucia quickly amended what she was going to say. "Jess appears to have sprained her ankle."

The elderly man showed surprising agility by jumping out of the hammock mid-swing and landing spryly on his feet. "Well then, let's get you on the table."

If her embarrassment was bad being carried by Lucia, it was ten times more humiliating to be carried by Lucia and an old, semi-retired doctor that had to be pushing eighty or more. "If you put me down, I could probably hobble in there on my own."

"Nonsense, my girl. Best you stay off it until we can get an x-ray."

"That hardly seems necessary," she protested.

The old man tutted. "Who's the doctor here? Don't worry, Miss Jess. We'll have you fit enough for the Big House soon enough."

His accent had a familiar Midwestern flavor. "Where did you go to school?"

"University of Michigan, why do you ask?"

"Oh! I'm from St. Seren. Small world."

He grinned, crinkling the corners of his deep-set eyes. "Sure is."

Twenty minutes later, Dr. K had treated her for a minor ankle sprain, then cleaned and bandaged two small scrapes. He wrapped the ankle, gave her a few packets of ibuprofen, and handed Lucia a canvas bag filled with enough instant icepacks to get her through the end of the month. It was overkill but Jess went along with it to get back to her room faster.

"You should probably stay off that for a minimum of twenty-four hours, more if the swelling hasn't gone down. If you're still feeling a lot of pain or the ankle remains swollen beyond that, ring up Lucia and have her bring you back to the clinic."

"Okay, thank you, Dr. K—what is your actual name?"

He held out his hand. "You can call me Jake or Jacob, whichever you prefer. It's my pleasure to meet you."

Jess made a face at the sketchy way he sidestepped the answer. But she figured that everyone was entitled to their secrets and shook his hand. It would be her luck if malpractice got him bounced out of medicine in the states. At least it was only a sprain and not something more serious. "Who do I give my insurance information to?"

Lucia laughed, low and musical. "Oh, you don't need to worry about that. All treatments on Paradise Island are part of your stay at the resort. We're all about total body enjoyment and wellness, remember? Are you ready to head back to your room? It's nearly dinner time. I can have guest services send someone over with tonight's special if you like."

Always conscious of her weight, Jess wasn't about to

admit to the goddess next to her that she was starving. Unfortunately, after walking the paths all afternoon, her growling stomach wasn't onboard with that plan. She clutched it and made a face. "Thank you. I guess I am hungry.

"That's great to hear. The feature this evening for the omnivores is steak and lobster. It seems a shame to miss out. Chef Azazel is very good at what they do."

An attractive, gaunt man walked up the path before Lucia could get in the golf cart and drive them away. He looked twitchy and his gaze never stopped on any one thing longer than a second or two. Lucia narrowed her eyes and addressed the man.

"Good afternoon, Mr. Staten. What brings you to the clinic today?"

At the sound of her voice, he glanced in their direction, but his gaze quickly skipped away again. It was as though he hadn't seen them sitting there. His voice was a bit nasal for Jess's taste. "Oh, hi Lucia. I've got some old back pain and I wondered if the doctor could hook me up with some pain meds."

Lucia frowned but nodded toward the clinic door. "Doctor K is just inside. Go in and explain what you need."

He swallowed and scratched idly at his forearms. "Uh, okay. Thanks." Then he scurried toward the clinic.

Jess watched him disappear with concern. "Is he okay?"

Lucia answered once they were safely down the path toward the guest suites. "Donovan came to Paradise Island because he's got a problem with prescription drugs."

Jess was surprised that Lucia would admit such a thing to her about another guest. "Uh, that's not good."

"No, it's not."

"Were some people forced to come here?" she asked, curiously.

"Not in the sense you're thinking. But life often has a way of choosing our paths for us." She waved a free hand toward the lush garden and fountain they drove past. "People come to Paradise Island from all around the world, all walks of life. Do you remember that long questionnaire you filled out before making the trip?"

"Vaguely."

"We use it to get a glimpse into the mind of our guests and tailor their stay in order to give them the best experience and outcome. When I said total health and wellness, I meant it. We do our best to help with whatever our guests are dealing with. You'd be surprised at some of the situations I've born witness to since taking over this resort from my father."

"Like what? Can you tell me?" Jess thought it couldn't hurt to ask since Lucia was already fairly loose lipped about Donovan's problem. They pulled to a stop in front of Jess's private bungalow before Lucia could respond.

"How about I get you situated inside and give guest services a call about dinner first? Then perhaps we can share a meal and chat if you would like the company." Lucia leaned over to bump her shoulder against Jess's.

The move wasn't a big deal, but Jess's natural instinct was to lean away just like she did when Lucia picked her up a short while ago. Her cheeks grew warm. "I'm sorry. I don't mean to be so…standoffish. I'm know I'm kind of an asshole sometimes and I'm working on that."

"You seem uncomfortable around me. Did I do something wrong?"

Jess frowned. On the contrary, Lucia had been beyond compare, but she wasn't likely to admit that to the woman. No way. Jess had her pride. "No, I'm just not comfortable being so physically close to strangers."

"Oh. Well, is there anything I can do to make it better? I'll try to keep my distance, but I must warn you that I'm a naturally social person and tend more toward physical contact as part of my communication method. As for keeping you company, I can simply make sure you've got your dinner and leave you to a quiet night of healing."

It was on the tip of Jess's tongue to send Lucia away, but something stopped her. Maybe it was the peacefulness of the resort, or the fragrant scent of blossoms on the breeze whispering through the trees. Either way, Jess was tired of being alone. She didn't want to be Fort Knox anymore. "No, dinner sounds nice, and I'd like to talk for a while. If you're sure you can stay?"

Lucia smiled. "I am."

"Then I would appreciate the company. Thank you."

"It will be my pleasure. Now, let's get you inside."

Jess was sitting comfortably on the small couch in her cabin fifteen minutes later. Her foot was propped up on an ottoman with a towel-wrapped ice pack draped over the ankle. The painkiller Dr. K gave her worked well but Lucia insisted she used the ice to help with the swelling. Jess called out her order to Lucia, who was busy on the phone with room service. "And I'd like the white sangria with that, please."

Her order was relayed, along with Lucia's own food request, then Lucia placed the receiver back on the cradle. "Miss Short said she'd have our dinner here within twenty minutes. Chef is doing a great job turning out the orders tonight. Apparently surf and turf is popular."

Jess rolled her eyes. "As it should be. Only weirdos don't appreciate a good steak."

Lucia sat down in the small lounge chair. "Are you telling me you don't have any vegetarian friends?"

She nearly snapped back, *none that she liked*, but remembered Jenn and frowned. Things weren't always black and white and maybe she'd become a little judgmental in her old age. "No, you're right. I suppose not all the folks refusing to eat meat are weirdos," she begrudgingly admitted. "My friend Jenn is pretty cool and she's a vegan. Even Stacy, one of my old college classmates that I still see once in a while is a pescatarian. But the rest, ugh!"

"What is it about vegetarians and vegans that you find so reprehensible?"

"Okay, so not everyone on a special diet is an asshole. But people like that Brittany chick? They're just doing it to be extra with no real physical or moral need, and they ruin it for others."

Lucia raised a dark eyebrow, an action that Jess tried her hardest not to find sexy. "Ruin?"

"Yeah. Take my friend Dar. She's really allergic to gluten. It's so bad she even has a service dog just to check all her food. But the popularity of people claiming gluten allergy means that a lot of restaurants and service staff don't listen to Dar when she explains she has a serious illness. And they're not always as careful with prep and cross contamination. Or they just flat out don't believe her."

"I can imagine that's pretty difficult to deal with. Especially with such serious consequences."

"Exactly!" Jess shifted her leg and the ice pack slid off her ankle. She frowned and tried to sit forward to fix it but became embarrassed by the fact that her paunchy belly kept her from reaching it. "Damn it."

"Here, let me." Lucia was out of her chair before Jess could even refuse the offer. Lucia's fingers were soft and warm against her cool skin when she adjusted the pack, eliciting a full body shiver from Jess. Of course, she noticed. "Are you cold? I can grab one of the throw blankets from the closet."

Jess looked up in surprise. "How do you know there's a blanket?"

Lucia grinned. "Every cabin has one. We want to cater to our guest's comfort."

She walked toward the closet door.

"Where were you last night?" Jess muttered.

"Did you say something?" Lucia draped the blanket across Jess's legs before resuming her seat.

"Nope, just muttering. Ignore me, please."

"That's patently impossible from where I'm sitting. I find you quite intriguing."

The bold comment took Jess off guard. "Me?" She snorted. "Oh, come on. Go sell that someplace else."

Lucia appeared quite surprised by Jess's outburst. "I don't understand. Sell?"

"I'm sure it's your job to make everyone feel welcome and special but you don't need to pretend with me. I prefer honesty from people and not lip service. I'm well aware how ordinary I am."

Lucia's expression grew serious and she leaned forward in her seat. "I can assure you that my job is not so base or pandering. The fact that you're here with us on this island proves that you've got amazing drive and the willpower to be better and do more with your life than what you left behind in St. Seren."

Jess grew suspicious, remembering the comments

from the shuttle bus on her way to the resort. "What do you mean?"

Lucia stood and moved over to sit by Jess on the couch. She picked up Jess's right hand and cradled it between her own palms. The motion was so surprising that Jess forgot to pull away. "I mean that you could have gone anywhere if you wanted a simple tropical vacation. Maybe even someplace with your friends. But you found yourself here. And from where I'm sitting, you appear to not only recognize your own faults, but wish to actively change them. It's only been a few days. That takes an enormous amount of bravery and perseverance."

"Now you sound like Doctor Dominion." She frowned. "Wait, he doesn't talk to you about any of the clients, does he?"

"Absolutely not. We respect the session privacy all our guests have. The counselor is only to help you work through your issues and fears, nothing more."

Jess blew out a relieved breath. "Good." She suddenly grew conscious of how close they were and the fact that her hand was still within Lucia's grasp. Jess's gaze moved upward along Lucia's smooth neck until it caught on and traced her sharp jawline. Then it was a quick trip to focus on a pair of dusky, full lips. Jess's breath hitched as a tongue peeked from between them. Lucia began to lean in when a knock sounded at the door.

"Room service!"

Lucia abruptly sat back and released Jess's hand. "Excuse me. I'll go fetch our dinner."

The sexy, professional, and all too put-together resort manager actually seemed flustered and Jess grinned. Maybe the flirting and spark between them wasn't all her imagination. Her brief but hopeful rumination was cut short as Lucia returned pushing a cart loaded with covered dishes.

"How is the ankle? Do you think you can sit at the table for a short while to eat? This will be difficult to spread out near the couch."

"I should be able to manage. It's much better already now that the swelling is going down."

"Jake did say it was a minor sprain."

Lucia helped her to the table and Jess took an appreciative sniff. The steak was easy enough to recognize, but she also scented butter, garlic, and spices. Her mouth watered and that traitorous stomach growled again.

Lucia laughed. "Trust me, the feeling is mutual. No matter how long I spend here, being able to have all my favorite foods whenever I like never gets old."

Jess groaned as she cut her steak. "I can only imagine. I'd be twice the size I am now if I lived here permanently."

"Oh, I don't know. It's a pretty active lifestyle. Especially if you have the right friends." She winked at Jess who promptly stuffed a bite of tender meat into her mouth to avoid answering. Jess diligently refused to acknowledge the heat in her cheeks.

They made small talk during dinner and Jess found herself having an unexpectedly nice time. She knew it wasn't a date but couldn't help comparing it to the last one she'd gone on nearly a year before. That was a disaster from the start. The woman refused all Jess's restaurant suggestions. Then when they met at the Bean Bag, rolled her eyes, and said she thought Jess would be taller. From there it went downhill as Tessa spent more time looking at her phone than literally anything else while they sat together.

Jess DM'd her later to say that she didn't think they'd be a good match, only to discover she'd been blocked on social media. A rousing success. She snorted at the memory.

"What's so funny?"

She looked up to see Lucia's tilted head, fork halfway to her mouth. "Oh, just remembering my last failed date. It's nothing."

Lucia finished her bite. "Failed?"

"When it fizzles out at the first meeting, I usually consider it a bust. Turns out Tessa wasn't interested in who I was, only who she thought I was online."

"What about you?"

The question threw her. "What about me what?"

"Were you interested in her?"

She shrugged. "I thought so. But I definitely had zero interest in the person that showed up for our date. She was pretentious and self-centered."

"Hmm. What do you consider a good date?"

Excellent question. It made Jess wonder about that exact thing. She thought back to her previous dinner or coffee dates she'd gone on after her divorce from Beth and found them all lacking. With the exception of her current company. "I guess if I'm looking to connect with someone romantically, attraction is important to me. Physical, mental, and emotional. I'm not really the wham bam thank you ma'am type. Never have been. There are exceptions of course, but for the most part, eh."

Lucia rested her elbows on the table and leaned her chin on top of her clasped hands. "Continue."

"This is embarrassing."

"No, it's incredibly fascinating. What else do you look for?"

"Well, besides good conversation, there should be some kind of connection." She met Lucia's dark gaze and was caught fast.

"Like chemistry?"

"Yes," Jess breathed out. "Chemistry."

Lucia gave her a broad smile, eyes twinkling. "I'd say that perfectly describes anything I've ever searched for. I'm afraid I don't have much luck in that arena either."

Jess burst out laughing. "Oh, please! You're gorgeous and you have an amazing job—"

"A job that, I'm not sure you've noticed, I'm quite married to. Paradise though it may be, it's hard to meet people that only visit for a short time."

"You can't leave and go to work somewhere else that's less remote?"

Lucia frowned and sat back in her chair. Her gaze became distant as she spoke. "My father actually owns this destination and others. I've been groomed my entire life to take over. Leaving would be next to impossible. I've spent years building this place up to what it is and to leave it now—" She looked back at Jess. "I'm afraid I'd be letting everyone down."

"And all the time you've worked at the resort, you've never met anyone who wanted to move here?"

Lucia gave her a wry smile. "Just one. But it turns out

we were too different in the end."

With just a few words, Jess knew who the other person was. "It's Lahash, isn't it?"

"Very astute, Miss Parker. You've won a prize." Lucia lifted her glass as if to toast, so Jess matched it and clinked the two together.

She finished the last few swallows of her sangria and set the glass down. Lucia stood and began clearing away their meal dishes back to the room service cart. When she was finished, she pushed it to the door and left it outside. She grabbed a cloth from the bathroom on her way back and began wiping the table where they ate dinner.

Jess gave her a curious look. "You don't have to call anyone about the cart?"

"No. They'll come around and pick it up later. Along with all the rules, we also have a system in place at the resort and it works quite well—" Lucia stopped speaking and a strange look washed over her face. She frowned and sighed as though she'd just thought of something. She glanced at Jess and looked...regretful?

"What is it?"

Lucia gave the table one last wipe and pushed her own chair in before responding. "It's nothing." She strode to the bathroom to rinse the cloth before returning and offering her hand to Jess. "Would you like help back to the couch?"

Jess allowed herself to be pulled up but didn't move once she stood on one foot in front of Lucia. She was feeling particularly brave after three glasses from the carafe of sangria. "And what prize do I win?"

Lucia sucked in a breath and Jess felt the arm beneath her palm tremble.

After a few seconds ticked by, Lucia answered. "I'd say that depends on you."

"Oh?"

"Yes. You're only here for a short time, Jess. Not only that, but I'm the resort manager. I wouldn't want to do anything you weren't comfortable with, or act in a manner you deem unprofessional. Propositioning guests is highly discouraged, something that is more for your protection than mine."

"Is this another of those resort rules you were talking about?"

"It is."

Jess leaned closer. "Sometimes we have to dive in to see what's below the surface."

Lucia laughed. "Now you sound like Lahash."

"I don't want to discuss Lahash right now."

"No? Why not?"

"You know why." Lucia glanced down at her lips. It was a move that Jess easily recognized, no matter how out of practice she was. "And my prize?"

Lucia faltered. "But you said you don't care for short term."

"I also said there were exceptions."

The other woman persisted with her questions. "You actually want this? I thought I annoyed you."

"Yes, and only right this second—"

The kiss cut off speech, thought, and the very air Jess was breathing. It was everything she'd expected and yet nothing at all. The moment was heavy and drew out for, what felt like, forever. Lucia offered her tongue and Jess gratefully accepted.

They stood there for a few minutes kissing and clutching at each other as waves of simmering heat ebbed and flowed through them. At least until Jess shifted her weight momentarily to the sprained ankle. She pulled away with a curse. "Shit, fuck, ow!"

Before she could register what was happening, Lucia scooped her up in those damnable strong arms and deposited her back on the couch. "I'm sorry. I let myself get carried away."

Jess laughed. "Shouldn't that be my line?"

"What?"

She gestured between them. "You literally just carried me back to the couch."

The wrinkles between Lucia's brows disappeared as she laughed. "Touché."

"So, what now?" Jess looked up at the unfairly attractive woman who, against all logic and reason, seemed to be interested in her.

Lucia stared down at Jess, then glanced at her watch

and sighed.

"Let me guess, you have to go back to work?"

"I've got a few things to wrap up," Jess frowned. "But I could probably get to them early tomorrow."

"I can see it on your face. Do you think you made a mistake?"

Lucia surprised her. "No. But I do think you need a little more time to decide."

Jess felt needy to ask but didn't want Lucia to leave just yet. "Will you still stay and keep me company for a while?"

"I—yes." Lucia broke another icepack and replaced the melted one. Then she settled on the couch next to Jess, but not so close they'd be tempted to spark whatever flame engulfed them a short time before. "Why don't I tell you about all my favorite places here on the island?"

"I'd love that."

# Chapter Six

Jess was on cloud nine the next morning. All the ice and one-on-one attention the day before certainly worked wonders because her ankle only gave a small twinge when she walked on it to the bathroom. Before Lucia left, she warned Jess that they'd need to be discreet if they engaged in any sort of romance between them. It made sense to Jess and she had no problems staying quiet as long as Lucia kept kissing her like that.

She dressed with a little more care than normal and pulled the breakfast cart into the cabin, planning to search Lucia out after her two morning sessions with Kam and Ronobe.

The ankle felt even better after taking two more ibuprofen. So much so that the walk to the main building where the classes were held didn't bother her in the least. Kam met her in the waiting room like normal, pointing out Jess's good mood right away.

"You seem happy today. Did something happen?"

"Well, I fell off a walking path yesterday, sprained my ankle, and got a few scrapes."

He looked non-plussed at her answer. "I see. Do you normally have such a response to pain?"

She laughed. "No, I just—" Lucia said whatever happened between them should stay private and Jess assumed that went for staff and guests alike, so Jess had to pivot. "Uh, I'm happy because I'm getting along better with others here at the resort."

Kam smiled and nodded. "That's great news. Now, let's discuss something we didn't touch on in our previous sessions."

Jess didn't want to touch on anything, unless they were talking about Lucia's body. "Sure, why not?"

"You've mentioned your past relationship, and the way the dissolution of it has affected you since. What do you feel is missing from your life that previously made you happy?"

She sat back in the chair and blew out a breath. "Wow, you don't start with the easy ones, do you? Are you referring to relationships, or—" Kam shook his head. "Okay. I'm not sure then."

"Maybe it would help to name things you did when you were with Beth that brought you joy. Ones that you don't do anymore. Would you like a pen and paper? Some folks prefer to make physical lists."

"No, I've got this." Jess gave the question serious thought. "Not everything went away because of my ex. I mean, I used to play a lot of different rec league sports but I kind of stopped once I hit my forties."

"Why is that?"

She patted her belly. "For one, I've put on forty pounds since I hit menopause that I can't seem to shake. My knees ache now, which means it's harder for me to run in the outfield. Volleyball is out because I apparently don't know how *not* to sacrifice myself to the hard floor when diving for a ball. It would take the entire week to recover after games."

He nodded. "Understandable. What else?"

"I don't live far from work and used to ride my bike daily when it wasn't cold, rainy, or snowy. I guess I let that go, too."

"What made you stop riding your bike? I'd imagine that wouldn't be hard on the knees."

Jess shrugged. It was a lot of things, but mostly just a general lack of drive and motivation for anything. When had she become so apathetic? Jesus, no wonder her friends got so mad at her. "I don't know."

He sighed. "I think you do."

She stayed silent for more than a minute. It was one thing to make the realization within her head, but to say it aloud to someone else? Ugh. "I think—no," She shook her head. "I know that I've been really down for a while. Low energy, no interest, and just…stuck. Instead of trying to do something about it, I've allowed myself to wallow. At least that's what my friend Shell says."

"Don't you want to be happy, Jess?"

"Of course, I do. That's a dumb question."

Kam made a note and frowned. "You'd be surprised at the number of people who don't want to be happy because it requires change, effort, and commitment. Others don't think they deserve it."

His comment made her thoughts catch and spiral. Did she enjoy her sadness? Why didn't she simply…go for a bike ride through the park? Her back yard wasn't far off one of the trails. She could even take herself to the movies. There was no crime against it. "I guess that makes sense."

"Happiness isn't a one-time game finish. Think of it like a journey of individual moments that you complete before continuing on to the next level. When you stop moving you become complacent and eventually stagnate. Sadness, depression, and sorrow, they breed in those stagnant waters like pests."

"So, what do I do about it?"

"It's in my professional opinion that most people need to understand why they've stopped in their journey. Sometimes it's internal or medical, others there is an external influence. There are a lot of reasons. Do you deserve to be happy?"

"I—I don't know." And she really didn't. She'd sat alone at home too many times wondering if there was something she did that drove Beth away. They'd been fighting more and more those last few years before the split. Beth blamed it on Jess's menopause and changing body. Jess had new fat, weird hairs that sprouted where they'd never been before, and a host of other ailments from achy joints to hot flashes. Who could blame Beth for cheating with all that going on? Jess thought about Lucia and swallowed. What did she have to offer anyone? Certainly not her old, pudgy body.

"Jess."

His comment startled Jess from her thoughts and she looked up. Kam was staring at her in a disconcerting way. "Sorry."

"You appear as though you went someplace dark. Care to share?"

"When you asked me if I deserve to be happy, it made me remember what led up to our divorce. I mean, cheating on me was shitty but it's not like Beth didn't have a reason. I'm not the same person she first fell in love with."

"Hmm," he made another note. "I think you've set yourself against an impossible standard. Change is inevitable."

"But—" Kam held up a hand and she cut off her protest.

"Are you telling me that Beth was the same person from the time you met to the time you divorced?"

Jess burst out laughing. "Not at all. She changed a lot. As a matter of fact—oh." His words finally made sense. They'd both changed and that fault wasn't on them. If Jess was guilty of anything, it was trying to hold onto a relationship that had gone too far off center. And Beth, well she was a cheating bitch.

"I can see that you've made the connection."

She nodded. "I think on some level I stopped doing some of the things I did when we were together because I didn't want to be that person anymore."

"What person?" Kam tilted his head.

"Someone that was unwanted. That wasn't worth the effort. Unlovable. I've always assumed she left me because I got old and fat." Jess sniffled and grabbed one of the stupid tissues, ignoring Kam's understanding gaze.

"Did she tell you that, or allude to that in some way?"

Jess's mind whirled at such a simple question. Did Beth ever say anything about her weight? Her most common complaints revolved about being bored and wanting to do new things. That and Jess's constant self-doubt brought on by her changing body. Oh. "She never mentioned my weight gain, only reassured me when I complained about it."

Kam said, "I'm going to say something that may upset you, or at the very least make you reconsider a lot about your mindset. Could it be possible you only assumed your weight gain was the biggest culprit in your divorce because it was already the thing you hated most about your life, your greatest evil so to speak? That, in all actuality, it's possible your weight gain had no bearing on your divorce or Beth's infidelity."

"No, that can't be. I, she—" Jess paused and took a shaky breath. Beth usually complained about Jess's lack of sex drive when they were fighting, but they'd been letting that aspect of their relationship slide for a few years prior to the divorce.

Kam cleared his throat and Jess gave him her attention. "Does size play a part in your attraction to other women, Jess?"

Her mouth dropped open and she sputtered. "Size, what? Of course not! I like intelligence, great smiles, energy, and ladies that are full of laughter. I've never once considered size…" She trailed off, caught again by Kam's logic. "Damn. I can see your point but that doesn't invalidate my own self-doubt and low self-esteem."

"I understand." He gave her a minute to collect herself before continuing. "Stepping away from the situation, from the experience of your divorce, what do you see?"

Jess's eyes watered at the thought that everything she'd come to believe about her past relationship and herself may have been skewed by her own shitty attitude. They had both changed but Jess built the failure up to be something more because she didn't want to see the basic truth. "I think we should have gone our separate ways long before she had the affair. But it's hard to admit defeat, even harder to let go of something that was once the best thing you'd ever had. We didn't start badly."

Kam smiled kindly. "Most don't. Relationships of all kinds follow the same journey of happiness, only you're walking with another. If one strays, or you both alter your paths, eventually you'll find yourselves lost and isolated. It doesn't mean you should remain alone. It merely means you'll have to do more work to get on track again."

He paused and she leaned forward. "And eventually, you will find someone who walks the same path. A person, if you're so inclined toward another relationship, who will grow and change *with* you instead of away."

"I am so inclined," Jess whispered.

"Let's circle back around to the question from earlier. Do you deserve to be happy?"

She sat up straighter in her chair, filled with a strange resolve. "Yes."

"Are you sure? Happiness requires work and you said it yourself that you've grown complacent over the past few years."

Jess ran her palms over her thighs. "Yeah. I mean, it's gonna take some work to get back into some of the things I used to love."

"And what if you find that you don't love them anymore?"

The question made her pause. She remembered seeing a bunch of videos on social media about little knitted animals and thought they were cute. A few of her coworkers did it and said they were fun and easy. "I've always wanted to learn to knit. And draw. I mean, I've always liked doodling and it would be cool to take classes or something."

"Keep going."

"I guess there are a ton of things I'm interested in but never tried because I was afraid to fail." She paused. "Or Beth said they were stupid."

He made another note and set the book down. "If you're not failing, you're not trying hard enough to grow." Kam glanced down at his shiny, black resort watch. "I'm going to give you some of your time back today but I have homework for you."

She rolled her eyes. "Oh joy."

Kam laughed at her and they stood at the same time. "It won't take long, I promise. You can even use the notepad in your cabin. The next time you come see me, I'd like you to bring two lists. One with all your favorite hobbies and activities that you've stopped doing. And another list with ten things you'd like to do but have always been afraid to try."

That sounded easy enough. She could make her lists that afternoon. "I can do that."

"Excellent. And I heard that the resort has set up a mimosa and bloody mary bar in the lobby until one. Perhaps you'll have some time before lunch to enjoy it."

"Maybe not the bloody mary before lunch because if it's done right, it's a drink and a snack. But a mimosa sounds delicious. Thanks, Doctor Kam. I'll see you tomorrow."

Jess wasted no time getting out of his office. Much like previous days, the session filled her with a maelstrom of emotions and thoughts.

Jess took time to pee and make sure her eyes weren't red before heading off to Ronobe's art class, where she was greeted warmly as soon as she walked in.

"Hi Jess, you're a little early."

"Yeah, but my previous session finished before time." She looked around. "What are we doing today?" After her talk with Kam, she realized that art was one of those things she used to love when she was a kid but never pursued after middle school. Her favorite was sketching but she took a pottery class with Beth once and had a lot of fun. Beth was less enthused.

"I've got blocks of polymer clay in a variety of colors for everyone. Today will be all about molding through emotion."

"What do we make with it?"

Ronobe walked over to a cabinet near the door. "I'll show you." She opened a drawer and removed a bin then took it back to the large table in the center of the room. There were stools all around the table, each with a little stack of colored bricks in front of them. Ronobe picked an empty spot and unpacked the bin while Jess watched.

"What is all that?"

"The nice thing about this kind of clay is that it doesn't require the heat of a kiln. I can bake it in the oven over there. It's also versatile, brightly colored, and once baked, very strong and durable." Ronobe removed a pair of earrings, three different necklaces, a bracelet, a picture frame, and two vases.

"Wow, that's pretty cool."

"So, you think you'll like today's session?" She winked at Jess.

Her words reminded Jess of the poor attitude she's had since she arrived at the resort. She glanced toward the door to make sure no one else was about to enter. "Yeah, I'm really sorry for being such a bitch. I've had fun doing these projects. Thanks for being so patient with us."

Ronobe nodded. "Of course. It's my pleasure to show people how much joy they can find in the simple act of creation."

She looked down at her black watch and gave Jess an

apologetic look. "Sorry, but I need to finish setting up before everyone arrives. Feel free to explore the room. Oh, and the paintings are dry if you wanted to take yours with you. You created something powerful and should be proud."

Jess's cheeks grew warm at the praise. "Thank you." Ronobe moved away to gather supplies and Jess picked a stool on the far side of the table where she could see everyone entering the room. Inspired by one of the items in the bin, she used the notebook and pencil at her station to sketch an idea for her project.

Once the session got started, Jess brought her idea to life. Her goal was to create a necklace from overlapping triangles. Each one pressed with a different pattern. The largest triangle in the center was deep blue. Then three more triangles moved up at a diagonal from each side, getting smaller as they went. Deep blue, then true blue, lavender-blue, purple, and violet.

"That's very striking."

Jess jumped. She looked down at Lucia's feet. "I don't see any bells yet."

Lucia laughed. "Sorry. I forgot how easily you startle."

"It's okay. I'm nearly finished but I don't know how to make the rest of the necklace. How do I attach a chain?"

Ronobe walked over. "We've got chain and clasps. Just make a small hole in each corner where you'll want the screw eyes. Once it's baked, we can affix the rest."

"Thank you."

Ronobe walked away and Jess made the little holes as suggested. When she was finished, she sat upright on her stool and tried to rub out the ache in her lower back where she'd been hunched over for nearly an hour.

"You know, Jake has some cream he can give you that will help with those little aches. You should pick some up before you head back to your cabin. Don't forget that the spa offers massages as well."

She gave Lucia a grateful smile. "Thanks. What are you up to? Did you come to check on the art class on a day you knew we weren't using a medium that could ruin your shirt?"

"Not at all. I actually stopped in to ask if you'd like to change your shell collecting excursion for a late-night stargazing experience."

Jess grimaced. "I've never been one to look at the stars."

"Not even if it involves a carafe of sangria and a *personal* guide to name all the constellations for you?"

Suddenly, Lucia's offer sounded a lot more intriguing. "Are we actually talking about stargazing here, or something more private?"

Lucia lowered her voice. "Which would you prefer?"

Jess did an internal happy dance because damn it, she *did* deserve to be happy. Conscious of other guests in the room, she whispered her response. "Definitely private."

"Well then. How about I pick you up in a golf cart at seven. If you'd like to skip dinner at the main building, I can arrange a picnic basket. We'll go to my favorite place on the island to watch the constellations. I'll make a star lover out of you before the night is over."

She smirked. "It sounds wonderful and I'll hold you to that promise."

"Until then." Lucia gave her a little two-finger salute and made her way over to speak with Ronobe before leaving the classroom again.

Jess put the tray containing her project on the bench that ran along one wall of the room before returning to her station to clean up the rest. She couldn't tamp down her excitement for later if she tried and knew she'd need a distraction. First stop after cleanup would be the main lobby for a mimosa or two, and then Jess thought she'd head for the pool for a few hours to read. Anything to distract herself from their impending date that evening.

She paused in wrapping up the clay like Ronobe showed them at the beginning of the hour. Date. She was going on a date later. Jess felt equal parts anxiety and excitement. It had been a long time but with any luck, maybe they'd end the night with more than sangria on their tongues. Jess shook her head. "From my lips to the goddess's ears." She wasn't religious but liked thinking that if there was a higher power of creation, surely, they had to be a woman, right?

To give credit where it's due, the mimosas were some of the best Jess had ever tasted. And lunch was lighter that day. She chose chicken salad and fruit. The rest of the afternoon passed in a blur. Jess finished one book and started another at the pool but couldn't begin to explain what either was about. She took great care showering and shaving her legs, spent some time lamenting her fat belly and thighs, and agonized over what would be the best outfit for the evening. She wanted something that was the perfect mix of comfortable and sexy, without making her seem easy. Romance was hard.

****

Jess had only ever seen Lucia in two different outfits. To say she was surprised when she opened her door would be an understatement. Gone was the usual business pairing of tapered black slacks and crisp white dress shirt. Instead, Lucia wore a pair of lightweight, cream-colored cotton capris, and a white linen boat neck Henley. Both made her skin appear even darker.

"Wow. You look amazing."

"So do you."

Jess's cheeks warmed because she knew it was impossible to match Lucia's good looks. She'd tried though. Jess wore her favorite black cargo shorts that came down to mid-thigh and made her legs look more muscular than normal. They had a high, elastic tummy-controlling waist. The shirt was a soft red V-neck that was tighter across the shoulders and loose near her waist. She remembered Lucia saying that red and black were her favorite colors.

Lucia glanced at her watch. "Are you ready?"

"Definitely."

They got into the golf cart and Lucia took them back to the main resort road. But instead of heading toward the airport, she went in the opposite direction. She glanced at Jess. "I noticed you weren't limping. How is your ankle?"

"I'd say it's good as new. I was pretty surprised this morning, but Doctor K said it was a light sprain and I remember how many times ice treatment worked wonders for me when I played softball. I'm just glad I didn't get stuck on crutches for the remainder of my vacation."

Lucia gave her a soft smile. "Me too. Speaking of your vacation, your request slip to extend the two weeks to four was received at the office. We already have your credit card on file so there is nothing else you need to do except relax and enjoy everything we have to offer for the rest of the month."

"That sounds like heaven. Thanks."

"I'm not sure about that. You still have the three class a day requirement and need to follow resort rules whether you stay two weeks or more. As far as the approval, I'm afraid you don't owe me any thanks. All the guest logistics are farther up the chain than resort manager. My job is merely to keep this place running to its fullest potential and take personal responsibility for all the guests' experience."

Jess rolled her eyes and playfully responded. "Merely, she says. Don't undersell yourself. I've seen how busy you are most of the time, and how much you legitimately seem to value everyone here." She paused as the cart bumped along. "For that matter, everyone else has that same drive and attention to detail. It must be a pretty amazing place to work."

Lucia turned them onto a narrow-paved path that made its way uphill through thick, tropical trees. "We're a family here as much as coworkers. Don't get me wrong, we're all far from perfect."

"Who isn't?"

"True. What I mean is that none of us are angels but my staff here at the resort are good folks who are great at what they do. I couldn't ask for a better team." Lucia clasped Jess's hand and gave it a little shake while she was speaking.

Since Lucia didn't release her hand, Jess naturally kept holding on. It would be rude to drop it, right? "I think that's pretty great for you. Not everyone is lucky to work with such a competent team." She looked around as they made their way farther up the hill. There wasn't much to see but trees and thick undergrowth. "Where are we going?"

"Just wait."

Jess opened her mouth, but no words emerged when they reached the top of the hill and broke free from the trees. There, in the middle of the clearing, was a two-story, minimalist house made of glass, concrete, steel, and some sort of timber. It was breathtaking.

"Holy shit. This place is gorgeous! You live here?" Lucia nodded. "By yourself?"

That elicited throaty laughter. "Yes. Now, let me show you the best part." Lucia pulled the cart up close to the house into a spot that appeared to be made for it. She led Jess toward the main entrance.

"There are so many windows. Is this even up to construction code in a tropical location? Don't you get hurricanes or tsunamis or whatever?"

Lucia laughed again. "Trust me, this place is as safe as you can get." She pointed out recessed sections that ran along the tops of all the glass panels. "Every window has steel shutters that can be lowered for protection. All I have to do is flip the switches inside."

"What if you lose power?"

"It's a smart home with a hybrid power system. If you remember from the brochure, the island is powered via solar and wave generators. Not only that, but nearly all buildings have wall batteries that we can run off in the event something happens to the underground power lines."

Jess shook her head in awe and followed Lucia through the door. "You've really thought of everything here."

"Trust me, it's mostly my father. He's very...thorough."

"You've never had any ideas for improvement?"

Lucia turned on the lights in the kitchen and set the basket onto the counter. "Well..." Her cheeks held the faintest hint of a blush. "I was the one who implemented the battery packs and wave generators. It was previously powered by solar arrays and gas generators, and a lot more rustic. I wanted to go full renewable."

There was something about Lucia's passion and drive when it came to the resort that Jess admired immensely.

After speaking with Kam earlier, she hoped that she could find some of the same regarding her own life. "I think it's great."

Lucia deflected the compliment by saying, "You know what else is great? Follow me." She picked up the basket and made her way to a set of stairs. Jess gamely followed along. The steps led up to a second floor that seemed as open as the lower level.

Jess glanced out the windows and gaped at the beautiful view over the treetops. She could see quite a bit of the island, as well as the surrounding ocean. She knew larger hills were on the other side of the resort, but this one was still pretty impressive. "Wow, this is gorgeous. I'm not sure what I'd do if I woke to this sight every morning."

"I'd like to say you never get used to it but to be honest, after years of the same thing, you do kind of forget what you have." Lucia glanced at her watch. "We're running out of time. One more level. How's the ankle?"

"It's fine."

They followed the stairs up two more short flights until they came to a door that exited onto a flat rooftop patio filled with comfortable furniture, tables, and plenty of greenery.

"I don't care what you say. I'd never get tired of this."

Lucia chuckled and placed the basket on a low table. "Never is a long time." She removed a sealed jug of sangria and poured them both glasses. "Care to watch the sunset with me? After, we can turn on the electric torches and eat dinner, then I'll show you something truly amazing."

Jess accepted the glass. "Lead the way."

They ended up sitting on a cushioned couch facing the setting sun. A warm breeze ruffled Jess's short hair and carried with it the smell of salt and sweet coconut. Closer still was the heat of Lucia pressed against her side and that delightful scent that belonged to the woman herself. It was more intoxicating than any of the delicious drinks she'd had on the island to date.

"What do you think?"

Jess answered quietly because she didn't want to ruin the mood. "I think this is one of the most amazing moments of my life." And it was. Jess didn't know if that made her sad, or lucky that she got to experience this at all. Perhaps both.

Lucia's voice was nearly a whisper on the wind. "I'll admit that being able to share this with someone whom I feel such a strong connection with is one of my more memorable moments as well." She turned away from the riot of colors in the sky to meet Jess's gaze. "Thank you."

The words were surprising. "You're thanking me? Why?"

"Because I appreciate your time and presence. I've rarely met someone who I find attractive on a multitude of levels."

"I—" The words got caught in a ball of emotion and Jess cleared her throat. "I don't understand why you're attracted to me. It feels like a cosmic joke when I think about it too hard."

Lucia pressed her lips together, then tilted her head. "You want reasons?"

Jess laughed self-consciously. "I mean, now I just sound desperate, like I'm fishing for compliments."

"It's okay. We've all got fears and past trauma and if explaining why I feel the way I do helps alleviate some of your fears, I'm more than willing." Lucia paused as if to collect her thoughts. Jess held her breath.

"To start, yes, I find you physically attractive. You've also got a dry sense of humor and an emotional depth that you don't find in many people. You feel things deeply, no matter how much you try to hide it." Lucia grew more animated as she described all her reasons and Jess sucked in a surprised breath. "And the painting, wow. You've got a creative mind and excel at bringing thought and feeling to life."

To say Jess was shocked would be an understatement. She expected a short declaration about Lucia finding her cute or something equally banal, but nothing like the flood that just washed over her. "I...I'm not even sure what to say to all that. Thank you?"

Lucia fidgeted for a second then she met Jess's gaze. "I'll admit that I know more about you than most people on first meeting because of my role here. I've read everyone's files and the questionnaires they filled out.

Jess remembered some of the information she had to provide and was a little mortified. "Oh, Goddess."

A warm hand closed around her wrist and she was the recipient of another of Lucia's heartfelt smiles. "It's all good, I promise. But what it all boils down to is that there is something about you that draws me more than I've felt in ages. I'm glad I get to spend this time with you."

That was something Jess could relate to. "We're on the same page. I'm not sure where the future will lead because I am only here for a limited time. But, Lucia... I don't want to let this go. I think I'll regret it for the rest of my life if I don't explore whatever this connection is we share."

For the first time since Jess arrived on the island, Lucia appeared hesitant. "Are you sure? Even if we part ways at the end of your stay, I couldn't bear it if you hated me."

"I'm certain." She considered some of the other topics she'd touched on with Kam. She leaned closer and took both Lucia's hands into hers. "I promise that I'll let you know if it becomes too much, okay?"

Lucia swallowed and she gave Jess a radiant smile. "Wonderful. Now, what do you say we eat the meal chef prepared for us?"

Jess looked up at her and winked. "Well, I am pretty hungry." She immediately felt stupid at her lame attempt to flirt but took comfort in the fact that Lucia sucked in a surprised breath before she licked her bottom lip. Maybe Jess wasn't so out of practice after all.

# Chapter Seven

Dinner was light but filling. Despite Jess's innuendo, all they did was talk while eating. Lucia asked about Jess's friends and her day-to-day routine in St. Seren. Lucia seemed fascinated by what she called normal life and had a million questions.

"Why are you so curious? I can assure you that my life is pretty boring."

"It's different. The island is truly a paradise but it's also stagnant. Things rarely change for good or bad."

Jess's attention caught on the word stagnant, and she considered the concept that even folks who seemed like they had perfect lives could also feel stuck in a rut. "Maybe you just need a vacation, uh, from this vacation paradise."

Lucia laughed. "Maybe you're right. Perhaps I could visit St. Seren."

Jess's cheeks grew warm thinking about Lucia coming to Michigan. It was fueled by equal parts interest and embarrassment. What would the goddess next to her even think of Jess's small house with her two acres ending at the metro park border? How would she react to Jess's friends? Or worse yet, what would Jess's friends think of Lucia? They'd probably say she was way out of Jess's league.

She was startled from her thoughts by a light touch on her wrist. The gesture was a familiar one from Lucia. "Hey, I was only joking. I didn't mean to make you uncomfortable."

"Oh, you didn't. I mean, well, I make myself uncomfortable most of the time. I got lost in my thoughts for a minute, but I guarantee that if you ever find yourself on my doorstep, I'll show you all the best parts of St. Seren. Though," she conceded. "I'd probably grin like an idiot first and ask how long you plan on staying."

Lucia leaned across the small table and lowered her

voice. The warmth of her breath caressed the edge of Jess's ear, causing a full body shiver. "I think that if I ever found myself on your doorstep, then I've already seen the best part."

There was no way that comment left Jess unaffected. She squeezed her thighs together and sighed. "You're pretty charming when you want to be."

"And you're charming regardless."

Jess rolled her eyes because that was ridiculous. "Should we clean this up so you can get to what you promised me?" While she was incredibly turned on, a state she found herself in nearly every second she was around Lucia, she also didn't want to rush into sex. She'd never been like that and wasn't about to start just because she was on some tropical freaking island with a practical Amazonian goddess across from her. On second thought, what was wrong with her head?

Lucky for Jess, Lucia accepted the pivot for what it was, and they cleared the remnants of dinner back into the large basket in short order. Then Lucia poured the last of the sangria into their glasses and led Jess to the far side of the roof where there was a large, expensive-looking telescope.

"This looks fancy. I don't want to break it."

Lucia smiled and pulled a remote from her pocket. "Trust me, you won't break it." She hit one of the buttons on the remote and every light shut off, bathing the pair in darkness. There was no moon in sight and the sky had filled with a sea of stars in the nearly two hours past sunset.

"Look up and tell me what you see."

Jess tilted her head so she could follow the line of Lucia's pointed finger. "Easy. It's one of the only constellations I know, besides the big dipper. Orion."

Lucia aimed the telescope and peered down into the view finder. Once she seemed satisfied, she stepped back and waved Jess closer. "Now look through the telescope and discover the world inside what you've always known."

"Why is the eye thing facing down, instead of at the end? I guess I've only ever thought of telescopes like one long tube that you hold up to see boats coming in or something."

Lucia snickered. "While a spyglass is a type of telescope, the modern ones are much more useful. And the eyepiece is set in a place that makes it more comfortable for use. Light comes in the top and reflects from a primary mirror to a secondary mirror, which brings the image to your eye."

That seemed simple enough. Jess moved closer and peered into the eyepiece. The sight took her breath away. "It's beautiful. What part is this?" She pulled back and gazed up at the sky again.

Lucia moved so she was pressed against Jess's back. She raised her finger to point again. "Notice how the belt is nearly vertical?"

Jess nodded and she tried her hardest not to lean into the warm body behind her.

"What you just saw through the telescope was the Orion Nebula. It's one of the brightest nebulae and visible to the naked eye in the night sky. But the beauty really shines when you peer at it through the telescope."

"That's pretty cool."

"I'm glad you like it. I'm going to show you Betelgeuse next."

Jess snorted. "Like the movie?"

Lucia smiled and shook her head. "Funny."

"Sorry. I warned you that I'm a bit of a smartass, and not very into staying up late at night just to look into the sky."

"And I promised I'd make a convert out of you." She pointed above them. "This particular star is one of the two brightest in the Orion constellation. It's near the upper left corner." She adjusted the telescope and Jess looked through the eyepiece.

"It's so red."

"Well, it's a red supergiant. Betelgeuse is actually a thousand times bigger than the sun. If it were in place of our sun, it would be large enough to engulf Jupiter."

Jess's jaw dropped open. "Shit." Never once had she found stars, space, or anything like it attractive. But she could honestly say that listening to Lucia recite astronomy facts was pretty hot. Maybe stargazing wasn't going to be so stupid after all. "Okay, you've sold me. What else have you got?"

They spent the next few hours looking at a multitude of twinkling stars, a few galaxies, and one more nebula. It was an entirely new world of beauty above that Jess had never given a second thought to. "What got you into—" Their evening came to a halt rather abruptly with a jaw-cracking yawn from Jess. She felt her cheeks warm, not wanting Lucia to think she was bored with her company. "Sorry. I'm not sure why I'm so tired."

Lucia looked down at her watch and frowned. "Probably because it's just after midnight. How have you been sleeping?"

Jess thought about it. "Great, actually. I thought I'd have trouble with the time difference but I acclimated pretty fast. Must be the fresh air and activity." She yawned again and tried to cover it with the back of her hand. "Ugh, shit. I'm sorry. Now I feel bad because I've stayed so late. I can just take the golf cart back by myself so you don't have to leave—oh, damn. Then how will you get to the resort tomorrow?" She scrambled to come up with a solution that wouldn't inconvenience Lucia.

"Hey, it's fine. I invited you over, remember?" Lucia removed the remote from her pocket and turned the LED torches back on but left the rest of the lights off. It was ridiculously romantic with the moon starting to rise above the horizon.

It was hard to stay worried in the face of such a setting, coupled with Lucia's kind presence and sheer magnetism. "True. I just didn't want to be a bother."

"You're not a bother. I promise." Lucia rubbed her bottom lip in thought, then startled Jess who had been a little too focused on the lip in question when she spoke. "Feel free to say no, but I have a spare room that you're welcome to. I know it would mean an early morning tomorrow, but I can take you back to your cabin on my way in."

"Hmm." Jess wasn't expecting that particular suggestion and tried to analyze Lucia's motivations.

Lucia tilted her head. "What is it?"

"I guess I'm surprised you didn't offer your own bed. Isn't that where all this was leading?" As much as she liked Lucia, Jess still carried a healthy dose of distrust for anyone that appeared interested. It was self-preservation at its finest. She didn't like feeling that way, but it was a hard habit to break.

"No."

Oh. Maybe she'd read her wrong after all and Lucia wasn't attracted in that way. Jess's heart pounded in her chest. "Fuck. I think I misread—"

"You didn't." Lucia held out her hands palm up and Jess took the invitation to grasp them. "I didn't lie. I am attracted to you, interested in you, and I've enjoyed tonight more than you can know. But I'm also trying to be respectful of the pace you said you prefer." She laughed. "I would gladly offer my own bed but I don't want you to regret it in the morning." Lucia pulled one hand away to scrub her face before meeting Jess's gaze. "I was being a gentlewoman."

It might be one of the nicest things anyone had ever done or said. Jess felt bad for each unkind thought and remark she'd directed toward Lucia in her first few days on the island. "I—I appreciate that. And I think I owe you an apology."

"It's okay—"

"No, it's not. I'm sorry that I made assumptions about you from the moment I got to the resort. I arrived with a major attitude that I'm learning was extremely negative and unhealthy. Thank you for understanding and looking past my bitchiness."

"Jess," Lucia sighed. "If you try to pet a wounded animal and they snap at you, do you blame the animal?"

"No. I suppose I wouldn't."

"I think it's my turn to apologize because I've got you at a disadvantage when it comes to our interactions. "I had an inkling about what I was getting myself into before you even arrived. That's not to say I was at all prepared when meeting you in person. Believe it or not, all that fire and personality, as well as those dimples, hit me in a place that's long been untouched. I've been inexplicably drawn from the moment I first saw you."

Fear. Jess's first emotion at that admission was anything but what she wanted. Despite the fact that Lucia had already said as much before dinner, this was closer and more visceral. She too felt drawn to Lucia since their first meeting and wondered what it would all mean when she had to go home at the end of her vacation. Was she just setting herself up for a broken heart? Lucia started to pull her hands away when Jess didn't answer so she tightened her grip. "I promise that I feel the same as you. I think that's why I was such an asshole. I just assume everyone who is fit, attractive, and so put together would look down on me. I've found that it's easier to reject people first, before I get rejected."

Lucia pulled her closer until Jess was forced to tilt her head up to look into the other woman's dark eyes. "Jess?"

"Yeah?"

"Does this feel like rejection to you?" There was no time to offer an answer before Lucia swallowed her breath like it was ambrosia. They stood in the flickering torchlight, shadows dancing all around them on the rooftop. Lucia began pulling away and Jess couldn't have that. She surged forward and was rewarded with a supple tongue parting her lips as well as a firm squeeze on her ass where Lucia's hands had wandered into sexy time territory.

They broke apart after too many minutes, yet at the same time not nearly enough. Jess blew out a breath and ran a hand through her short hair. "Jesus!"

"Was not the one kissing you." They both burst into laughter at the unexpected comment.

"No, definitely not. Something tells me that if Jesus were real, he wouldn't be so handsy."

Lucia snickered and pulled Jess into an embrace. "I like that you make me smile so easily."

Jess gazed up at her. "You do?"

Another sigh. "I'm not just worried about your feelings and emotions. I fully admit that being so drawn to you, to someone who is as impermanent as a guest at the resort, has the power to... I don't know. I haven't felt this way so quickly in a very long time."

"Yeah," Jess admitted. "I was thinking the same thing."

Lucia looked up at the stars, then back down to Jess. Her expressive eyes nearly took Jess's breath away. "But it's worth risking for me. It's worth bending the rules here if it's something you're interested in as well."

It's not like she was saying anything Jess wasn't already thinking. But it did make Jess stop and take stock. Realistically she had a little more than three weeks left at the resort. Was pursuing some sort of short-term relationship with Lucia worth how she'd feel after? What was that saying? It's better to have loved and lost than never to have loved at all. Even though they weren't discussing love, the sapphics were nearly all the same in Jess's experience. Emotions happened fast once the sex got started. But was it worth the risk?

"Jess?"

Startled, Jess met Lucia's worried gaze. "Yes?"

"What are you thinking about?"

Fuck it. Kam and Shell were right, she deserved to be happy. It was stupid to continue through life expecting everyone else to be worth no more than that one person who thought she was worth less. She smiled back at Lucia and tightened her embrace. "I'm thinking about how much I'd regret walking away and never kissing you again." She shrugged. "I'm thinking that you're worth the risk and we'll deal with any fallout when it happens."

As if to seal the promise they'd both made, they kissed again until Jess was forced to pull away and stifle another yawn. "Oh my god, that's embarrassing."

"It's fine. After all, a yawn was what prompted this entire discussion and I don't know about you, but I feel better about where we stand."

"I do, too. Now, is that offer for a bed still good? Because I'm dead on my feet right now. Turned on, but too exhausted to do anything about it even if the offer were for your own bed."

They laughed and Lucia stepped back and held out her arm. "Sure. I have some toiletries and light sleep clothes you can use as well."

"Oh, you don't have to bother with the clothes. I sleep in the nude." Jess took a lot of pleasure in the little stumble she caused with her words.

****

Hours later, Jess woke from a sound sleep in Lucia's spare room. She checked her smart watch. "Witching hour." The bed was one of the most comfortable she'd ever slept on. There weren't any odd noises in the house, but something pulled Jess out of a string of weird dreams. She was thirsty so thought maybe that could be the cause. It seemed weird to pull on her underwear and V-neck shirt in the middle of the night, but it would probably be weirder to wander around someone else's house naked, looking for a glass of water.

Jess quietly made her way downstairs to the open first level where she knew the kitchen to be. She stopped in the middle and stared at the array of cabinets. "Eeny, meeny, miney, moe..."

"Are you looking for something or just naturally curious about other people's kitchens?"

"Holy fucking shit!" Jess jumped and spun around, catching sight of Lucia's silhouette framed in the moonlight that was streaming in through all the windows. She leaned back against the counter while dramatically clutching her chest. Jess took a few deep breaths and willed her racing heart to calm. "Bells, dammit."

Lucia laughed and made her way to the kitchen. "Hard to wear bells when I'm not even wearing socks.

Jess moved her gaze down to take in the wiggling toes. She was fine until her traitorous eyes made their way back up smooth, toned legs. Heat suffused her face, lower body, and practically everywhere else. Lucia stood in front of her wearing nothing but white panties and a thin, white tank top. "Oh, God."

"Also, not him."

That broke some of the sexual tension and both women burst into laughter. Jess averted her eyes once she got control of herself and gestured in Lucia's direction. "But seriously though, are you trying to kill me?"

That only made Lucia shake her head and chuckle. "Don't you know? Here at Paradise Island Self-Help

Resort, we're only in the business of saving people. Besides, I'm wearing more clothes than you said you sleep in. Talk about giving me something to think about while trying to nod off." She paused. "Did I wake you? I tried to be quiet coming downstairs."

"No. I had odd dreams about being in a hospital that was also my work, and all my coworkers came to visit me. Then I was staring at a man who turned into a donut and started singing. It was just a series of weirdness after that, but I'm not sure why I woke. I realized how thirsty I was once I was up."

"Weird dreams?"

"Yeah, not nightmares but not great either. I was also dreaming about my ex, Beth. She was—" Jess shook her head as if she could shake all the thoughts of that disaster free. "I don't want to think about my ex. It's just that our conversation earlier must have stirred up some things in my head. Anxieties, maybe. What about you?"

Lucia appeared startled. "Me?"

"Yeah. You were awake when I came down. Is something wrong?"

"No. I think I'm having similar thoughts. My last relationship didn't end the way yours did, but that's not to say it wasn't disappointing in its own way. It's been a long time since I got close with anyone, not wanting to make any connections when I couldn't meet all my heart's desires."

Jess sucked in a breath. "Oh. And now?"

"Well, I suppose it's better to have a partial meal than no food at all. Lobster without the steak if you will."

"Am I lobster now?"

Lucia tapped her chin with an exaggerated motion. "Let's see, tender, juicy, delicious—"

Jess groaned and gave Lucia's shoulder a shove. "Stop already. That's awful but I'll forgive you if you show me where the glasses are so I can get some water."

"It's a deal." Lucia held out her hand and Jess gave it an exaggerated shake with a goofy grin.

A few minutes later, they'd both sated their thirsts. "You think you can sleep now?"

Jess took stock of her body and felt strangely keyed

up. "Honestly, I don't know. Apparently, I only get tired when you're holding me. Sorry again about that."

Lucia grinned. "If you promise to keep your clothes on, you can join me in my bed. That way I can hold you and you'll be sleepy enough to finish your night."

"Is this another deal that we need to shake on?"

"It can be."

The thunk of the glass hitting the countertop sounded especially loud in the quiet house. "No deal necessary. I accept." They started walking toward the stairs when Jess stopped, and Lucia stopped with her. She wasn't sure how to admit the next part without coming across as dismissive. "It's weird how comfortable I am around you. It's rare I feel this way about anyone, let alone someone who I'd never even heard of a week ago." Shell would say it was a miracle she'd opened up to a stranger.

The smile she received from Lucia removed all worries. "You say weird but I think it's kismet."

"Destiny? That seems kind of deep."

Lucia shrugged. "We all have our beliefs. Now, let's get to bed. The moonlight waits for no one, and I don't want you tired for your activities tomorrow."

Jess grinned and waved for Lucia to go ahead of her up the stairs. Was it to look at her ass in those panties? Maybe. Jess discreetly ogled as she responded. "Some activities more than others."

Lucia turned and winked at her. Caught out, Jess's cheeks burned the rest of the way to the second floor.

After a trip to the bathroom for both, Jess snuggled into Lucia's side. She couldn't remember the last time she spent the night with someone, with sex or no sex involved. It was nice. She drifted off thinking about ringing bells.

****

Jess woke alone the next morning and she wondered if it were all a dream. Then she looked around and realized she was actually in Lucia's bedroom. She smelled coffee and smiled. A melodious voice called from somewhere downstairs. "I know it's early but I made us a quick breakfast before I need to head back to the main building."

Jess dressed and stopped to use the bathroom and gifted toiletries before walking downstairs. Lucia didn't mess with the big table that was set apart from the kitchen space. Instead, she had the plates of food sitting on the countertop that ran along the window side of the long island.

Seeing the crispy bacon, eggs over hard, and iced milk, Jess looked at Lucia in shock. "How did you know what I like?"

Lucia blushed. "I may have called and asked what your usual breakfast order is. I hope that's okay."

Jess stepped closer and gave her a kiss on the cheek. "It's more than okay. Thank you."

Lucia snorted. "Oh, now you're thanking me for doing my job?"

Once again, Jess felt bad because she remembered giving Lucia and Lahash so much grief about that exact thing. Then she noticed the smirk threatening Lucia's full lips and shoved her shoulder. "I've already said sorry. Do I have to keep apologizing?"

"That depends on your method of apology."

"The only thing you'll get now is my wish for you to suffer an eternity of torment being Rick-rolled by someone singing bad karaoke."

Lucia made a face. "Never mind. That's weirdly specific and decidedly less fun."

Breakfast continued with plenty of teasing and laughter. Jess had to concede that it was officially the longest, and best, date she'd ever had. And they hadn't even slept together. Well, slept-slept together.

"What are you thinking about that put that look on your face?"

She glanced up to see Lucia watching her intently. "Oh, uh, just that this is the best date I've ever had." Lucia tilted her head and Jess panicked. "I mean, I assumed this was a date. If it's not, then—"

"Definitely a date." If the words didn't satisfy her, the kiss certainly did. Lucia pulled away and Jess could only give her a stupid grin. She was so screwed but what an adventure it would be.

****

They returned to the resort thirty minutes later and Lucia drove Jess right to her cabin. Jess looked around and let out a sigh of relief. "Looks like we got lucky and nobody is up yet. Strange not even seeing the groundskeepers."

Lucia blinked at her then shrugged. "Eh, it happens. We'll call this a win."

"Will I see you later?"

"If you'd like."

Jess sighed and looked around again. "I don't suppose we'd be able to eat lunch together, would we? Not if we're keeping this a secret."

"There is nothing saying we can't be friends, Jess."

"Oh."

"How about this. One of the activities today is listed as A Culinary Adventure and put on by Chef Azazel himself. I've tagged along plenty of times because there is something about the preparation of unique foods that intrigues me."

Jess didn't have a diverse palette but her mental state since coming to the island prompted her to make more choices to live adventurously. "That sounds great. While my counselling and art sessions are standing appointments, I never got a chance to fill out a card for the third activity. Will it be too late to sign up?"

"No worries. Leave the logistics to me. Do you know where the kitchen entrance is located?"

Jess nodded.

"Good. Meet me there when you're finished with Ronobe's class. I'll even have an apron waiting for you."

She growled and it came out sounding more like a disgruntled kitten. "Seriously? My assholery is going to follow me forever, isn't it?"

Lucia snorted. "Not forever. It's a good thing you have such a cute face. It makes you easy to forgive."

"Oh, and yours isn't?"

Lucia hummed and shook her head. She looked around, leaned forward, and gave Jess a quick kiss then jumped in the golf cart. Lucia winked. "See you later, Tiger," before speeding away down the path leading to the main building.

# Chapter Eight

"Good morning, Jess. You seem in a chipper mood. Did you get a chance to work on those lists last night?"

At first Jess panicked, thinking she had forgotten about her assignment from their previous session. Then she remembered completing the lists while sipping her mimosa. She pulled out her phone. "Sorry, but I didn't write them on paper. I hope that's okay."

Kam smiled. "It's quite all right. After all, the lists are more for you. Would you care to share with me?"

His phrasing was odd. "Isn't that what I'm supposed to do? You're the one who gave me the homework."

"As I said, the task was for your knowledge and introspection. If you don't feel comfortable sharing, I will accept that."

"I don't mind telling you, but some of them seem stupid."

"Doubtful but continue please." He gestured toward her phone.

Jess looked down at her first list and grew sad. It represented the negative changes in her life and the beginning of that spiral that led to her current situation. "Let's see...I stopped playing all sports. Softball, volleyball, uh, bowling, and frisbee golf. I was even on a cornhole league for a few years but once Beth left, I lost my partner and didn't ask if anyone else wanted to join me."

Kam made a note. "And would you say you were passionate about sports?"

She shrugged. "I mean, not necessarily watching it, though I do love to catch the big games with my friends. But I'd played softball for more than twenty years. I started rec league just out of high school. I wasn't good enough to play college but I prefer the low pressure of community versus school teams. Bowling, I picked up when I had to quit playing volleyball."

"And did you quit all sports immediately after the

divorce, or did they fade away?"

Jess thought back five years. "We split in the fall, just after softball ended but right before bowling leagues began." She frowned. "We were also on the same bowling team so I quit that immediately. And normally I'd be raring to go every spring when softball season began but that following year—" She swallowed and looked out the window. "I'd put on ten pounds that winter and just didn't have the motivation to play when my old team asked."

"That sounds rather abrupt in the grand scheme of your breakup."

"Yeah."

She moved her gaze back inside the room and watched as Kam made another note. He looked up., "And you didn't pick up anything in the subsequent years?"

Jess shrugged. "I mean, once I'd stopped everything, I also stopped riding my bike. I gained more weight every year and after two years had gone by, I didn't feel like I had anything to offer on the field anymore."

He put his pen down. "Forgive my ignorance, but those community softball leagues, are they all the same skill level?"

Who hadn't heard of rec league softball? Non-lesbians, probably. It took effort, but Jess held onto a snarky response and just answered his question. "No, St. Seren is big enough that we have three leagues, A, B, and C. My team always played in B league. I've done A and B, but the middle league is definitely a better time."

"Why is that?"

"Well, A is super competitive and sometimes you don't have fun even if you win. But I've lost plenty of games in B league where both teams had a blast. It's a different atmosphere."

"And were you the best player in your league?"

The snort came unbidden. "Hardly! I was one of the cleanup hitters but my fielding skills were just okay. What difference does that make?"

"You said that not playing sports for a few years meant your physical fitness was less and you felt as though you didn't have anything to offer."

"Yeah."

"Did you think you were worse than all the other players on your team? Would you not be able to hit a ball while carrying more weight? Or throw?"

"Um," She paused, surprised that she never gave it much thought. She just quit and assumed she wouldn't be able to play again. "I don't know. I think it's like that one Newton law."

"You're talking about number one. An object at rest will remain at rest, and an object in motion will remain in motion and at a constant speed, blah, blah, blah. That one?"

"That's the one." She made a face. "You remembered more than I did."

"Are you saying that once you stopped playing, that it was easier to remain sedentary?"

As usual, his questions stirred up way more stuff than the answers themselves touched. She sighed. "I think there were a lot of reasons I didn't come back to softball. Bowling, cornhole, those were simple. Beth was my teammate and I wanted to be as far away from that stuff as possible. But softball..." Her breath hitched.

"Jess?"

She met Kam's soft gaze. "Yeah?"

"This is a safe and non-judgmental place. It's okay to be open and honest here."

"You know, it's funny you used the words safe place. Because that's kind of what softball was. I played with some of my closest friends. They were people I'd known forever it feels like, before and after Beth."

He picked up the pen again. "Did you think they wouldn't understand?"

"No. I knew they'd understand too well and I didn't want their pity. The first couple years were pretty dark. I wasn't in a good place emotionally. I ate my feelings and stopped doing all the stuff I thought was fun."

"Punishing yourself."

Jess shrugged. "Maybe. But it was also because I thought that if I came back to softball, I wasn't going to be the same person they remembered. I didn't want to let them down."

"That hardly seems fair."

His comment sparked a flame of anger. "What the hell does that mean?"

"You didn't give them a chance, simply made an assumption that you would be a disappointment. None of us are an island—"

"He said while sitting on an actual island."

Kam smiled at her joke but continued. "And there are points in our lives where we simply cannot go it alone. A crutch is a necessary tool. Only when you use it beyond actual need does it pose problems."

"I know." And the truth was, she did know. But that didn't stop the fear of how they'd see her, of being rejected yet again.

"Is there anything else you stopped doing after the divorce?"

Jess glanced back down at the forgotten phone in her hand and turned the screen on again. "I started going out with my friends less. But to be honest, my closest friends had a baby a few years ago so they rarely go out now. Other friends are coupled up and I felt like a third wheel tagging along. I stopped riding my bike to work because I didn't have the motivation to leave my bed early enough to do it."

"Does riding your bike take a lot longer?"

She scrubbed her face with the hand not holding the phone. Kam's questions sucked but she understood why he asked them. "That's the thing, it doesn't. Between traffic, and the bike lanes all around the city, it's an easy ride. Doing nothing every night became the norm and the lethargy kind of took over the rest of my life. The less active I became, the angrier I got, and it spiraled from there."

"It happens like that sometimes. Perhaps you're one of those people who needs a lot of activity for their mental health."

Jess closed her eyes and thought of all the years she'd lost to Beth's actions and her own reactions. "I'm pretty fucked up, aren't I?

"Not at all. There is nothing done that can't be undone at this stage. Let's start by discovering who you are, and the motivations behind your current state. After that, you can decide who you want to be."

Kam wrote down a few sentences and Jess wondered what exactly his notes said. Before she could question him about it, he moved the discussion along. "Let's put the things you've left behind aside for a moment. The other list I had you fill out should be all those things you've wanted to do but have never gotten or taken the opportunity to try."

"I'll give you this, you're right in that this was the easier of the two lists. The other one brought up a lot of not great memories. I mean, I'm probably too old to do this stuff but at least it's a more positive list."

He inclined his head slightly. "Go ahead."

"Well, I've always wanted a dog. I was too busy when I was younger then when I got together with Beth, she was allergic. After, I could barely take care of myself let along another living thing in my orbit."

"I don't see how that's unattainable, nor does your age preclude you from pet adoption. Carry on with your list."

"Let's see, I'd love to take cooking classes. I like those cooking shows on the Food Network." She made a face. "Even if they always make me hungry. Uh, I've always thought swing dancing was cool. Lessons would be fun, but my knees probably wouldn't agree. Maybe if I dropped some weight..." She lost her train of thought for a second imagining swing dancing with Lucia. Kam cleared his throat and she felt heat warm her cheeks. Luckily, he didn't ask why she got distracted. "Um, I'd like to see a few musicals, travel more, and take a hot air balloon ride."

He looked up from his notepad. "Your form said you were afraid of heights."

She nodded. "Oh, I am. But I think it would be beautiful. Take the paragliding I did the other day. I never in a million years thought I would have liked that, but Lucia helped me realize that a changed perspective could be beautiful."

"Interesting. And are you getting along with our resort manager? The friction between you two at the orientation meeting was obvious. Not to mention, the staff have to report on guests' progress and apparently, you two seemed tense on your snorkeling excursion."

Damn that blush. How was she going to keep her little

romantic exploration a secret when she couldn't control her own reaction to the mere thought of Lucia? "Uh, yeah. That's one of the people I was referring to when I said I was getting along with others better."

"What about your fellow guests?"

She rolled her eyes. "Most of them are grade A assholes."

"And what do you think their opinion of you would be?"

That elicited honest laughter. "Oh, I'm sure they'd say the same thing. But you know what?"

He shook his head.

"It's weird but I can already feel like I'm changing here. Maybe it's like the hot air balloon and I needed to distance myself from life back home to get perspective. I may have arrived an asshole but I don't want to be that person anymore because I don't like her and I'm pretty sure I never did."

Kam grinned and slapped a hand on each thigh. "That's excellent. You've cracked a code that many never even see. Nobody can change, evolve, or improve their place in life unless they want it. I know I've asked you this before, but do you want to be happy, Jess?"

"I think I do."

"And you want to do the work that will get you to the place you need to go?"

Ugh, the work. "It's going to suck but so did college and I got through that, so, yeah."

Kam glanced at his watch and stood. Jess looked down at her cell phone and wondered where the hour had gone.

"Jess, I think you've made great progress today. I do have another assignment for you before our next session."

"More lists?"

"No, this one is pretty easy, or maybe the hardest thing I've had you do."

Dread pooled in her belly. "And?"

"I want you to respond with kindness to one person you normally wouldn't."

"But what if they're mean to me? Or an ass—"

He shook his finger and smiled. "I didn't say you need to befriend them. Just...don't respond with anger. It's the first step toward getting your emotions under control and rewiring your brain to healthier habits."

Jess thought of all the people she'd had actual contact with since arriving on the island and groaned. This wasn't going to be easy but he did say it only had to be one person. "Fine. I'll try."

"That's all I ask. Now, I'm going to graciously give you four minutes back."

She snorted. "You're very kind, Doctor Kam. I can do so much with those minutes."

"Maybe you'll make some friends, yeah?"

"Riiight," Jess responded. Then she gave him a little salute and donned her bag before leaving his office.

****

Kam's four minutes gave Jess enough time to use the bathroom and try to remove the evidence of her tears. She hated the emotions her therapy session pulled to the surface but in a weird way, she did feel better with every day that went by at the resort. Jess was thinking about all the things that came up in therapy when she rounded the corner of the hallway containing the art room and ran right into the last person she wanted contact with. She grabbed Brittany by the arms to steady the smaller woman, but Brittany jerked herself from Jess's grasp.

"Watch where you're going, cow!"

"Listen, you b—" Jess immediately stopped speaking. Kam's words rolled over her and she pulled back and took a deep breath. Brittany also stepped back and eyed her warily. Jess held up her hands. "I'm sorry. You're right, I wasn't watching where I was going. I guess I was distracted by my session with Kam. It was—" She shook her head and drew in a shuddering breath.

"That good, huh?" In a weird turn of events, Brittany actually smiled. "I get it. I, um, my sessions with Doctor Berg are bringing up a lot of stuff for me I never considered before."

Jess sighed. "Yeah, it's been rough but good I think."

"Uh huh, pretty much. Anyway, I'm sorry I've been a

bitch. Doctor B says–" She made air quotes. "It's a defense mechanism that stems from my fear of rejection. Or whatever." She dropped her hands and Jess saw Brittany's cheeks pinken. "I don't know why the fuck I just told you that." She shuffled nervously.

"Hey, I get it. Kam says a lot, too, but it's been spot on so far. Apparently, I've been stuck and blaming everyone else for my self-doubts. So, I'm sorry for being bitchy, too." Jess scrubbed a hand over her face and gave Brittany a sheepish look. "God, we're a pair, huh?"

That elicited a giggle from Brittany and Jess thought maybe they'd reached a truce of sorts, based on their shared therapy trauma. Brittany gestured down the hall in the direction Jess had just arrived. "Anyway, I was just running to pee before class started so..."

Jess stepped out of the way. "Sorry."

The younger woman gave her a grateful smile and hustled around the corner.

Well, that went better than she thought it would.


****


Her hour of sketching in Ronobe's class practically flew by and Jess was ready to see what Lucia had in store for her with Chef Azazel. Lucia met her as soon as she pushed through the doors.

"There you are. Prompt I see."

Jess patted her gut. "Much like a Labrador, I'm food motivated." She looked around the bustling kitchen. "I'm learning to cook in the middle of all this...this, chaos?"

"Hardly. We're meeting Chef in the test kitchen. The regular kitchen crew can handle lunch for staff and guests without him. Come on."

Lucia led the way around the side of the busy kitchen to another exit. They walked down a short hallway until Lucia pushed through another swinging door. The kitchen inside was much smaller and quieter. Azazel was a little shorter than Lucia but shared her darker complexion.

He clapped his hands and smiled at their arrival. "Ah,

I see Lucia has brought with her the new chef-in-training. Excellent to have you here, Miss Jess." He held out a hand and Jess gamely shook it.

"Thank you for taking the time for this class. I'll admit that I'm okay at cooking most things but I'm no professional."

Azazel pointed a thumb at Lucia. "Better than this one. She never cooks at all."

Jess caught herself before she could rush to Lucia's defense. Blurting out that she makes a tasty breakfast is not the way to keep their more personal acquaintance a secret. Instead, she smiled. "Well, maybe she can learn something today, too."

Lucia snickered. "Maybe."

"Okay, I'm Azazel, as you already know. Introductions made, tell me what your best dish is."

Jess felt a little on the spot. "Besides Jell-O shots?"

"That is alcohol, no?"

"Yes. And I was kidding." She thought about it for a minute until she could come up with a dish that she was fairly proud of. "I used to make a mean lasagna."

Azazel tilted his head one way then grinned. "Did it throw rocks?"

"Uh—" His question threw her off guard and Lucia snickered. "What?"

"Your lasagna," He had a way of speaking that made him sound like an authentic Italian, but she didn't think he was. "You said it was mean."

Lucia full on laughed and Jess groaned at his terrible joke. "No, not mean. It was something I'd make when I had guests coming over for dinner years ago. It tasted awesome and everyone raved about it." She paused. "I haven't made it in forever but I can still remember how it tastes."

"Why did you stop making it?" That question came from Lucia.

Jess glanced toward Azazel and figured it wasn't too embarrassing to admit. "When my ex and I split up, I stopped having dinner parties at my place. After that, it was just easier to go to other people's houses and bring my famous shots. And it's silly to make a dish like lasagna for just one person."

Azazel touched her shoulder. "Loved food is always worth the effort, but I understand that perhaps one person doesn't want the same meal for many days in a row."

She nodded in agreement.

"How about this. I shall teach you an easy Italian dish, one you can tailor to a small number of guests."

"Oh?" Jess's ears perked up at that. She loved pasta but rarely indulged for multiple reasons. But she figured once in a while wouldn't be too bad for her post-menopausal waistline if it was delicious and homemade.

"*Si.*"

"What is it?"

"Today we shall make *Cacio e Pepe*, a dish that originated in Rome and contains only three ingredients."

Even Lucia looked surprised at that. "How?"

He wagged his finger. "I will explain as we go. First, I will warn you that for this particular cooking lesson, we will need more ingredients because you'll make the pasta from scratch. But it is a quick and easy meal option if you use the dried pasta from boxes."

He spoke about boxed pasta like it was something you'd scrape off the bottom of your shoe. Jess smirked. Perhaps it was to an Italian chef. "I'm game. Where do we start?"

Azazel waved toward the nearest wall where a row of white aprons hung on hooks. "First, proper kitchen protection. Neither of you have long hair so I won't ask you to pull it back. I'll bring the pasta ingredients to the prep station."

Chef Azazel walked them through the ingredients and steps a few minutes later. After he finished his explanation, Jess asked, "Wait, two different flours?"

"Yes. It is best with a fifty-fifty mix of finely ground and durum wheat flours. Now, pour your flour mixture onto the board and make a mound with a hole in the middle. This is where you put your eggs."

Jess performed each step called out by Azazel while Lucia either watched or fetched tools and ingredients. He explained that you could make good pasta in a stand mixer while she was kneading the dough and she nearly threw the ball at his face. Lucia clearly read the look on her face and hid a smile behind her fist. She wrapped the dough tightly to prevent drying and set it aside to rest.

"Next you will prepare the ingredients for the sauce. It is very easy."

"I thought you said there were only three ingredients. That implies easy."

He tutted, "Never assume less ingredients means less challenge or skill. Some of the easiest dishes can be the most difficult to prepare properly."

She gave him a curious look. "Like?"

"Scrambled eggs. It takes real skill to produce something that is light, fluffy, and moist. It's all about technique. Too much heat means a rubbery, dry texture. And if you use a whisk, they break down too much."

Jess had no clue there was a process behind something so stupidly easy. "Well, that's probably why my scrambled eggs suck. Good to know. Thanks, Chef." She looked at Lucia, who shrugged.

"I had no idea either but I'm going to try making scrambled eggs tomorrow to test it out. I should see if someone wants to be my taste tester…"

She left the statement open and Jess's face grew warm. It was obvious what Lucia implied. Breakfast that morning was tasty but would waking at Lucia's home a second night in a row be too soon? Would Lucia expect more than the simple night of sleep they'd had the previous evening?

"Miss, Jess, are you with us?"

"Erm, yes." Her face warmed again and she scrubbed her cheeks with her hands. Lucia snickered. "What?"

"You've got a little—" She reached up to wipe Jess's chin. "A little flour."

Jess groaned and turned back to the prep table, ready for more instruction from Azazel.

"First we start with pecorino Romano."

She finely grated it as directed while Lucia retrieved the peppercorns. After she finished with the cheese, Jess used an honest to gods mortar and pestle to grind up the peppercorns. She looked at Azazel when she was finished. "Now what?"

"Now you prepare the noodles."

Lucia brought over a pasta machine and Jess learned how to make proper pasta for the first time. She made handfuls of something Azazel called tagliolini but looked a lot like linguini to her. Then, he gestured toward two pans on the cooktop. One was a stainless-steel skillet and the other a cook pot filled with the boiling water Lucia had started a few minutes earlier. "Our Lucia has already salted. You may add. You will cook only halfway because the pasta will finish in the sauce."

The smell of black pepper filled the kitchen as the noodles cooked. "Now what?"

"Put a ladle of pasta water into your skillet with the pepper. Then add the pasta to the pan. Move it around with tongs and shake the pan to finish cooking. You want the starch to release."

She clumsily moved the pasta around. "Why? I was always told the starch was bad for you."

"Nonsense! That is the basis for the best sauces. Americans and their food ignorance. Well, except for you, Miss Jess. I appreciate your willingness to learn." He gave a disdainful sniff and she grinned at Lucia.

"Now, while the pasta is cooking, add a small bit of pasta water to your pecorino. Use a fork to mix it together until you make a paste."

"Done," she said a minute later.

"Good, good. Now set aside and check your pasta. You're looking for *al dente*."

"Firm, right?"

"*Sì.*"

Jess tested a noodle and nodded.

"Okay, now you remove the pasta from the heat." She did as directed. "Add the pecorino mix to the pasta pan and quickly stir with your tongs."

Another minute and Lucia leaned closer. "Ooh. That looks good."

Azazel pointed to the dish. "Yes. You see how the creamy consistency forms between the pecorino and the starchy liquid?"

Jess nodded and took a sniff and her stomach growled. "As good as it looks, it smells even better." With the dish thoroughly mixed, she looked over her shoulder at Azazel.

"Now what?"

Azazel grinned and clapped his hands once before rubbing them together. "Now we eat! Lucia, be a dear and fetch us three place settings while I slice some of the fresh bread that I made this morning."

All in all, it was the best pasta dish that Jess had ever eaten. She couldn't believe it was so simple. Well, if you discounted actually making your own freaking pasta. The rest was easy. She looked longingly at the last bite twirled around her fork. "I predict this will be a regular meal going forward. It's so light and the flavor is like nothing I've had before."

Chef nodded in agreement. "Yes, it is exceptional. You did quite well." He looked at Lucia, whose plate was already empty. "You see what you are missing when you refuse to come to any of my classes."

Lucia shrugged. "I guess I'll have to depend on Chef Jess to keep me in well-made Italian food."

He rolled his eyes. "*Leccaculo.*"

Jess had no idea what he called her, but Lucia snorted as she gathered the empty plates.

# Chapter Nine

Azazel went back to the main kitchen to check on his staff after they finished eating and cleaning up. That left Jess and Lucia alone in awkward silence. Jess saw a nearby bin full of dirty aprons and tucked hers inside. Lucia followed suit.

"So…that was more fun than I expected."

"I'm glad I could talk you into the class. You're a very good cook."

Jess felt her cheeks warm at the praise. It had been a long time since she'd heard anyone compliment her cooking. "Thanks, but it wasn't much. You heard Chef, there are only three ingredients and he talked me through every step." Lucia smiled and tucked a short strand of hair behind Jess's ear. She sucked in a breath at Lucia's nearness.

"I also heard him say that sometimes the easiest dishes were the hardest to make. Don't discount your achievements, no matter how insignificant they may seem." Lucia glanced around then moved so there was less than an inch between their lips. "I want to kiss you right now."

Jess held her breath for a few seconds, not expecting such a bold statement from a woman who wanted to keep their less-than-professional acquaintance a secret. She grew nervous, wondering yet again about Lucia's intentions. "Oh?"

Lucia brushed their lips together. "Is that okay?"

She didn't trust her voice. Instead, Jess surged forward and caught Lucia in a searing kiss that left them both panting once they separated a few minutes later. Jess licked her lips. "Wow. You taste delicious."

"I can assure you that how I taste is a direct reflection on the chef that's controlling the heat."

The innuendo wasn't lost on Jess, and she found herself wanting Lucia in a way she hadn't wanted anyone in a long time. "You know, this class filled my third requirement of the day."

"Is that so?" Lucia smirked and Jess grew annoyed because the other woman was going to make her ask.

"It is. I find myself with the rest of the day free and it's," Jess glanced down at her watch, "only a little after one. What time do you finish work?"

"Technically, I can get off whenever I like. I have an extremely under-used assistant manager who owes me one or twenty favors. Would you like to spend time together?"

Jess huffed. "Are you seriously asking me that?"

Lucia put up her hands. "Fine. Let me call Amy and let her know I'm taking the afternoon off."

"Won't she get suspicious?"

"Not at all. The upside to living in so secluded a location is that it's still a paradise island. She understands the notion of taking a little time to play now and again."

Jess sighed. "Must be nice."

"Eh, we've already discussed the pros and cons of this place. It can get stale after a while. As for the afternoon, would you like to take a bike ride around to the far side of the island? The trail has a great view of the ocean and the smaller islands farther out."

It had been years since Jess rode a bike. She didn't want to make a fool out of herself in front of someone she was attracted to, someone who admitted to being attracted to her in return. "I don't know..."

Lucia nudged her arm. "Come on, it'll be fun. The resort bikes are comfortable and easy to ride. There is a basket so you can bring one of the cameras."

"You're making it hard for me to say no."

"So, don't. Say yes instead. And after, if you're not opposed, we can go back to my place and I'll make you the only dinner I've mastered."

Jess gave her a curious look. "Which is?"

Lucia stepped back and crossed her arms. "I can't tell you. It would ruin the surprise. Are you interested or not?"

She conceded. "Fine. But I'm going to blame you if I can't walk tomorrow."

"Well then," Lucia grinned. "Maybe we should use the hot tub after dinner to make sure your leg muscles are properly loosened up."

They were standing in an air-conditioned kitchen, but Jess began sweating when she thought about how warm it would be to share a hot tub with Lucia. At least if she were going to die of heat stroke, she'd probably die happy. "Fine. You want to go now?"

Lucia glanced down at her black watch and hummed. "Give me half an hour to arrange the bikes and camera. I'll meet you outside your cabin at one forty-five."

"Okay." Jess was at a loss on how to part so she gave a little wave. "See you then." She turned to walk away but stopped at the sound of Lucia calling her name.

"Jess?"

"Yes?" She turned and her lips were caught once again in a steamy kiss. She pulled back with a gasp and touched her lips, then shook a finger at Lucia. "You're going to kill me. How will I pedal if you keep making my knees weak?"

"I'm sure you'll be fine. Until then." Lucia gave her a little salute then disappeared through the double doors back into the corridor, leaving Jess with a racing heart and her stomach whirling in anticipation.

****

Jess heard a quiet click from the cabin next door as she held up her own key to scan the lock. Each cabin had tall fronds that protected the front of the door from casual view from the side. They could still see the cabins across the path. She leaned back to see who it was because as far as she knew, Brittany was assigned to that one. It definitely wasn't Brittany because Jess had passed her in the main building minutes before.

It was the shifty guy from the bus ride to the resort. Stephen. Jess stepped closer to her door to hide and peeked through the fronds. He glanced around before sticking his hand into his pocket and scurrying away. That was odd behavior for anyone, but especially for someone coming out of a cabin that wasn't theirs. Maybe he and Brittany were more than friends and she'd given him her key.

Whatever was going on, it was none of Jess's business. A

few pleasant words outside art class didn't mean she and Brittany were suddenly friends. Jess shook her head and scanned into her own room.

The first thing she did was pee and check her appearance in the bathroom mirror. It wasn't her favorite outfit, but it would have to do. One thing Jess refused to do was compromise her comfort when doing any kind of sporting activity. And bike riding definitely counted, even if it was just casual. She debated on what to bring when she re-entered the main room. If they were ending the bike ride at Lucia's place, does that mean she should bring a change of clothing for dinner? An even better question was whether she'd be staying the night again.

She mulled over the dilemma before throwing all cares to the wind. What happened would happen and it didn't do any good to plan. After all, Lucia had a bathroom and a shower that Jess could use to clean up if any romance were to occur later.

Jess still had ten minutes before Lucia would arrive, so she checked the schedule for the next day. She'd signed up for an evening spa and massage as her third requirement. She'd need it if the bike ride wiped her out. And if the night happened to include a little vacation boom-boom, she'd definitely need it. After all, she'd gone without sex longer than she'd gone without riding a bike.

Her daydream of what Lucia would be like in bed was interrupted by a sturdy knock. She jumped before clearing her throat. "Just a second!" Jess fanned herself then went to the door and took one last look around her cabin. As a precaution, she had gathered all her valuables and locked them in the safe for when she'd be out. It seemed the best course of action given Stephen's behavior earlier.

Lucia stood on the other side of the door wearing deliciously tight bike shorts and a tank top. It was enough to make a straight girl swoon, let alone poor Jess. Two bikes rested on their kickstands just off the path. Both sported sweating water bottles in the holders, and one bike had a camera bag in the basket. Jess grew excited thinking about the adventure ahead.

Lucia smiled and gestured toward the bikes. "Ready?"

"Definitely. Maybe." She paused and grimaced. "I'm

pretty sure I am. I hope I didn't forget how."

That drew a laugh from Lucia. "Impossible. Riding a bike is like…well, riding a bike."

Jess walked over to the bike with a camera and shook her head before grabbing the handlebars and raising the kickstand. "That was pretty bad."

"It was, wasn't it?" Lucia mounted her own bike. "Well, you may not appreciate my humor, but I think you'll like this path. Don't fall behind," she called out, after she pedaled away.

"Son-of-a—" Jess raced to catch up.

****

As promised, the afternoon was one of the best Jess had experienced in a while. She'd missed the freedom of a good ride and was surprised to discover that her usual aches and pains were practically non-existent. Jess had heard that warmer climates were good for things like arthritis but had never experienced it herself. Until now. Maybe moving away from Michigan wouldn't be such a hardship as she grew older.

The last overlook they visited was one of the prettiest sights Jess had ever seen. She took photo after photo of the blue-green surface of the bay far below, as well as the small islands dotting the water beyond.

"Was I right?" Lucia walked up and wrapped an arm around Jess's shoulders once she'd put the camera away. They hadn't seen anyone else in hours. She assumed most would stay closer to the resort if they weren't doing an official excursion.

Jess leaned into her. "You were definitely right. Thank you for suggesting this. I didn't realize how much I missed riding. It's invigorating."

"That it is."

She glanced up at Lucia. "I, uh, stopped riding after my divorce. It's something I've been speaking with Kam about, and he suggested I make an effort to get back into those things I used to love. He was right."

"I'm glad I could help get some of your joy back. Are you okay to go a little farther? My house isn't much beyond this section." She pointed to the west and Jess could just make out Lucia's home shining in the sun through the trees of the tall plateau they were on.

"I'm going to be pleasantly sore tomorrow but sure."

"I can treat you to a leg massage later if you ask nicely."

Jess looked up to see Lucia smirking. "Ask nicely, hmm? Let's see how dinner is before I offer to let you put your hands on me." Lucia sucked in a breath and Jess was proud of the reaction she'd elicited. Two could play at Lucia's particular game of innuendo.

"You may be disappointed in the meal. It's not exactly up to resort standards."

"Didn't you say it was the only one you mastered?"

"I did. But that doesn't mean it's any good." They both laughed.

Jess walked over and mounted her bike. "I'm not worried. I've worked up quite the appetite and I think I'll appreciate anything of yours I put into my mouth."

Lucia's cheeks darkened and Jess knew she'd scored another win. "Fine. The sooner we get there, the sooner we can sate your hunger."

Jess imagined doing exactly that and licked her lips. Lucia was quick, she'd give her that. Perhaps they'd both scored a win.

As promised it was a short distance to Lucia's house. They dismounted next to a golf cart that was plugged into the outdoor charger and Jess grabbed the camera from her bicycle basket. "How did the cart get here?"

Lucia led the way to the main door. "I asked facilities to drop one off for me earlier."

"Did you know I'd say yes about the bike ride?"

"No, but I had the idea of it this morning and thought I'd take a chance. I figured I could always ride a resort bike home so I wasn't stuck with two carts."

Jess tilted her head. Lucia was still too cocky but she appreciated all the effort. "Good thinking." She followed Lucia inside, once again marveling at the high ceilings and view provided by the glass walls.

"Dinner is a little while off. You're free to take a shower while you wait."

Jess moved to stand right in front of Lucia and wrapped her arms around her waist. Her nearness was intoxicating. She admired a few sweaty tendrils of dark hair stuck to Lucia's forehead. "I didn't bring a change of clothes."

Lucia tucked a loose strand of hair from the top of Jess's head just behind her ear. She seemed to enjoy doing that...or the hair annoyed her. "I have something you can wear."

"Funny, but I thought you'd be talking me out of clothes, not into them."

"That can be dessert." Lucia leaned in and Jess's breath caught in her throat. Then a second later they were kissing. Jess wasn't sure if she was out of practice and touch starved, or if Lucia was just that good. She was an amazing kisser. When they pulled apart, Lucia rested her forehead against Jess's. She said exactly what Jess had been thinking. "I don't know what it is about you, but your kisses are like ambrosia. They only make me hungrier for more."

Jess drew in a deep breath and gave herself a mental shake. "Ditto." Her stomach gurgled loudly before she could resume kissing. She grabbed it and made a face. "Ugh. How soon did you say dinner was?"

Lucia grinned. "I've got something I can put out while I cook. Let's get you in the shower so I can start dinner."

They went upstairs where Lucia left Jess in the bathroom with toiletries, a pair of loose shorts, and a tee shirt. "Thanks."

"I'll have sangria and a snack waiting when you're finished."

Fifteen minutes later, Jess felt human again. She sat at the kitchen island with her drink and a plate full of sliced tropical fruit while Lucia stirred mushroom risotto. Sure, most folks would say it was just rice. But it was fancy, creamy rice and Jess loved it. Lucia served the dish with toasted French bread.

Jess offered to clean up while Lucia ran upstairs for her own shower. She was standing at the tall window wall looking out toward the ocean when Lucia snuck up and wrapped her in an embrace from behind. Jess looked over her shoulder and Lucia kissed her. It was deep and Jess nearly dropped her glass. She pulled back after a minute.

"Hold on, let me set this down." She placed the glass on a nearby coaster then stepped back into Lucia's embrace. "So…"

"So."

Jess sighed, suddenly feeling shy. "You've shown me gorgeous views, lured me back to your house, then fed me an excellent meal. One would think you had an ulterior motive."

"Oh, I do."

The comment startled Jess and she felt a little tendril of doubt creep in. "You do?"

"I've adored getting to know you. Seeing your face as you take in the beauty all around. But if I have to pretend for one more minute that I don't want to see your face under different, more intimate circumstances, I'll probably go mad."

Doubt was assuaged. "I think this is the part where I admit that I'm insanely attracted to you."

"What was it you said to me earlier? Ditto." They laughed but it died off quickly when Jess met Lucia's gaze and tension rose between them. "Would you like to go up to the roof?"

The offer took Jess by surprise. "Not your room?"

Lucia shook her head. "There is something special about the smell of the ocean and scent of blossoms on the breeze. Come on. Let's pour ourselves another drink to take upstairs."

Jess's butterflies came back in earnest on their way to the roof. Lucia took a seat on the couch and placed her glass on the table. Jess sat next to her and did the same. Then she turned to Lucia and blurted out her confession. "I haven't had sex with anyone since my ex. I—" She swallowed and looked away. Admitting that was mortifying enough. She wasn't about to tell Lucia that one of the reasons she hadn't gotten intimate with anyone in years was because of her abysmal self-image.

"Hey," Lucia placed a warm palm on Jess's cheek and

turned her so they could look into one another's eyes. "It's been years for me, too. It's just...never been a priority. Not to mention the lack of good partners available. Then there's my father. He has offered to set me up with suitors from the big island, which is embarrassing in and of itself. But..." She trailed off, seemingly embarrassed by her admission.

"What?"

Lucia shook her head. "Nothing ever clicks for me. They're all lacking in some way." She paused, then added, "Until you."

"Oh." Jess ducked her head shyly. "Well, I will admit I hated you at first. You were so, so, insufferably attractive, and perfect."

Lucia burst into laughter. "What? I'm hardly perfect! And I could definitely tell I annoyed you. It became a game of sorts for me, eliciting a reaction. I enjoy seeing you flustered and blushing."

"I knew it! And truthfully, I think I was madder at myself than you. I assumed my libido had died years ago then I come along to this random paradise island and see you. It was like every sexual nerve sat up and screamed howdy."

"I'm, uh, sorry?" Lucia tried and failed to hide her grin.

"I'm sure you are."

Lucia shifted closer on the couch and wrapped her arm around Jess's shoulders. "So, what you're saying is that we're extremely attracted to one another, neither have had sex in a while, and we've got this entire evening to ourselves with no interruptions?"

Jess gave her a curious look. "You mean nobody will call you with some stupid request like missing towels?"

"I gave the phone to Amy. I'm all yours, Miss Parker."

Jess growled and lunged at Lucia, pushing her back onto the couch. "I thought I asked you not to call me that."

Laughter met her frustrated statement. "Oh, you did. I was hoping to push your buttons a little. I'm glad it worked. You're quite the tiger when provoked."

"I'll show you tig—" The kiss cleared all conscious thought from Jess's head. The only thing left going through her brain was the feel of Lucia below her, strong hands holding Jess close, and the sensation of Lucia's tongue caressing hers as the kiss went deeper and deeper.

Jess moaned and moved against Lucia's raised thigh. Sure, strong thighs were nice to look at but Jess found a better use for the solid muscle. She shifted and Lucia gasped into her mouth. Was she about to come with someone else for the first time in years while making out on an outdoor lounger like some hormonal teenager? Jess began to overthink, at least until Lucia dug her fingers into Jess's ass and pulled her mouth away.

"Jess?"

She was panting but managed to answer. "Yeah?"

"Turn it off. Let things happen as they will."

Jess met her dark eyes. "You mean go with the flow."

"Exactly."

Lucia pulled Jess against her thigh and Jess moaned again. She was so close when her mental spiral caused them to stop kissing. "Oh, God."

"Not him." Lucia moved her lips down to Jess's throat as Jess rode her thigh in earnest. "Let yourself go, Jess."

Jess's pleasure twisted higher with each delightful slide along the length of Lucia's leg. Her borrowed shorts were soaked through, and she knew that Lucia would be able to feel how wet she'd become. The end, when it came, was fast and abrupt. "Oh! Fuck." She jerked against Lucia as her clit pulsed with her release. Jess shuddered through the climax, Lucia adding pressure by raising her thigh even higher. Suddenly, Jess collapsed to Lucia's chest. She was panting like she'd run for miles.

Lucia lowered her leg but continued to play with the hairs at the nape of Jess's neck. "Your face... you come beautifully," she whispered reverently.

Jess chuckled tiredly. "I think you mean abruptly. I'll admit that surprised me. It was embarrassingly fast and I've always been slow to wind up and finish." She rose up just enough to see Lucia's confused look.

"Wind up and finish?"

"Yeah. It usually takes me a long time to get there."

Lucia grinned. "Really? Should I feel special then?"

"You definitely should. Now, what about you?" Jess

moved so she was next to Lucia on the couch, her back to the ocean view. "I think I left you hanging."

"I wouldn't object to a little more attention." Lucia's gaze was heavy with want.

"Can I touch you?"

"Please."

Jess had easy access to Lucia's body with the way Lucia was lying on her back. She slid her hand downward from Lucia's belly. The anticipation had her breathing hard and she'd already gotten off. Her finger's skimmed the top of the loose shorts that Lucia had donned after her own shower. Jess watched Lucia's face as her fingers dipped beneath the waistband. Her breasts were pressed against Lucia's arm and side of her chest, and she felt Lucia stop breathing at the first touch of fingers to her wet folds.

Lucia's eyes fluttered shut. "Yes."

The heat on either side of Jess's middle two fingers was incredible. She split the fingers so she could lightly massage each side of Lucia's clit at the same time. Breath stuttered as Lucia lifted her hips for more pressure.

Jess slid her fingers all the way down until the pads of her fingertips touched Lucia's hot entrance. It was molten, like an inferno burned inside her. "Can I—"

"Please. Start with two, then add another."

Jess smiled into Lucia's neck as she tasted the sweat on her skin. "Pushy. I like it." She didn't enter Lucia right away. She slid up and down a few more times before going inside the tiniest bit whenever her fingers reached the bottom of the stroke.

"Please," Lucia whined.

Unable to reach the way she wanted, Jess had to abandon Lucia's neck to slide lower on the lounger. On the next stroke, Jess slid up to the second knuckles. She worked her for a minute, spreading the wetness around her fingers before pushing all the way in. Lucia abruptly leaned forward and pulled Jess into a kiss, forcing her hips down. Jess licked into her mouth then grew dissatisfied with that alone. "I want to taste you. Is that okay?" She was a little nervous because it had been a long time, but Jess was determined to go all the way after imagining

Lucia on her tongue.

Lucia gasped. "Yes, please." She shuddered and fell back. "I should warn you that I probably won't last long."

"It's okay. We have all night." Jess removed her hand and Lucia groaned. "You're wearing too many clothes for me to do what I want." She stood from the low couch while Lucia sat up and removed her shirt. While she wasn't as perfect as Jess first thought, she still looked delicious.

"What about you?"

Suddenly, Jess felt less sure. "I don't look anything like you."

Lucia smiled. "That's a relief. I'm not attracted to myself, Jess."

Jess laughed nervously. "Heh, good point." She played with the hem of her shirt then threw caution into the wind. "Fuck it. I want to taste you more than I don't want you to see my pudgy body." She quickly removed her shirt and tossed it off to the side. Then, as an afterthought, Jess glanced around. "Uh, nobody can see us up here, right?"

Lucia stood as well and wrapped her arms around Jess. Their breasts slid together and Jess whined.

"Hey," Lucia met Jess's gaze. "Trust me when I say we have complete privacy in my home."

Jess sighed with relief. "Okay. Now, I'm pretty sure you owe me something."

"What?"

She grabbed Lucia's shorts and underwear together and bent her knees to slide them down those long legs. Jess winced in anticipation of her regular knee pain but they seemed to be holding up well despite bike riding all afternoon. Lucia kicked the fabric away while Jess stood again and walked Lucia backward a step until her calves hit the couch and she sat down.

Lucia reached forward and tugged the leg of Jess's shorts. "What about you?"

Jess tried to remember if she trimmed that morning when she shaved her legs. She couldn't. She supposed it was a little late to worry about it now. Impatient to get to her reward, Jess shimmied out of the shorts and moved so her knees were on the couch between Lucia's legs. "Now, where were we?"

"I think you were kissing me."

"Like this?" Jess leaned over Lucia's reclining form but held herself up, not wanting to rest her full weight on her.

Their tongues slid together and Jess moaned as her hips pushed against Lucia's out of pure reflex. It had been too long since she felt this. Turned on, exhilarated, excited. Lucia tried to tug her closer, but Jess resisted with shaking arms. She pulled her mouth away. "I don't want to crush you."

A chuckle met her admission. "I'm pretty sure I picked you up and carried you all the way to a main trail. I'm a lot stronger than you think and I want to feel every inch of your skin." Jess met her gaze. It was dark-eyed and pleading. "Please, *microbino mio*?"

"Do I want to know what that means?"

"It's Italian."

Jess snorted. "I bet it has to do with food, doesn't it?"

"No. Are you saying you want a food nickname?" She growled at the suggestion but Lucia only grinned and gave another tug at Jess's shoulders until she relented and relaxed onto Lucia, chest to chest.

Lucia's skin was hot. Jess wasn't sure if it was because they were outside in the tropical breeze, or because it had been too long since she'd had sex, but the sensation of them sliding together was highly erotic and she moaned into the kiss. Jess felt her own wetness increase but her gaze was caught by Lucia's dark nipples when she pulled away from those addicting lips. Giving in to her craving, she slid down and took one in her mouth. Lucia sucked in a breath before holding Jess's head between her hands.

Jess worked at Lucia's breasts for a few minutes, her hands stroking and kneading every place she could reach while Lucia's moans grew in volume and frequency. Jess licked and nibbled her way down Lucia's body until she could part puffy lips with her thumbs. The first taste was a little salty, but each one after grew sweeter.

Lucia writhed beneath her, mouth open and panting. Jess tasted every bit she could reach and then introduced her fingers when she thought she'd teased Lucia enough. First two, then a third after a few full strokes, exactly as Lucia first requested. The skin beneath her tongue tightened when Jess curled her fingers up to rub that little rough spot just inside.

"Jess."

She mumbled around Lucia's clit. "Yes."

"Jess, Jess, Jess…" Lucia's head thrashed back and forth, and she threw an arm over her face.

That made her stop licking. "What do you need?"

"Oh, don't stop!"

Jess immediately began running her tongue from the place where her fingers were thrusting inside all the way up and around Lucia's engorged clit. Lucia moaned and her thighs began to shake. Jess knew she was close so redoubled her efforts. When the skin of Lucia's mons got especially tight, Jess took that nub into her mouth and rhythmically sucked, while flicking the tip with her tongue.

Lucia's back arched off the couch as she screamed. Jess rode it out with her, feeling the walls clench around her fingers over and over. It was intoxicating to bring so much pleasure to someone. She'd forgotten what it was like to connect with another person in such a physical and deeply personal way.

Lucia abruptly lost tension as she sank back onto the couch. Jess carefully slid her fingers out, apologizing when Lucia shuddered. "Are you okay?"

Lucia's arm was still thrown over her face. "I—I'm…"

She sighed and Jess smiled and wiped her fingers on her own thigh. She already wanted to taste her again. "You're what?"

The arm moved to show Lucia's flushed face. Her eyes looked dark and wild. "That was amazing. You were amazing. I forgot what it was like for someone else to take care of my needs for once. It's been too long."

Jess moved so she was lying on the couch next to Lucia, back where she'd originally started touching her. "I was just thinking the same thing. I didn't realize how much I missed being able to touch someone else." She shook out her right hand to ease the cramp in her forearm. "I'm a little out of practice but hearing you come was totally worth it."

"Good. I'm happy you said yes to this."

"Yeah?" Jess closed her eyes when Lucia's left hand reached up to play with her hair.

"I was prepared to be a professional and keep my distance, but I'm glad I didn't have to."

Jess smiled. "Me, too."

Lucia leaned up and kissed Jess. "Now that I can feel my legs again, what do you say we grab some water then take this to my bedroom."

"That depends."

Lucia tilted her head. "On?"

"On whether or not your bedroom has any toys."

Laughter met her condition. "Oh, I think I can find something for us to play with. Do you like giving or receiving?"

Who knew getting in touch with her sexy side again could be so fun? Jess whispered into Lucia's lips. "I like everything."

It didn't take long for Lucia to lead them down a level to the bedroom, where they continued their exploration long into the night.

****

Jess woke the next morning sore but sated. She could only imagine what she'd feel like if Lucia didn't have an abundance of lube in her drawer. Menopause really was a bitch. Jess wasn't sure if Lucia was up yet, so she turned and came face to face with her dark-eyed gaze. "Oh, you're here."

"I am." Lucia paused, then asked, "Are you a cuddler?"

"Oh, generally not while I sleep. But I do like cuddling when I'm awake. What about you?" Lucia straightened her arm in clear invitation and Jess wasted no time sliding over. It was nice. Lucia smelled like her cologne and sex. She was warm without being sweaty.

"Are you comfortable?"

Jess tilted her head so she could meet Lucia's eyes. "I am. Um, thank you for last night. Well… all of yesterday really. It was the most fun I've had in a long time."

"Trust me when I tell you it was my pleasure. And honestly, it was the same for me. I don't know what it is but conversation with you is delightfully easy."

"Once I got over my annoying attraction and we got to know each other, I realized how comfortable you make me feel."

Lucia smiled. "Yes, that's exactly it."

"So, what now?" The sun was up but it was still early from what Jess could tell. She glanced around but didn't see a clock. "What time is it?"

A tan arm came into view sporting the black resort watch. "We have about an hour and a half before your first session."

Jess sighed. "Are you sure I can't play hooky?"

"Sorry, *ma petit chou*. I'm already bending the rules by having relations with a guest. We can't break them or you risk getting kicked out."

"That's not Italian."

"It's French."

"Is this one food?"

Lucia only grinned.

"Fine. I'll be good and go to my sessions today." Just the thought of having to leave so soon after experiencing this new and exciting connection with Lucia caused a tendril of anxiety to form in Jess's gut. And just that reaction alone told Jess that parting at the end of her vacation was going to be hard no matter how much she said it would be worth it.

"I'll tell you what the words mean later. But speaking of food, are you hungry?"

The previous evening was amazing and Lucia had already fed her one meal, it seemed rude to expect the woman to cook again. "I'm sure I'll be fine until I get back to the—" Jess's stomach rumbled and she clutched it dramatically. "Scratch that. I seem to have worked up an appetite."

"I can't imagine how."

"Don't laugh. Last night was really… special to me."

Lucia leaned close and gazed deeply into Jess's eyes. "I promise I'm not. It was special to me too, *chuisle*."

Jess let the seriousness of the moment sink in, then hit Lucia with a pillow. "Stop teasing me with words I don't know." She narrowed her eyes at the laughing woman. "Just how many languages do you speak?"

"We get guests from all over. I've picked up a few of this and that during the years."

"Fine. Be a showoff then."

Lucia sat up and swung her legs off the bed to the floor. She glanced over her shoulder and winked. "We better get moving if you want to shower before you see Kam."

Jess made a face. "Ugh, I reek of sex. A shower is definitely in order."

A twinkling dark gaze met hers. "Hot or mild shower?"

"Mild. Why?"

"Want to share?"

Jess didn't need to be asked twice. She hopped out of bed, heedless of her own nudity in Lucia's presence. It was freeing to feel so confident with another person. They had to leave the bikes and take the cart back to the resort after Lucia cooked breakfast, but at least they were clean and fed. More importantly, on time. Jess wondered what the new day would bring and if Lucia would be a part of her next adventure.

# Chapter Ten

Her hour with Kam breezed by. He covered a variety of meditation exercises and assigned more homework but other than that, it was pretty light. Jess was glad she didn't have a session like some of the previous days. She didn't want heavy emotion bringing her down after such an amazing night. Perhaps he sensed her upbeat mood and purposely kept things easy.

Jess walked into Ronobe's art studio wearing a smile and her instructor gave a little wave while setting up easels around the room.

"Are we painting again today?" Jess didn't see any aprons out yet so hoped not.

Ronobe placed a tote on the center workbench and popped the lid off. "Nope. Today we're going to use pencils only."

That perked Jess up even more. She used to doodle when she was a kid but didn't pursue any art classes in high school. Jess's guidance counsellor stressed how important it was to fill your electives with beneficial classes and not things like art and cooking. The joke was on her because the high school stuff didn't mean much once she got to college. She should have just taken the electives that made her happy.

"Hey, Ronobe, have you seen my watch? It's a Gucci."

Jess rolled her eyes at the brand. Of course, it was.

Unlike Jess, Brittany strode into the art studio wearing a frown. "I couldn't find it this morning and thought maybe I left it in class yesterday when I was cleaning up."

"I haven't, and I went through the entire room, clearing counters and putting everything away after class. You should check with Vassago. He's in charge of facilities and most lost items end up with him."

"Damn. I checked first thing this morning but nothing had been turned in yet. I was hoping it would be here.

Thanks anyway." She looked genuinely upset at the news.

"Sorry, Brittany."

Jess suddenly recalled what she'd witnessed the previous day, before her bike ride with Lucia. "Hey, Brittany, do you know Stephen?"

She tilted her head at the question. "Not really. He's the guy with a thin mustache, right? Kinda shifty?"

"Uh, yeah. That's him."

"I think I've caught a glimpse of him a few times since the first day, but we've never spoken. Why?"

Jess wasn't sure how to answer. On one hand, she didn't want to implicate someone who was innocent. But on the other hand, what reason would Stephen have for coming out of Brittany's room? "I saw him coming out of your cabin yesterday and thought maybe you two had become...er, friendly."

"Ew, no." Then she paused when Jess's words sank in. "That little fucker!"

"Is there a problem, ladies?"

"Jess is in the cabin next to mine and she saw another guest come out of my room yesterday. And now I'm missing stuff. Who do I report that to?"

Ronobe appeared genuinely dismayed. "Oh no, that's not good. Class is about to start but you can report it directly to the manager, Lucia, when we're finished. If she's not available, then you can tell Amy."

Brittany huffed. "Why can't I go now?"

"Unfortunately, you can't miss your class now that you've signed up. Your things won't go anywhere. It's not like the thief can get off the island. Once you lodge a complaint, Saleos will have his team check the security cameras. They have views of all buildings and cabin entrances. If someone other than resort staff entered your room they'll be discovered."

Brittany's eyes watered and Jess didn't know if the watch held actual meaning, or if it was just because of the value. After all, Brittany threw the brand out there with an air of expectation when asking Ronobe, like that was the most important thing. "I can go with you after class if you'd like. I don't have anything else until my spa session this evening. I mean, since I was a witness and all."

Brittany looked surprised by the offer but gave Jess a tentative smile. "Okay, thank you."

Ronobe clapped her hands. "Now that you've got a plan, class is about to start. Please take your places at an empty easel and we'll learn how motion and emotion can be found in simple lines."

Jess enjoyed the class but given their task after, she decided to leave the completed sketch rolled up in her studio locker. The painting was still there since she'd yet to decide what to do with it. When she was done, she turned to see Brittany standing at the edge of the room biting her nails. "Are you ready?"

"Yeah." They left the studio and Brittany gave her a sidelong glance. "You probably think I'm just being a big baby about some fancy Gucci watch, but my dad gave it to me for my sixteenth birthday. He died a few months later so it's the last thing I have to remember him by. Like, it reminds me that time is short and I should enjoy what I can with the people I care about."

"I'm sorry. That really sucks." Jess felt guilty for assuming the worst, but Brittany had been hot and cold since their meeting. To be fair, most of the other guests could probably say the same about Jess herself.

Brittany shook her head. "Honestly? I don't know how I got to this place."

"The resort?"

"No, like, this mental place. It's funny but I never used to care what other people thought about me. I'd just be the kind of person I knew my dad would be proud of. I guess as I got older, everything on the TV and Internet kept telling me that I had to do more or be more to be important. And somewhere during the past few years I went from being that real girl whose dad taught her how to make pancakes to some plastic facsimile that doesn't dare eat carbs because she might gain weight and disappoint all her imaginary friends, her followers."

Jess had no idea what to say to that. Truthfully, if someone told her that today would be the day a previously stuck-up bitch would unload her deepest truths on Jess before lunch, she'd have said they were whacked. But at the same time, she felt like she and Brittany were kindred in a way. Both of them lost and searching for a better path forward. "I feel you. I think I've fallen into a negative spiral myself. This trip has opened my eyes in a lot of ways and I don't think I like what I see."

"Jesus, we are a pair, aren't we?"

Jess glanced sideways and saw Brittany make a face. She laughed along with her. As luck would have it, they found Lucia and Amy having a conversation near the main desk outside the administrative offices. Lucia stopped speaking when they approached and gave them a broad smile. "What can we do for you ladies?"

Brittany looked nervous so Jess spoke for her. "Brittany is missing a watch and I saw another guest come out of her cabin yesterday before I left for a bike ride. Her cabin is right next to mine."

Lucia narrowed her eyes. "And this person wasn't someone you'd given permission to enter your room?"

"No. I've never even spoken to him, except maybe on the shuttle from the airport."

"Who did you see leave her room?" Amy asked Jess.

"Stephen. I don't really know him either, but we were on the same excursion a few days ago so I know his name from that."

Lucia and Amy shared a significant look before Lucia turned her gaze back to Jess and Brittany. "Okay, thank you for the information. We will treat this matter with the utmost priority. I'll have security look at the cameras. Once we ascertain what happened, we'll track down your stolen watch"

"It's Gucci and has the words *for my little girl* written on the back." Brittany supplied.

"That sounds special and I promise we'll get it back. Please, try not to worry and enjoy the rest of your day. Either Amy or I will keep you updated on our investigation."

Brittany gave Lucia a grateful look. "Thank you." Then she turned to Jess. "And you, too. I wouldn't have known what happened to it if you hadn't come forward."

"It was nothing, really. I hope they find your watch." Jess looked at the three of them then pointed with her thumb in the direction of the dining room. "I'll just get out of your hair and grab some lunch. Good luck." She hurried away, doing her best not to look back at Lucia before turning down the hallway.

Jess lingered over lunch, secretly hoping she could get Lucia alone after but her new lover didn't seem to be in the main building. Logically, she knew that Lucia had a job to do and couldn't spend all her time with Jess. Rather than dwell on it, Jess checked out another bicycle and grabbed the camera from her cabin. The previous day had reminded her of all she'd given up years before and it was time to take back her joy.

To keep it fresh, Jess rode in the opposite direction she'd gone with Lucia. There were a number of overlooks that made for some gorgeous shots. She found one hiking trail that led to a secluded beach and, despite her previous mishap of falling down an embankment, carefully made her way to the water.

Once she got her fill of photos in the cove, Jess sat in the sand to take in the beauty of the secluded place. The breeze gently pushed her bangs around and smelled of salt, coconut, and the ever-present blossoms she'd come to associate with the island. The call of sea birds rode the wind above and the sun was warm without feeling like it would cook her.

She scooped a handful of sand and let it slowly trickle through her fingertips. Widening and narrowing the gap between her fingers to slow or speed the flow. Time was a lot like that. Jess's life was full of gaps where all her little joys previously existed, and time simply got away from her. She'd been lost in a haze of depression for too long. All of the sudden, she woke up one morning and found that she didn't like the woman in the mirror. Unlike Brittany, Jess had stopped caring about everything. There had to be a healthy balance between the two.

Jess thought about that important question Dr. Kam had asked in her third session. She abruptly stood and yelled into the wind. "I want to be happy!"

The circling gulls didn't care. And Jess knew it wouldn't be as easy as all that. Returning home would be hard, weighed down by an ocean's worth of self-realization she'd attained at the resort. Realistically, Jess knew that she'd struggle not to fall into her old habits. But more than that, she'd have to prove to herself and to everyone else that she was actively changing. Her bad attitude and outlook on life didn't occur overnight. It was built on layers of disappointment, self-loathing, and sadness. Jess made a mental note to ask Dr. Kam about something that would help her with accountability.

She heaved a sigh at the low position of the sun and grabbed the camera case from its perch on a nearby rock. Then with one last look over her shoulder toward the blue-green expanse, she made the laborious trek back up the embankment to the bike path.

Staying at Lucia's the night before meant her smart watch was dead and she'd left her cell back in the cabin. Jess had texted Shell a few times since her arrival but had yet to hear anything back from her friend. She assumed Shell was busy between work, softball starting, and Rory, and didn't want to bother her. But with no watch or phone, she didn't have a way to tell time and didn't want to be late for her last session at the spa.

Jess parked the bike outside her cabin and ran inside to grab clothes that weren't full of sand. She glanced at the clock by the bed. "Oh shit! I'm late."

In an effort to save time, Jess cut through the main building to the spa, rather than follow the paved trails outside. The lobby was dim, but Jess heard voices coming from Lucia's office.

"Mister Johnson, we have video evidence of you entering Miss Coleman's cabin, which in and of itself is a breach of etiquette and resort rules. We had legitimate reason to search your room."

"I didn't put that stuff there!"

Jess needed to get to her spa session, but she found herself rooted to the spot out of sheer human curiosity.

"I'm afraid you opted out of room service which means the only security scans in and out of your cabin have been your own."

She could just make out Stephen's agitated form standing in front of Lucia's desk through the cracked door. His hands were clenched at his side and Jess wondered if he would take a swing. "This is such bullshit! The watch doesn't even work."

Lucia continued. "Be that as it may, nothing you can say now will buy you more time. I think you're finished here at Paradise Island."

Jess was surprised to see the man's face crumple. It was like a switch had been flipped. A look of fear washed over Stephen's face as he sobbed. "No, please! The resort was my last chance."

Jess found the abrupt change in attitude alarming. She wondered if he'd been sent there as part of a program. She knew some places did that.

Lucia closed her eyes briefly. "I know and I'm sorry." She looked at someone out of Jess's view. "Take him back to the transfer point."

A male voice answered. "Will do, Boss."

Jess stepped behind a large decorative planter full of thick bamboo growth right before two men wearing resort uniforms exited the office with a crying Stephen walking dejectedly between them.

Then Amy moved into the place he'd previously been standing. "Sorry about that, Luce. I know you hate it when they don't make it through and have to return."

"It happens. You can only do so much but ultimately, it's on them to do the rest."

"How was your visit with Mister C at the big island?"

Lucia sighed. "It was fine. It's always good to get back though. I asked him again for a break from this place but he ignored my question. Instead, he took me out to a series of dinners. I'm glad to be in my own bed again. Sorry for getting back so late, I lost track of time."

Amy laughed. "It always happens there."

"True enough."

Amy glanced out the window and Jess used the opportunity to sneak the rest of the way through the lobby so she could get to the spa. Her heart raced at the thought that Lucia was trying to get away from the resort. Her hopes were tempered by the fact that Lucia's father apparently said no to her request.

Jess explained away her lateness to the spa session by saying she lost track of time on her bike ride. Which was the absolute truth. They didn't need to know she could have made some of that time up again had she not stopped to eavesdrop. She closed her eyes during the deep tissue massage a short while later, grateful that they'd at least found Brittany's watch.

****

Jess arrived back in her cabin later feeling loose and relaxed. Her sore muscles from the morning were a distant afterthought, but not so for the memories of how it felt to touch and be touched by Lucia. She ordered room service for dinner rather than returning to the dining hall in search of food. Jess figured she'd have just enough time to shower and pull on some sleeping clothes before the food arrived and she was right.

The knocking at the door was loud. "Just a minute," she called out, while pulling a resort robe over her tank top and shorts. Sure, she was dressed, but she didn't like anyone to see her without a bra unless they were a lot more intimate.

"Sorry for the late order—" Jess's apology cut off when she swung the door open.

"No worries. It was an honor to deliver your meal."

"You're here."

Lucia suddenly looked unsure. "Yes, I am. Is this okay?"

Jess rolled her eyes and pulled Lucia inside. She went to shut the door after, then remembered her food and wheeled the cart through the doorway as well. "Can't forget this. I'm starving."

"Don't let me stop you." Lucia helped Jess unload her dinner tray to the table then took a seat opposite her.

The evening special was seafood paella and Jess's mouth watered at the smell alone. She felt a pang of guilt, then glanced up at Lucia before digging into her plate. "Oh, sorry. Are you hungry?" She gave her dinner a mournful look. "I can share if you are."

Lucia caressed the back of her hand. "It's fine, *schatz.* I've had plenty today."

Jess rolled her eyes at the new nickname before asking, "Did today keep you busy dealing with the missing watch?"

Lucia shifted in her chair. "No, actually. I let Amy handle that one. My father called me to the big island and saying no to a request from the boss isn't an option."

"Oh? Something important?"

She shrugged. "Mostly logistics. I asked him again for a vacation and was denied. Same old thing."

Jess swallowed her bite of savory rice. "Wait, so he called you there at the drop of a hat and Amy handles the stuff here, yet you can't take even a few weeks away? I don't get it."

Lucia put her elbows on the table and rested her chin on her hands. She let out a tired sigh. "It's complicated."

"You've told me a lot about the amazing improvements you made to Paradise Island Resort, but if you have a capable person as your backup, it sounds more like your dad is less afraid things will fall apart without you and more afraid you won't want to come back." She stabbed a shrimp and stuffed it into her mouth before she could give any more unsolicited opinions.

Lucia stiffened in her seat and her mouth opened with surprise. "Jess, you're brilliant."

"Hardly."

She looked deep in thought and Jess continued to eat while Lucia rambled aloud. "Perhaps if I sign a contract stating I'll return by a certain time."

"A contract, for vacation? That seems extreme."

Lucia frowned. "You don't know my father."

"Is he one of those overly controlling businessman types?"

"Something like that."

It didn't take long for Jess to finish her meal. "I don't know if the special tonight was better than normal or if all my activity lately has my appetite increased."

That earned her a smile. "Maybe a bit of both. What did you do today that caused you to work up such an appetite? Laps in the pool, maybe?"

"I decided to skip the pool today. I knew my spa session wasn't until this evening, so I went for a long bike ride in the opposite direction to what we took yesterday. I can't wait to see some of the shots I got."

"Oh?"

"Did you know there is a secret little cove down an embankment from the main bike trail?"

Lucia smirked. "And I see that you made your way there safely." She craned her head around to search Jess's body for injury. "No scrapes or sprained ankle so I'd say you're doing well."

Jess looked at her with mock affront. "Rude! I'm not nearly as klutzy as I probably led you to believe. I may be a whale now, but I've got athletic bones."

"I'm not sure which is more ridiculous. The fact that you are comparing your size to a whale, or that such things as athletic bones exist."

Anger and annoyance washed over Jess at the tail end of that statement. Was she just fucking with her? "Luce, I'm not blind. I've never been a scrawny girl, and I'm aware of just how much weight I've gained during the past few years. You can't say I'm skinny by any measure of the word. We don't all have bodies like yours."

"I never said that. I'm only saying you aren't a whale. I think our perceptions are skewed from a young age. Society, expectation, and self-image turn every mirror into a fun-house image. We become a caricature of ourselves, only seeing partial truths."

"I..." Jess wasn't sure how to respond. She could tell that Lucia wasn't just saying it for her benefit either. The other woman seemed especially passionate on the subject.

"Nobody is perfect, *minha paixão*. You've seen all of me there is to see. I've got scars on my back from an accident years ago, a few burn marks, and a variety of other blemishes to prove just how normal I can be."

Guilt churned the food in Jess's belly. "I didn't mean to imply you were anything other than you are. I'm sorry if it came across that way."

"It's fine, and you didn't. I just wish you could see yourself the way I see you." She shrugged. "And who knows, maybe my attraction is nothing more than personal taste but if that's the case, then one could definitely say you're my flavor."

Jess burst into laughter. "Now who is being ridiculous?" She stacked her dishes back on the cart then leaned against the counter with her glass of water. "So..."

"So?"

"Do you have to get back to your place or can you hang out for a while?"

Lucia tapped her bottom lip. "Hmm, I'd say that depends."

"On?"

Dark lips curled upward with a smirk. "Whether or not hang out is a euphemism."

Jess sucked in a breath at the sudden image of the two of them sharing her giant soaker tub. "It can be."

"What are we waiting for then? Let's get your meal cleared away so we can hang out."

The evening was definitely looking up.

Jess started the water while Lucia wheeled the dinner cart outside. One thing she noticed the previous evening was that Lucia let her initiate everything they did together. Sure, she actively participated once things got started, but it seemed as if she were being careful not to pressure Jess. It made sense given the power imbalance between them, with Lucia being the resort manager and all. But Jess liked a little pressure and wanted Lucia to be less careful and polite.

Between the tub filling and Jess's deep thoughts, she never heard Lucia enter the bathroom. She was startled when strong arms wrapped around her from behind.

"You're staring into the water like it did something to personally offend you. Is anything wrong?"

Jess stiffened at first, then relaxed into the embrace. "Nothing is wrong. I'm just thinking about last night, us. Are you normally more dominant in bed?"

Lucia burst into laughter and let Jess go. "Whatever made you think of that?"

She shrugged at the question. "I'm sporty and I've always been with sporty women."

"And that means what exactly?"

She struggled to explain what she was thinking. "Well, I mean... I guess there's a give and take involved. One ex called it switch. I like trading control during sex, but I notice you seem to defer to me every time last night."

Lucia tilted her head. "Hmm, is that a problem?"

Jess held up her hands. "No, not at all. I guess I expected you to be a little more dominant and..." She swallowed and looked away, afraid that she'd screw it all up between them. But dammit, life was too short not to tell someone what you want. Communication was important, right?

"Jess,"

She turned her head away from the running water to meet Lucia's gaze.

"Do you want me to be more dominant? More asser-tive?"

"Maybe?" She paused then changed her mind. "Yes. I mean yes."

Lucia chuckled and ran a hand through her dark hair. "I was trying to be respectful of your will, given our unique circumstances here. Permission is important and I didn't want to take a chance of doing something you didn't explicitly request."

"Well, if we're having *this* conversation, I'm not into anal but other than that, you can do whatever you want. I'm game."

The smile curling Lucia's lips could be described as sinful. "Well then, I think I can accommodate your wishes. Because I also like most things, and I'm very comfortable being in control."

Lucia stepped into Jess's personal space and Jess swallowed. It didn't matter that Lucia was still wearing the crisp white shirt and black dress pants. If anything, that made it hotter. Jess could feel her body warm as their breasts brushed together. Lucia's unique scent and her nearness drowned out everything else in the room. She took a stuttering breath. "Aren't you going to kiss me?"

Lucia lowered her head and brushed her lips along Jess's ear. Her whispered "No," caused a full body shiver.

Jess's eyes opened all the way. "What?"

"I'm going to shut off the water before the tub over-flows. Then the two of us are going to undress and get in that bath."

"When you put it like that, it's a lot less sexy than I

imagined."

"Less talking, more undressing." As if to press her point, Lucia reached down to untie Jess's robe. She gently pushed it off her shoulders where it slid down Jess's arms and pooled on the tile floor. Her eyes moved to Jess's loose breasts beneath her lightweight sleep shirt. Hands followed the heavy gaze and Jess closed her eyes as pleasure washed across her.

"Wha—what about you?"

Lucia ignored her. Instead, she moved her hands down to the hem of Jess's shirt and lifted it over her head. Then she helped her step out of the shorts. Jess felt self-conscious at first, at least until Lucia's long fingers caressed her abdomen before sliding down to put pressure on her pubis. Jess moaned and her knees nearly buckled.

Lucia wrapped her free arm around Jess's waist. "I've got you."

"Wait."

Lucia stopped her ministrations. "Yes?"

"You're wearing too many clothes."

That earned her a laugh and Lucia pulled away. "Fine." She swiftly unbuttoned her shirt and tossed it aside. Then she kicked off her shoes and socks and unclasped her pants, letting them puddle at her ankles, before kicking those away from the tub as well. Rather than go back to what she'd been doing, Lucia stepped into the tub and held out a hand. "Are you coming?"

Jess blinked in response. Between Lucia's talented hands and the quick strip tease, Jess's arousal was thick and pulsing. But she was able to snap out of her daze long enough to utter "hopefully" before climbing into the tub after Lucia.

# Chapter Eleven

Jess woke later than normal the next morning and was surprised to find Lucia had already gone. She felt hurt at first, but quickly realized it was a lot different staying overnight together here at the resort than in the privacy of Lucia's house. Lucia probably had to go home and shower before coming back for the day. Despite Jess's logical mind telling her it was normal and expected, there was a bigger part of her that wanted to wake in Lucia's embrace again.

Jess sighed and threw an arm over her eyes. "I may be in trouble here." Shell would say to just enjoy the experience and go with the flow. But no matter how much she tried to convince herself otherwise, Jess wasn't built like that.

Her cabin phone rang, and Jess reached across the bed to pick up the receiver from the cradle. "Hello?"

"Sorry I had to leave you this morning. I miss cuddling with you already."

Oh. "You didn't even say goodbye." Jess pouted.

"We were up late so I thought I'd let you sleep."

"You could have at least given me a kiss," she said.

You could hear the smile in Lucia's tone of voice. "Next time I won't be so nice. I'll rudely wake you instead."

"See that you do. Rude kisses are always better than no kisses."

Both women broke into laughter at how ridiculous the conversation had gotten. They talked for a while until Lucia reminded her. "Don't you have your session soon?"

Jess looked at the clock. "Oh shit! Sorry, Luce. I have to go. Will I see you later?"

"Count on it. Until then, *schatje*."

She couldn't even complain about yet another word she didn't know. All Jess could do was scramble around getting dressed, before heading out the door for her session with Kam. Jess realized belatedly that she'd begun using the nickname other folks working at the resort had for Lucia.

Jess rushed into Dr. Kam's office a few minutes later, out of breath and disheveled. She took off her baseball hat to straighten and tuck her hair behind her ears, then put it back on. "Sorry! I overslept."

He glanced at his watch, then met her eyes. "It's fine. A little tardiness is acceptable if it means you show up looking lighter of spirit." Kam waited until she took a seat before speaking. "What put you in such a good mood today?"

All her thoughts of the past few days, and the high emotion she'd only just begun to realize, barreled to the forefront of Jess's mind. As a result, she rather abruptly unloaded the most significant thoughts. "I've been thinking a lot about all the things I left behind when I tried to distance myself from the pain I associate with my ex."

"Please share with me what precipitated all this introspection."

"I went for a bike ride a few days ago and had so much fun, I repeated it yesterday in the opposite direction around the island."

Kam nodded. "Excellent. Did you do anything else?"

"Well, I checked out a guest camera and got a lot of good shots. Not only that, but there's a trail that runs down to the beach from the bike path. If a person is careful, they can hike down to a secluded little cove. It was..." She shook her head, at a loss to describe the beauty of such a place. Even her words to Lucia the previous night had been insufficient.

He smiled. "I've often found beauty in its many forms to be particularly enlightening. Some of my deepest thoughts have been born of nothing more than peaceful solitude and a good view."

Jess leaned forward in her chair. "Yes, that's exactly it! I thought about all the progress I've made since I arrived at the resort. I mean, at first, I thought it was complete bullshit. But deep down I'm pretty sure I was looking for any excuse to get out of the dark place I'd fallen into."

Dr. Kam made a few notes on his notepad. "That's excellent news, Jess. I'll admit that you've made faster progress than most I see come through Paradise Island. That can only happen if the guest really wants to change their life. Congratulations on your perseverance."

Jess's cheeks grew warm with his praise. "I mean, I had a lot of help from you. Sometimes you don't realize you're lost until someone asks where you are and you can't answer. That was where I stood when I got here. It's funny, but I can tell it's not just me changing. The other guests were total assholes when we all arrived, but some are noticeably nicer now. So, I think it's working for other people, too."

Kam shifted and crossed his legs before resting the notepad on his knee, tapping the pen against the paper. "Have you considered that we get out of social interactions what we put into them?"

"What do you mean?"

"Haven't you heard the old saying that you can catch more flies with honey than vinegar?"

She snorted. "Yeah. I mean, I'll admit that if someone is shitty to me, I'm more likely to be the same way in return. Maybe that's part of it, but I'm genuinely connecting to some people I never thought I could. Like Brittany."

"I'm not familiar with that name."

"Oh, that's because she has her sessions with Dr. Berg. Anyway, we've had a couple random conversations and it made me realize that despite how different we are, we have some of the same struggles—no, that's not right. We don't have the same issues, but we have the same responses to struggle."

"Like what?" Kam asked.

She groaned. "For one, we both turn into raging, defensive bitches."

"Jess," he chided. "Remember what we discussed about disparaging yourself?"

"I mean, we're both better now. I even helped Brittany recently when she had something go missing from her room."

Kam frowned. "Ah yes, I heard about Mr. Johnson. It's a shame. I didn't connect your friend Brittany with the one whose item was stolen. Anyway, we try to help everyone but not everyone wants to help themselves. It makes those wins we see even more special."

Jess picked at the hem of her shorts. "It wasn't that much work to help myself. I'd say you did the brunt of it by pointing me in the right direction."

He slapped the notepad on his thigh to get her attention. "Never discount the amount of work you put into yourself. It's vital, important, and emotionally taxing. Your next homework is to accept your own self-worth."

Jess snorted and made a face. "I'm afraid that will take longer than I have here at Paradise Island. But speaking of my time here, my introspection made me realize that my real challenge will come once I return home. I'm afraid I'll fall back into the same patterns I was in before. Do you have anything that will help me stay accountable?"

"Before I answer that, did you do the homework I assigned yesterday?"

"Eh..." Jess grimaced. "I didn't know what to say. What do you mean by goals for myself? Like, learning to knit or getting another degree?"

Kam held up his hands. "No, nothing like that. Think smaller. Smaller steps and goals are easier to meet. Give me one goal for yourself, just off the top of your head."

"I want to lose weight?"

"Okay, that's something. Tell me why."

Jess considered that very thing, attempting to distill the question down like she was doing a five whys problem solving session. Five whys was a repetitive questioning technique she learned when getting her engineering degree. It was a way to explore the cause and effect of relationships underlying a particular problem. Why did she want to lose weight? "I want to be healthy and for my knees to hurt less."

"And why is that?"

"Because when my knees hurt my mood is low and I snap at everyone."

"And?"

"I mean, the pain itself is a good enough reason. But the pain usually means I can't physically do the things I like to do, which also affects my attitude."

He poked one more time. "What does that mean for you?"

She shrugged. "I used to be a pretty happy go-lucky kind of person. But I'll admit that sometimes I spiral when I'm not happy and take it out on other people. I don't like doing that. I don't like being a constant downer, spreading negativity everywhere. I want to keep moving forward with my progress to be happy."

Kam grinned at her. "So, what is your simple goal?"

Her simple goal. Could it be that easy? Maybe it was. "I want to be better tomorrow than I was today." She met Dr. Kam's dark gaze. "Does that make sense to you?"

"Jess, it doesn't need to make sense to me. It's your goal. But to answer your question, yes. It fits how you're changing and how you want to continue to change. Accountability begins by using that statement as an affirmation of sorts. Remember your goal, find new things, or old ones, which bring you joy, and start exploring your world again."

Jess blew out a long sigh. That last part really hit home. "I totally stopped engaging, trying new things, and meeting new people."

He nodded. "My other suggestion is to find someone to talk to when you get back."

"Like another therapist?"

"It certainly can't hurt. But even just confiding your struggles to a friend can help. I'm going to hazard a guess and say that you feel changed since coming to the island and you're afraid that others won't see the person you've become. Expectation can be a burden, especially if it's negative. People will live up or down to your expectation."

"It's true. I deal with that a lot at work."

He jotted another note on the tablet. "Unfortunately for you, you've created this pattern of negativity and established yourself in the eyes of all the lives you've touched. It will be on you to reform those pathways and teach people about the person you are now. Perseverance is the real key to continued progress, but I have the utmost faith that you can do this."

"You think so?"

"I do. But ultimately, it's not my belief in you that will pull you from the abyss."

Jess's shoulders slumped. "You're going to say it's

having faith in myself, aren't you?"

Kam chuckled and pointed at her with the pen. "You got it in one."

"Okay. You've given me even more to consider but I feel a lot better about what will happen when I return home after this vacation. Thank you."

"It's my absolute pleasure. Guests like you, with so much willpower to change for the better, make everything I do here all worth it." Dr. Kam looked at his watch. "Oh, that's our time for today. I'll let you go a few minutes early so you can get to your next session."

Early was good. She'd have just enough time to pee before Ronobe's class. "Awesome, thanks. I have to say, one of the unexpected joys I've found since coming to the island is a love of art. I plan to look up local classes when I get back home."

Kam gave her a wide smile. "See? You're already working on finding those joys. Well done." He shook her hand before walking with Jess to the door. "See you tomorrow."

Brittany rushed to her as soon as Jess walked through the door of the studio. She held up her wrist. "I got it back, look!"

Jess wasn't a fan of gold, but she thought it was cute, if expensive looking. What caught Jess's attention more than the returned time piece was the smile on Brittany's face. Jess wasn't sure she'd ever seen the young woman truly happy since they arrived at the resort. "Hey, that's great. I'm glad they could get your watch back."

"Yeah. Apparently, he'd taken a few other things. I'm glad he's gone."

Jess remembered how stricken Stephen had been when they were leading him out of Lucia's office the previous night. "Yeah, but I kinda feel sorry for him too. I hope he finds a better path when he returns."

Brittany thought about it for a second before nodding in agreement. "I guess you're right. It's too bad he didn't get more out of the resort. I know I am for sure." She gave Jess a quiet smile, one that radiated sincerity. "I can't wait to get home."

"To reconnect with your friends and followers?"

"No," she shook her head and looked down, shyly. "To reconnect with myself. Dr. Berg says it's an important next step. Doing the things that I need to do when I get home to keep moving forward."

"Yeah, Dr. Kam said something similar. I need to hold myself accountable to my small goal, to be a better person every day." She paused, then added one of her favorite statements from Kam. "We deserve happiness."

Brittany gave her a regretful look. "Do you honestly believe that? I've been kind of... shitty. To a lot of people. Doesn't that require, I don't know, more restitution or something before I can be happy?"

"It seems to me that the attitude we give others is a sign of the misery inside. In a way we created our own prison and punishment while committing the crime. I don't know about you, but I'm tired of living half a life." Jess smiled and gave Brittany's shoulder a little push. "Go ahead, say it aloud. It doesn't feel real until you do."

Brittany looked around, maybe checking to make sure nobody was close by. Then, in a quiet voice, she said, "I deserve to be happy." She shook out her hands after and her watch made a metallic clacking sound.

Jess nodded with encouragement. "Go ahead, try it again. I'll even say it with you. Ready?" Brittany nodded. "On three. One, two, three—"

"I deserve to be happy," they intoned, as one.

"Yes! Up top." Jess raised her hand to accept Brittany's high five.

"Okay, you may be kinda old." She looked at Jess with more than a little panic, "I don't mean that in a bad way! Okay, so I'm not good at this but I'm just trying to say that you slay for someone who is middle-aged."

"Uh, thanks?"

Their strange bonding moment was interrupted by Ronobe calling from the other side of the room. "We're about to start, ladies."

Jess responded, "Sorry." Then she noticed the familiar looking resort cameras at all the stations around the large workbench in the center of the room. "Ooh, photography?"

Ronobe broke into a wide grin as Jess and Brittany walked over to take their places. She seemed equally excited about every new type of art she introduced to the class. "This will be a two-day project. Today we start a photography challenge I call Above and Below and tomorrow we'll assemble albums with the images."

One of the other regulars in the art classes, Kyle Kirgan, raised his hand. "What if we don't know anything about photography? Even the pictures on my cell phone are blurry."

A few people chuckled and Ronobe quickly reassured the young man. "Not to worry, Kyle. The cameras are very easy to use. Point and click. They auto focus so you don't have to do anything fancy if you're unfamiliar. We'll cover the basics so you can head outside and get started. But," she added. "Most people that turn their phones sideways to text don't realize that they're smudging the lens with the way they hold the phone. Start cleaning off your lens with a soft shirt or cloth right before using the camera and I think your selfies and other pictures will improve."

His mouth dropped open in surprise. "Huh. I never thought about that. I *do* text a lot."

"What's the Above and Below theme about?" Jess asked.

"It's mostly as it sounds. I want you to find things you can focus on from multiple viewpoints. You see a blossom hanging down from a tree? Take a photo from two different perspectives. It works especially well for items on the ground, hence the name of the session. You may have to get right down in the grass though so anyone that wants to borrow a smock is free to grab one from the hooks on the way out the door. Just return them and your cameras at the end of class."

"That's all?"

"Not quite. I'll give you each a printed list of easy to photograph everyday things. Flowers, signs, flora, fauna, and more. Your job is to take pictures of each today. I'll download and print everyone's pairs and put them in folders for you. I want to know what your natural eye sees. You can crop down images as you see fit tomorrow when you work on your albums." A few comments murmured around the room then Ronobe continued. "Are you all ready? Excellent. Gather round and I'll show you how to use the camera."

"I've been taking pictures all week with the resort camera. Can I just get started?" Jess said.

"Go ahead, Jess. Good luck!"

"Thanks." Jess went off in search of adventure. She was more excited about this one than the sketching from the previous day and that was saying a lot.

Jess wasted no time grabbing the sheet Ronobe handed her and heading out the door. She looked at the list as she made her way through the main building. Jess decided the gardens would be a great place to get many of the assigned items. She ran into Lucia before she could make it outside.

Lucia raised a single, dark eyebrow. "Aren't you supposed to be in Ronobe's class right now?" Then she snapped her fingers. "Oh, is today the Above and Below session?"

"It is." Jess glanced down at her page then gave Lucia a mischievous smile. "I don't suppose you'd like to help me out, would you?"

"Sure, what do you need?"

Jess looked around, searching for something that would give her a height advantage. There was a bench near one of the walls of tropical planters. "Let's go over here."

Lucia gamely posed for Jess. First Jess had Lucia stand with her legs shoulder width apart and her arms crossed. Jess lay on the ground between her feet with the camera aimed upward. It made for a very intimidating shot.

The second photo involved Lucia leaning against a nearby wall, turned slightly away from Jess's position atop the bench. Lucia still had her arms crossed but looked over her shoulder up at Jess. The smile Lucia wore was perhaps a little telling, but Jess still thought it was a gorgeous shot. She scrolled back on the screen to look at the little pictures then hopped off the bench. "That's perfect, thanks!"

"Do I get to see them?"

Jess grinned at her. "Nope. I have to go get the rest of the pictures on the list before my session is up. Maybe if you stop by the art studio during tomorrow's class you can see our albums."

Lucia winked. "I'll do that. Just make sure there's no

wet paint on your hands."

Jess was still laughing as she pushed outside and made her way down the garden path.

She had a ton of fun during the next hour, even going to the dock for photos of one of the sailboats moored there. Jess walked to the end of the pier and took a picture from one side, then stood on shore and got a shot of the opposite.

One of her favorite pictures was of a large tropical bird she'd never seen before. Her first shot was taken while lying on the ground directly below where the bird sat on a low branch. It made a strange warbling sound and Jess sincerely hoped it wouldn't shit on her before she could take the picture. It was bright red with blue and purple accent feathers. The beak was a startling orange. Jess was used to the more muted colors of native Michigan birds. Maybe that was why she always loved the rare sightings of cardinals and bluebirds at her backyard feeder.

It didn't move, even when she carefully crept out from beneath it. Or when she stepped up on a nearby bench to get more height, much the way she'd done when taking pictures of Lucia. The green grass below made all the colors pop and Jess was especially pleased with that perspective.

She continued working her way down the list throughout the course of the hour-long session. While the morning light wasn't as nice as afternoon and the golden hour of early evening, the beautiful setting and blue skies meant nothing captured would turn out bad. One thing she made sure to do before turning in her camera was to delete all but the pairs of photos she wanted to submit. Jess figured it would be easier on Ronobe that way. She couldn't wait to see them printed out the next day.

****

Lucia found Jess after a leisurely lunch. "What's on the agenda today, another bike ride?"

Jess shrugged. "I'm not sure, actually. I signed up for

the poetry class with Penemuel at three today, so I don't have as much time as usual to explore."

"Have you done that before?"

"Not at all. Not even when I was younger. I was more into sports than writing angsty poetry, but I figured what the hell, you know? I like trying new things."

Lucia's eyes twinkled. "Oh really?"

Jess glanced around to make sure they were alone then shoved Lucia's shoulder. "I'm not talking about that! But–" She tilted her head and gave her a naughty smile. "I do in that regard, too."

"Good to know." Lucia's lips were parted, and she began to lean forward before catching herself and glancing around. Jess was glad to see Lucia was as affected by their insane chemistry as she was. "So, since you've got an earlier third session, would you be interested in a long dinner cruise?"

"Cruise? Like, on a boat?"

Lucia snickered. "Yes, Jess. On a boat. The *Pair O Dice* to be more specific. As a warning, it won't be just the two of us because we still need to safely operate the boat."

"Who else?"

"Don't worry, it's only people I trust implicitly. Amy, Berith, Gusion, Zepar, and Lahash."

Jess knew the assistant director of the resort but two of the names were only vaguely familiar from orientation on the first day. "No Captain Eem? And who are Berith and Gusion?"

"Eem has plans and isn't usually part of our group. Berri runs our yoga and meditation sessions. Gus is the activities director."

"Oh yeah, that's right. There are no other guests going out?" She asked.

"Just you." She must have read something on Jess's face because Lucia added, "I told you that I trust them all. We're breaking the rules but I've known those five for a long time. They've seen a lot over the long years we've worked at Paradise Island. It will be okay, I promise. Oh, and I asked Azazel to put together a spread of food and drinks for dinner and general entertainment."

Jess grinned. "Dinner, sunset, and you? Count me in."

She didn't know if Lucia expected her to say no, but Jess was surprised by the look of genuine pleasure that transformed Lucia's face.

"Excellent! I'll see you at the dock at five thirty. And—" The chirping phone on her hip interrupted whatever else she was going to say, and Lucia mouthed *Sorry* before turning away.

"Bye, Luce," Jess whispered before heading back to her cabin. With only two hours before her next session, Jess thought it was a great time to get a few laps in at the pool and read a short fanfic. She wondered about Lucia's decision to make such a big statement by inviting her on a cruise with all her closest friends. Did that mean she was interested in more than a short casual fling? And how would that even work out with Jess set to return home in a few weeks? Jess didn't know but she was going to do her best not to think too hard about the situation and simply enjoy her time. She deserved to be happy, damnit.

# Chapter Twelve

There was a slight breeze that evening when Jess got ready to head down to the docks, so she stuffed her Scion hat and a hoodie into a larger drawstring tote bag she pulled from her suitcase, along with her kindle and the checked-out resort camera. Jess looked around to make sure she wasn't missing anything. She saw her phone on the desk and decided to lock that in the safe with her wallet and passport. Everything else should be secure enough now that Stephen was gone.

Jess did a headcount when she got to the dock and saw everyone but Lahash and Lucia waiting. Her attention shifted to movement on the deck of the *Pair O Dice*. Jess was too far away to hear anything but could clearly see that Lucia and Lahash were engaged in an animated discussion. Lahash gesticulated, first pointing at Lucia, then vaguely toward shore. Lucia responded with something that made Lahash throw her arms up in the air and stalk away toward the pilot house of the boat.

Lucia turned and saw Jess's approach on the dock and gave a smile and a wave. Whatever issues Lahash had clearly didn't impact Lucia wanting Jess on the trip. A small part of her was concerned about their relationship. Was Lahash jealous, or maybe warning Lucia away from fooling around with Jess because of the risk? Jess had no clue. One part of her wanted to know but the other, bigger, part wanted to keep her head in the tropical sand a little longer.

Zepar bounded over as soon as she joined the main group near the gangway for the boat. "Jess, hey! You remember me from the snorkeling expedition?"

She laughed and accepted his exuberant hug. It was a way different reception than the professional one she'd witnessed the day of their big water adventure. "Hard to forget you, my dude. Good to see you again."

"Yeah, same. It's great that Luce found a click this

round, you know?" She merely nodded back to him, not having the slightest clue what a click was. She made a mental note to ask Lucia about that later, too.

Lucia came down the gangway. "Jess! Have you met everyone yet?"

She shook her head, suddenly feeling shy around all the people she'd had little to no interaction with since arriving at the resort.

"Let's get that out of the way then." Lucia walked down to the dock and put an arm around her shoulders. "For those of you that haven't met her yet, this is one of our guests, Jess Parker. Jess, you know Amy and Zepar." She gestured to the others. "Those two are Berri and Gus. Now, let's get aboard. Food was delivered a short while ago and Lahash went up top to get the engines going."

The trip out was a little awkward at first, despite the fact that Lucia didn't leave her side. It was clear by the conversation and general comfort level that the group knew each other well and spent a lot of time together. Jess felt a little like an outsider, but they were great about including her by asking her plenty of questions. She figured it was probably weird for them, too, because she was a guest and not a resort employee.

Once Lahash had deemed them far enough away from the resort, which to Jess meant she couldn't see Paradise Island anymore, she brought the big boat to a stop. The waves of their wake caught up and sent it rocking a bit while Zepar dropped anchor. "It's not as deep as you'd think here. I just don't want us to drift off the shelf," he explained, when he saw Jess watching.

Jess nodded despite having no knowledge of boating on the sea. She just assumed it was all super deep. Hell, even Lake Michigan was too deep for anchor. At least she thought it was. Her knowledge of boating began and ended with day drinking on Caleb and Richard's pontoon boat a few holiday weekends every summer.

Once they were secured, Lahash joined them on the back deck. Amy handed her a drink. "Thanks, Captain." They all chuckled and Lahash took a sip of her sangria.

She looked over to Jess and raised her glass. "Great to have you aboard, Jess. Luce has nothing but good things to say about you."

Jess didn't know Lahash well enough to tell if she were lying but nodded. "Thanks for being the driver. It's so beautiful out here. Maybe I should sign up for another excursion."

Apparently, that was the correct thing to say because Lahash's smile got looser and actually made her eyes crinkle. "I'll admit that it's my favorite of any other place in the world." She raised her face to the waning sunshine and closed her eyes. "There is something about the freedom of the open water…it's exhilarating."

Zepar chucked her shoulder. "Yeah, yeah, we all know you're a water fiend."

Lahash moved her drink away with the other hand to keep his antics from spilling it and rolled her eyes. "Whatever, it's not like you have any room to talk. We're cut from the same skin, my friend."

"But I make my love of the water much cooler." He looked over at Jess, searching for confirmation. "Don't you think?"

She held up her hands and laughed. "Oh, I'm not getting in the middle of this. I can tell it's a regular argument."

Lucia leaned close. "Good call. They'll keep going for the rest of the night if they think someone agrees with them."

Jess wandered around the boat with the camera while laughter and conversation continued on the back deck. She got some good shots of a few small islands farther out, and the low light of the sun sparkling on the water. She paused to enjoy the view when someone wrapped their arms around her from behind.

Jess stiffened until she realized it was Lucia. She glanced over her shoulder, more than a little panicked. "Aren't you worried about what your friends will say?"

"They're aware of our situation. I told you I trust this group. Do you trust me?"

Jess's heart slowed and she nodded. "Sorry, I just know you wanted to keep this quiet because we were technically breaking the rules."

Lucia laughed. "If anyone knows a thing or two about

breaking the rules, it's the ones on this boat."

She shook her head at Lucia's statement. "That seems so wrong coming from their boss. Shouldn't you be a better influence?"

Lucia moved her mouth closer and whispered. "I'm a great influence. Perhaps you'll need a little convincing later." Her lips ghosted over the edge of Jess's ear and Jess shivered.

Her voice, when it came, was breathy. "Convincing is good. Your place or mine?"

"Mine." Jess's knees went weak at that single word answer. The timber of Lucia's voice and the way she held Jess so tight from behind conveyed more than the obvious meaning. Not for the first time, Jess wondered exactly what they were doing and if either of them would make it through the aftermath of Jess's return home.

They were interrupted when Amy called, "Food's ready. Come inside before Zepar and Gus eat it all."

Lucia snorted. "Not on my watch. We'll be right there." She stepped back from Jess. "Are you okay? Are you having fun?"

Jess turned around and leaned against the railing, the gentle bobbing of the boat making her feel at ease. "I am, actually. Thanks again for inviting me."

"I'm just glad you said yes."

She took a chance and brought up the argument between Lucia and Lahash before they all boarded the boat. "Is everything okay between you and Lahash? Is she mad that you brought me along?"

Lucia sighed and looked away for a few seconds before meeting Jess's gaze. "We'll be fine. And she likes you, Jess. La is just…she's concerned for both of us when the time comes that you have to go back."

"She's worried this will bite us in the ass, isn't she?"

Lucia snickered. "That's one way to put it."

"I'll admit that I've had a few concerns as well."

"Oh?"

"I like you. Probably more than I should and definitely more than anyone else in a long time. I don't know what the future will bring for us, but I'm still committed to enjoying my time here as much as possible."

Lucia swallowed and looked sad. "Are you sure? Completely sure?"

"I am." Jess grabbed Lucia's hand and gave it a squeeze. "This is worth it. Kam told me that I deserve to be happy, and I think I've begun to agree with him."

"And when you go back?"

"Then I'll have plenty of happy memories to tide me over until I start to make new ones. One day at a time."

"Hey, are you two going to eat or not?"

Lucia squeezed Jess's hand in return before pulling her inside the cabin. "On our way."

There was something that looked like the world's largest charcuterie board set up where they'd had their food on the excursion. Slices of bread and condiments meant they could make sandwiches, or just have crackers, fruit, cheese, and vegetables if that was the preference. There was a cooler of drinks nearby, as well as a jumbo container of the resort's special sangria. Jess and Lucia each fixed their plates while Gus, Zepar, and Berri all went back for seconds. It could have been thirds though based on the speed they were eating.

"So, Jess, what's your favorite thing you've done at the resort so far?"

"Probably Luce," Lahash joked, and everyone laughed.

Jess glanced up at Lucia to see her face a little darker than normal. She should have expected the question and the teasing. After all, she wasn't one of their normal group of friends and didn't have the history to join regular conversation. But they all knew Lucia. "Honestly? I've loved everything here. The bike riding and view are unbeatable. Classes with Ronobe have introduced me to a new love of art, and even my one other excursion on the *Pair O Dice* had me trying things I never thought I'd do in a million years." She paused and shrugged. "Oh, and Luce is great, too."

That sent the rest of the group into laughter again. For her part, Lucia took the joking in stride. "You're all hilarious."

"Poor Luce. She has it so rough trapped on a paradise island while working for her daddy."

Lucia threw a grape at Berri. "Rude."

"Tell us about the real world, Jess. What's it like where you're from?" Gus looked as excited as the rest for information about something other than the island.

"Cold." They looked at her in shock and she elaborated. "Okay, not right now and not all the time. We have four seasons. Our Michigan winters give us temperatures below zero and an abundance of snow." More wide eyes met her words and Jess remembered that only three places in the world used standard units of measurement. "Uh, what's zero Celsius? That's freezing, right? That's thirty-two degrees in Fahrenheit so, um, carry the one..." She was bullshitting. Jess had no idea what the conversion between the two was.

"Negative six degrees in Michigan would be negative twenty-one Celsius."

"Nope." Zepar held up his hands. "That is not the climate for me."

"Same," Lahash said.

"I've seen the US map. Aren't you surrounded by giant lakes or something?" Zepar asked. "What do people do with all that water in the winter?"

She shrugged. "Me? Nothing. I prefer staying inside with a warm fire going and a good book. But other people drill holes in the smaller frozen lakes to fish, go skiing, snowshoeing, or sledding."

If anything, that made the big redheaded man look even more horrified. He glanced around the group. "Remind me to never go anywhere that's not tropical."

They laughed again and the questions continued. Amy asked if she had any pets or siblings.

"No to both. But I'm considering adopting a dog when I get back. I've read a lot about the senior program and think that may be the way to go."

"Senior program?"

"It's where you can adopt an older dog or cat. One that would usually be considered unadoptable because of its age and would typically be euthanized. Folks don't want a pet with a shorter life span, or one that may have medical issues. I figure everyone deserves a second chance."

"But won't that make you sad if you lose your pet

after a short amount of time?"

Jess looked at Lahash and understood the point she was trying to make. "It should be sad. I think the loss of someone should result in sorrow if they brought true joy into your life. And real happiness is worth the pain of loss."

Berri raised her glass. "Good answer, Jess."

Everyone followed her lead and shouted their agreement.

The conversation eventually turned away from Jess and her life. Lucia used the lull in their attention to whisper in her ear, "You're worth the pain of loss to me as well. I hope you know that."

Jess gave her a hopeful look. "Maybe we'll meet again at a later date."

Lucia sighed and a defeated look flickered across her expressive face before she hid it with a sad smile. "I don't think that will happen. I'm trapped on this island, Jess. It doesn't seem likely my father will ever let me escape."

Jess put her arm around Lucia's waist and pulled her close. "Well, then I guess we should make the most of our time together."

The smile Lucia gave her caused butterflies to fill her stomach, but her words and the timber of her voice made things flutter farther south. "I guess we should."

The sunset ride made Jess feel a lot of unfamiliar things. She never thought she'd be so comfortable with a group of relative strangers. But they were extremely inclusive without being prying. Not to mention, Jess had plenty of time to snuggle on the deck, wrapped in Lucia's embrace. Once she had her fill of sunset photos, Jess didn't have much else to do but put on her hoodie and relax next to Lucia while the water churned out behind the boat as the sky turned purple with the oncoming night.

Everyone went their separate ways back at the resort. There was a two-person crew waiting to take care of the catered food, so Zepar and Lahash stayed aboard to supervise and stow the rest of the gear for Captain Eem.

The rest shared electric carts and went off, presumably to wherever they lived on the island. That left Jess and Lucia to walk back to the main building alone.

"Sorry, *ya amar*. I should have brought a cart down for us before we left."

Jess snorted at the new nickname. "It's fine. A little exercise is good for me. My knees haven't hurt in days. I think it's the warm air and company I've been keeping lately."

Lucia gave her a sly look. "Oh really?"

She shrugged. "I mean, I can't say for certain. It could be Chef's cooking." She laughed as Lucia pulled her into the darkness next to the paved path.

"Maybe you need something a little warmer than the air to convince you?"

Jess stepped into Lucia's embrace. "Maybe something hot even?"

"Oh, that can be arranged—"

"Don't move!"

Jess looked over to see Donovan Staten standing on the path holding a large kitchen knife. The overhead lights cast a rictus of shadows across his face making him look more sinister than attractive.

Lucia immediately spun around and put her body between Jess and Donovan. "Mr. Staten, is there something I can help you with?"

His arms and face featured scratches and sores where he'd clearly been picking at his own skin. Donovan's hands shook but he didn't drop the knife. "I don't want to hurt you, but I need the keys to the drug cabinet in the medical clinic."

"There's nothing in that cabinet for you, Mr. Staten. Why don't you put the knife down?"

"Don't tell me what to do you fucking bitch! Give me the keys, now!" He stepped toward them and sliced the knife through the air. Everything that happened after was almost too fast for Jess to follow.

Lucia rushed Donovan and Jess was afraid he'd actually hit her with the blade, but there was no blood or cry of pain. Instead, the knife was knocked from his hand right before Lucia grabbed him by his belt and the front of his shirt and lifted with his forward momentum. He careened over Lucia's head right before she slammed him to the ground off the path. His back hitting the soft grass was loud and probably painful, but not nearly as bad as the paved path would have felt. It was an impressive show of strength but then Jess knew Lucia was strong from the day she fell from the walking path and sprained her ankle.

The move stunned him for a minute and Lucia wasted no time grabbing her cell phone to call for help. Jess kicked the knife farther away while Lucia spoke with security. She'd barely dropped the phone back into her pocket when Donovan scrambled up and made a lunge for Jess. "I'll kill you!"

Lucia grabbed him by the collar and spun them both around so Jess faced Lucia's back. Lucia's voice lowered to a growl which did nothing for Jess's poor racing heart. Every word was enunciated perfectly. "You will not touch her."

Jess wasn't sure if it was Lucia's tone of voice or the strength of her grip, but Donovan suddenly grew quiet and afraid. "Please..."

A scooter careened around the bend in the path, followed closely by a golf cart. Jess recognized Saleos on the scooter, the resort's head of security. The other two were the same ones she'd witnessed escorting Stephen out of Lucia's office.

Saleos had a weirdly deep voice. "What's the problem, Luce?"

Lucia shoved Donovan toward the big man. He stumbled and fell to the ground before Saleos righted him again. "Return him. Immediately." Her voice radiated fury and Jess could only guess the expression on her face.

"No review?"

Lucia shook her head. "Not for this one. He attacked me and another guest."

He nodded once. "As you wish, boss," before handing over the man to the other two security guards. Then he picked up the knife and dropped it in the basket on the front of the scooter. Once Donovan was secured in the back of the golf cart, Saleos remounted his scooter and gave a little wave, then they all took off down the path. They were out of sight in less than a minute.

The adrenaline hit Jess all at once. She gasped and bent forward at the waist, resting her hands on her knees while she breathed hard through her racing heart. "Holy shit. Did that seriously just happen?" Once she got her breathing under control, she stood again and noticed that Lucia still hadn't turned around. "Hey, are you okay? He didn't get you, did he?"

She saw as much as heard Lucia take a deep breath then slowly let it out. "No."

Jess moved closer and put her hand on Lucia's shoulder. "I'm sorry you had to deal with that. Not exactly the way I pictured this evening going but we're not hurt and that has to count for something, right?"

Lucia spun around and pulled Jess into a tight embrace. She shuddered in Jess's arms. Then before Jess could ask her what was wrong, Lucia kissed her hard and fast. Her heart began to race for another, less terrifying, reason. Lucia's tongue was strong and insistent when she begged for entrance into Jess's mouth. The fear and surprise from Donovan's attack faded away in the onslaught of Lucia's passion.

When Lucia pulled away from the kiss, she rested her forehead against Jess's. Her eyes were closed when Jess opened her own. Lucia panted for a few seconds before swallowing thickly and meeting Jess's gaze. "I'm so sorry, love. He should have never gotten this far. We have a system in place to catch people that may be falling outside the program." She shook her head. "I knew he was on the edge. The signs were there days ago outside the medical clinic. I was a fool to think he wanted to help himself here."

Jess reached up to place her palm against Lucia's cheek. "Hey, it's not your fault. You can't know what someone else is thinking, or how they're going to act. What you can do is protect yourself and innocent guests and for that I'm extremely grateful."

That brought Lucia around. "Innocent guests, hmm?"

She shrugged. "I mean... I have my moments. Do you need to fill out any paperwork or can we get back to your place? I don't know about you, but I'm ready for a drink."

"I think that can be arranged. Come on." Lucia took Jess's hand and led them farther down the path toward the main building where Jess knew a group of carts were parked.

Lucia turned to her after they got into one of the carts. "Thanks for being so understanding."

"I'm learning that not everything happens the way we want. Ultimately, we can only deal with stuff as it comes along and control what we can."

"That's pretty wise."

Jess laughed. "Don't be so impressed. I'm picking up a lot of great advice from Dr. Kam. He's good."

That earned her a gentle smile. "So are you, Jess. I hope you know that."

She shrugged at the tender statement. "I think I'm learning."

"Excellent."

****

It took them less than fifteen minutes to drive back to Lucia's house on the darkened paths. There were solar lights low to the ground every ten feet, but they didn't illuminate much, just enough to not stray.

Throughout the trip, Lucia kept Jess in a constant state of arousal with her strong grip high on Jess's thigh. She never knew something like that could be a turn on. Hell, Jess didn't realize she could even be turned on to that extent anymore. She chalked it up as a delayed response to the physical altercation. There was no denying that Lucia's strength and forceful words to Donovan were like an aphrodisiac.

It was a new feeling for sure. Jess was sporty, some had called her butch, others described her as femme, but the truth was that Jess was somewhere in the middle. She was lucky to have never witnessed or been part of any kind of violence like that before. But that meant Jess had no idea how it would make her feel until it happened. She never once thought she would be the kind of woman to swoon over an aggressive display. Part of her was disturbed by the revelation but a bigger part of her wanted to enjoy the new kind of stimulation.

"You've been pretty quiet on the ride. Are you sure that you're okay?"

Jess jumped when Lucia spoke and she turned wide eyes toward the woman who had dominated her thoughts since Jess had arrived at the resort. "Me? Yeah, he didn't touch me. I should probably ask you that."

"It's understandable if what you witnessed left you shaken up. We can just have a quiet evening with that promised drink. Or I can take you back to your cabin if you need to decompress by yourself for a while."

Lucia squeezed Jess's leg. She probably meant the gesture to be comforting but all it did was make Jess gasp as she found herself wound inexplicably higher. "I'm not shaken and definitely don't want to be alone right now," Jess said through clenched teeth.

"Then what—oh." Lucia took in Jess's expression, then looked down to where her own hand rested on Jess's taught thigh muscle.

"Lucia,"

"Yes?"

"If you don't take me inside in the next minute, I'm going to do something that this cart probably wasn't meant for."

As if thinking about that very thing, Lucia looked from Jess to the steering wheel, then smirked. "I guess we should go inside then. Give me a second to plug in and I'll meet you at the door."

Jess whined at the stupid delay but hastily left the cart and strode to Lucia's front door. Once there, she leaned against the solid surface and watched Lucia plug in the charge cable and sling both their tote bags over her shoulders. Jess had forgotten hers in her distracted state. Lucia stopped a few feet from Jess and just stared.

"What are you waiting for?"

"You look good there, framed in the moonlight."

Jess tugged self-consciously at her oversized hoodie. "I doubt it. My sweatshirts are chosen for comfort, not sex appeal. I'd be equally as attractive in a burlap sack."

Lucia shook her head and stepped closer. "I'm not looking at your clothes, *mia kara*. I'm looking at your smile, the way your eyes watch me approach, and the way your beautiful soul shines through everything."

She grew shy at Lucia's admiration. "I don't know what to say to that. Are you even real? Because nobody says that kind of stuff outside of a romance novel."

Laughter met her skepticism and Lucia closed the distance between them. She took Jess's hands and raised them over her head before leaning down to kiss Jess's neck.

Jess arched into Lucia's lips and moaned. "Oh, God."

"Definitely not him." Then Lucia worked her way up Jess's neck and across her jawline before taking her in a searing kiss. Just the touch of Lucia's tongue against her own left her with weak knees. Lucia abruptly let go of Jess's hands and moved down to run hot palms up underneath both the sweatshirt and Jess's T-shirt.

"Fuck. You're going to kill me before we even get inside." The hands suddenly left her overstimulated skin and Jess sagged against the door.

Lucia winked as she met Jess's gaze. "We can't have that now, can we?" Then she reached around Jess and entered the code to the door lock. It swung open and Jess would have fallen backward to the floor without Lucia's quick intervention and strong arms. "Careful. I want you in one piece before I take you apart."

Jess got her footing and groaned, Lucia's words turning the functioning part of her brain to mush. "You *are* trying to kill me, aren't you?"

Lucia's voice grew serious for a second. "Never," she whispered as she shot Jess a mischievous grin. "Come on. I have a promise to keep."

"Promise?" Jess's brain definitely wasn't fully firing. "The drink?"

"Drink?" Truthfully, the only thing Jess wanted to drink at that point was Lucia.

Lucia chuckled and pulled Jess into the kitchen. She removed two recyclable bottles of water, then gestured toward the stairs leading up to her bedroom.

"Finally," Jess muttered. They hit the bedroom minutes later. Jess wandered over to the bed as Lucia followed and put the waters on the night stand. She faced Lucia. "Are you—" Her question was silenced by another toe-curling kiss.

Lucia made short work of Jess's hoodie, then her shirt beneath. Jess shivered as she was left standing there in shorts and her bra. Not wanting to be the only one who was half nude, Jess began unbuttoning Lucia's loose linen shirt while the kiss continued. Her hands faltered when Lucia trailed the kisses down to her chin, then back across the jaw until she could nip at Jess's neck.

"Shit," Jess hissed.

Jess redoubled her efforts until she could push the shirt off Lucia's shoulders.

Lucia let go of her long enough to free herself from each sleeve. Then she wrapped her arms around Jess again and promptly unclasped her bra. Lucia replaced the fabric with her own hands and Jess moaned.

"I love the way you sound."

"So-sound?" Lucia massaged her breasts then moved her fingers up to pinch Jess's nipples. Jess moaned again.

Lucia licked her way up to Jess's ear. She nipped Jess's ear lobe. "The noises you make when you're aroused. They're real and raw and you make me feel grounded."

Jess could barely think at that point she was so turned on. "You're wearing too many clothes," she managed to say, as she untied Lucia's linen shorts. Then she slid them down until they pooled at Lucia's feet. Jess reached around to dig her fingers into each fabric-covered ass cheek.

Lucia groaned and pulled away from Jess's neck. If Jess thought Lucia's hands were everywhere before, it was nothing compared to her speed and urgency removing Jess's shorts and underwear. Their footwear had been left by the door downstairs, so Jess was left completely nude and very wet. Lucia quickly removed her own underwear then guided Jess backward onto the bed and settled between her open thighs. Jess canted her hips upward, hoping for a little friction to take her over the sharp edge she'd been teetering on since the front door.

Lucia moved her hands into a pushup position and lifted herself out of Jess's reach. "Not so fast, love."

Ignoring Jess's frustrated whine, Lucia got onto her hands and knees and started shuffling backward on the king size bed, only stopping to lavish attention to Jess's breasts and nipples. "I've been wanting to kiss you all over, to taste you, since you walked onto that dock earlier."

"I won't last," Jess warned.

Lucia grinned at Jess once she was poised right above her mound. "That's the great thing about quick bites…you can have as many as you like until you're sated." Then she settled onto the bed between Jess's legs and gently parted her lips. "You're so wet." The declaration was done with whispered awe. A sacred utterance.

That comment elicited another whine and Jess threw her arm over her face. "Please…" She shuddered at the cool breath whispering across her open labia and clit.

Before Jess could beg again, Lucia leaned down and swiped her tongue through Jess's folds.

Jess rode Lucia's mouth for all she was worth. It could have lasted seconds, or hours, she wasn't sure. All Jess knew was that she was close before Lucia worked two fingers inside. After that, she may as well have signed the warrant for her sexecution.

Lucia held Jess's abdomen in place while she continued to lick up and around Jess's clit at the same time those long fingers kept at their unceasing pace. Jess closed her eyes as little sparkling spots danced across her vision. A great pressure grew in her head and chest then broke like tidal water crashing over her, drowning, cleansing, and freeing. Jess cried out as she clenched around those powerful fingers, riding wave after wave of her pulsing orgasm. It lasted longer than she could ever remember. Then with one last shudder, Jess collapsed blissfully limp onto the bed.

Lucia stopped all motion before depositing a sweet kiss to Jess's clit, making her twitch. At least she was considerate enough not to remove her fingers. "How was that?"

Jess was unable to move, and her power of speech had abandoned her minutes before. "Buh."

"I'm afraid I don't speak that language. Can you translate?"

Jess moved her arm and stared stupidly down her torso

toward her lover. Lucia's eyes twinkled with mirth.

"If you don't answer, I'll be forced to punish you."

"Hu" Jess cleared her throat. "How will you punish me? I've already come—oh, fuck!"

Lucia began thrusting again mid-question. Only that time she curled her fingers upward in such a way they pushed forcefully on that sensitive spot inside. Jess went from sated to needy almost immediately. She'd never come twice in a row during sex before, but it literally took mere seconds of aggressive sucking on Jess's twitching clit for her to come screaming again.

The second orgasm left Jess shaking and muttering and she knew she was bordering on incoherent. Lucky for her, Lucia let her rest properly after that one.

"Are you ready?" Lucia asked, a few minutes after Jess stopped clenching around her fingers.

She nodded and prepared herself for the simultaneous overstimulation and empty feeling as Lucia carefully slid her fingers out. That was the point that Jess would have said she was done, fully tapped out for the night. But the sight of Lucia licking her fingers clean filled Jess with a new burst of sexual energy. She pulled Lucia down and kissed her passionately. "How the hell did you do that?" Jess asked when they came up for air.

Lucia shrugged as she sat up enough to grab their water bottles. "It was the easiest thing in the world. I just listened to your body. Every reaction, the way you taste and how wet you got...it was as though you spoke to me and told me everything you liked best. I love how respon-sive you are during sex."

Jess sighed after quenching her own thirst. "I've never done that before."

"Really?" The look on Lucia's face said she didn't believe Jess in the slightest.

"I swear it's true. I've never been able to come twice like that, didn't even know it was possible for me, to be honest."

Lucia smirked at her and put the bottle back on the nightstand. Then she leaned over and took Jess's as well. "I'm honored. What do you say we explore more things you've never done before?"

As a response, Jess hooked her leg around the back of Lucia's thighs and pulled her down. Lucia caught herself with her hands on either side of Jess's shoulders but got the hint and put her talented mouth to work on Jess's neck again. The night was just getting started but Jess had a feeling her heart and body would never be the same. Lucia had already ruined her.

# Chapter Thirteen

Awareness washed over Jess slowly like a rising tide. She tried to go back to sleep but once her mind began racing with a million thoughts it was impossible. Jess took in her surroundings with her eyes shut. The bed was comfortable and the temperature perfect, but the air was pungent with more than the usual blossoms and salt breeze. They'd stayed up too late, but Jess felt strangely refreshed, if sore in places she'd long forgotten about after such an intense night. She sensed Lucia in the bed nearby, her breathing even and deep.

Jess shifted slowly to stretch her calves. The darkness in the room told her that it was still early but she had no idea why she was awake.

Lucia stirred next to her. "Is something wrong?"

"No. I just woke and was taking in the moment."

The exhalation of a yawn tickled the hairs around Jess's temple. "Aren't you tired?"

Jess tried to answer. "I am, but—" Even with her eyes shut, Lucia's yawn proved contagious. "But I woke and started thinking about all the things I want to do when I get back. Then I wondered what I was going back to." Jess opened her eyes and turned her head to peer at Lucia through the darkness.

Lucia rolled so she was lying on her side and met Jess's gaze. "What do you mean?"

"I mean, I've been going through the motions for years. What if I don't just need a change of attitude, but a complete change of scenery?"

Lucia was silent for a minute. "You think you need to move?"

"I could definitely see myself living someplace like this. It's just…different. There's work to be had but it's a different pace. Like time doesn't exist here and the world merely revolves around who you can touch and the beauty you create."

"Jess—"

"I know, I know, you all talk about how trapped you are on Paradise Island. That it's stagnant here and lacks the diversity of life experience and all that, but sometimes familiarity and safety are good things to have. It's certainly idyllic."

Lucia sighed and rolled to her back, then scrubbed her face with both hands. "I know what you're getting at, *elskede*."

"But do you though? It doesn't have to be about this place. I'm just thinking that if you and I both agree we have something that *could* work, maybe we could try to make a go of it if I were closer. Maybe another island or resort nearby even if this one isn't hiring?"

Lucia looked at her. "First, do you even have any experience working in a hospitality-based industry, or in a remote location? And what about your friends and family? You'd be leaving everything behind for the slim possibility that we wouldn't end up hating each other in a few years."

"Is that what happened to you and Lahash? You seem to get along pretty well."

"No, I'm not saying that exactly. I think there is a bigger issue, besides the fact that there is no way for you to emigrate from your home to Paradise Island."

Jess caressed Lucia's arm. "And that is?"

"As much as I'd love to pretend like my life is my own and I can break free at any time, I'm tied to this place for the foreseeable future. I'm stuck here and there is no changing that."

Jess sat up and clutched the sheet to her chest. "But why? Is it because you just don't want to leave, or that you don't want to disappoint your dad?"

"You don't understand. I can't leave. My father—it's just not possible unless he lets me go. I made a promise a long time ago and I'm responsible for the work we do here, for all the people on Paradise Island, temporary and permanent alike. I can't let them down."

"I see." The news wasn't surprising. Jess expected that it wouldn't be as easy as all that. Hell, she knew this thing between them was always going to be short-lived, but she felt something special about Lucia that she'd never felt for anyone and she had to try. Even though it felt as though she had a lead weight sitting on her chest, Jess met Lucia's expressive eyes. "I'm sorry, Luce. I didn't mean to pressure you into something you couldn't or don't want to do."

"You have nothing to be sorry about. I'll admit that I've found a connection with you that I've never experienced before. But the situation is more complicated than I can explain." Lucia reached over to tug at the sheet in Jess's hands and Jess followed her direction to lay back and put her head on Lucia's shoulder. "I wish I could make everyone happy, myself included. I'm just…stuck."

Jess let out a long sigh. "It's okay. I meant what I said last night on the boat. You make me happy and that means this is worth it." She hugged Lucia around her waist. "I have a feeling the memories we're making will be bittersweet but even so, I'll gladly take them with me to the grave."

"There's a local saying that the grave is a hole for the body and heartache is a hole for the soul."

She snorted at Lucia's depressing declaration. "That's decidedly less than inspirational. I guess I was hoping for, hell, I don't know what I wanted out of this. I thought maybe I could find some happily ever after here but maybe I need to take care of myself first." She turned to see Lucia staring at her from a few inches away. "According to Kam, if I don't resolve my internal issues, they'll follow me wherever I go."

"That's very true," Lucia said quietly.

Jess tried to be hopeful about it all. "Who knows, maybe we'll meet again someday."

Lucia caressed her cheek and tucked a lock of Jess's longish bangs behind her ear. "Maybe we will. But no matter what happens after you leave Paradise Island Resort, I will never forget you. For good or ill, you've left an indelible mark on me."

If you had asked Jess at any other point in her life if it were possible to simultaneously be overjoyed and filled with sorrow, she'd have said no way. But at that moment, everything changed. She kissed Lucia and poured everything she'd begun to feel into that intense connection. The sun broke over the horizon and was on its way to another beautiful morning, but Jess was determined to steal a few more minutes of Lucia for herself before life and the island pulled her away.

****

They'd just stopped in front of Jess's cabin when Lucia's phone rang. She held up a finger playfully, indicating for Jess to wait, then answered.

"Hello?"

Lucia's indrawn breath said that whoever was on the other end wasn't expected. A gamut of expressions flickered across Lucia's face, surprise, panic, anger, and sadness. It was weird for sure. When she hung up, she sighed.

Jess put her hand over Lucia's free one where it rested on the seat between them. "Is everything okay?"

Lucia shook her head and pinched the bridge of her nose. "Mostly. That was my father. I'm being called to the big island. I was going to ask if you wanted to take a bike ride and have a picnic tonight, but I don't know how long I'll be gone."

"Well, that sucks. I still need to speak with Gus before I go to lunch today since I forgot to sign up for a third activity last night. If you're busy, I'll just see if I can get an early spa session."

"What about another creative writing class with Penemuel?"

"I realized after the poetry session that it's not really my thing. Not like art is. Why?"

Lucia shrugged. "I was just throwing options out." She snapped her fingers. "Gus is running a group hike today. You may like that a lot more. I recommend taking your camera because some of the places you visit on the trip are particularly beautiful."

"That sounds fun. I'll look into it. Where does the hike take you?"

"There are trails that lead toward the center of the island. A lot of uphill there but worth it when you see the view at the top. The way back is much nicer."

"Will I be able to see your house?"

"Probably, if you're wasting your time looking farther inland rather than toward the much nicer ocean view. Regarding later, what about this? Like I said, I don't know how long I'll be gone but I'll let you know as soon as I get back."

Jess smiled shyly, touched that Lucia would think of her before potentially a lot of other people and things at the resort. "I'd like that, thanks."

Lucia glanced down at her watch and frowned. Then she leaned over and gave Jess a quick kiss. "Okay, I'll let you start your day. Wish me luck."

Jess got out of the cart. "Luck?"

"Eh, every visit with my father is like a high-stakes negotiation. Trust me, I'll need it."

She laughed at Lucia's over-the-top explanation. "Okay. Luck then. Bye Luce."

"Until later, *lyubimaya*."

Jess watched her drive away, before entering her cabin. She had just enough time to call activities and request a spot on the hike, then change. She was able to shower at Lucia's house but didn't have any fresh clothes there. She got to Dr. Kam's office with just two minutes to spare.

He met her at the door as soon as she pushed into the waiting room. "Good morning, Jess. How is your day going so far?"

They took their seats. "Not bad actually. I'm going on a hike this afternoon and I'm pretty excited about it. I heard the views are great, so I'll take the camera I've got checked out from the resort."

"Excellent. I'm happy to see you out and active in the fresh air."

She laughed. "There's fresh air by the pool, too. But I used to like hiking so decided I'd give it a shot."

He nodded. "Have you thought about your return, or made any definitive plans for your future?"

"I've been able to try so many new hobbies and activities since I got to the resort. I think the first thing I'm going to do is take my bike in for a tune-up. Just the small amount of riding around the island I've done has made me want to get back into it."

Kam's pleased smile conveyed his thoughts on her declaration as much as his words. "That's wonderful! Anything else?"

She nodded. "After speaking with Ronobe, I've got more of an idea about the type of art classes I can look up back in St. Seren. I've seen ads for stuff before, but I want to pick the right one first, you know?"

"Understandable. What are your favorite things you've done in your art sessions so far?"

That was a hard question because she enjoyed most of the different classes. The painting was interesting, but ultimately a lot more of an initial investment and extremely messy. Clay molding was fun, too, but another investment just to make a bunch of stuff that would ultimately clutter up her house. "I think my favorites have been photography and sketching."

She shrugged. "The sketching I can do anywhere, any time. I just need to get a sketchbook and a nice pencil set. But I'm for sure looking up some photography classes when I get home."

"Have you done any photography before? Or is this a new hobby?"

"I didn't do it seriously like I have since coming to the resort. But I have a decent camera back home that I got on eBay a few years ago. Who knows? Maybe if I enjoy it enough after I take a few classes I'll upgrade to a better camera."

Kam wrote something on his notepad then gave her a smile. "I like your drive and vision. You've taken your experiences here and made plans to continue the most positive ones when you go back. That's admirable. Is there anything else on your future Jess agenda?"

She thought about it for another minute and shook her head. "I don't think so. I figured I'll start with just a couple smaller things and try to build my joy up from there. Then I'll take each day as it happens. If opportunity comes knocking, I won't turn it away again." She rubbed the palms of her hands on her shorts. "It's exactly like you said, I deserve to be happy, so I just need to learn what that looks like back in St. Seren and not on some island in paradise."

Her thoughts suddenly touched back to the conversation in Lucia's bed just a few hours before. She frowned. Even if she knew it wasn't a possibility, it still hurt to shut the door.

"What's going through your head right now?"

Jess sighed. "I woke this morning thinking I needed to get away from my old life completely, rather than just change a few things. Like…maybe I need to move far away, perhaps even someplace tropical."

He tilted his head. "From the way you're speaking, it sounds as though you already discounted that option. Why?"

"You've told me often enough that running away from my problems wouldn't solve them, especially if my problems were internal more than external. I guess I realized that moving away isn't actually fixing my issues because they'll still be there wherever I go."

Kam nodded sagely. "Very astute, Jess. If this were a class, I'd give that answer an A plus."

She rolled her eyes at him. "Very funny."

They spent the rest of their time together with more talk of her fears and expectations involved with returning home from her vacation getaway. Once her session ended, Kam followed her to the door and held out a hand. "I have to say, it's been a real pleasure helping you in your journey."

Jess found the handshake odd but gamely accepted. "Yeah, well, I appreciate all your help with this stuff. I couldn't have made it this far without you."

"I'm not so sure about that. You've got a magnificent strength of will."

She shook her head. "You don't understand. Willpower will only get you so far. I didn't have the tools to do what I've been working on with you since arriving. You can't hit a homerun without a bat or drive a race without a car. For that I will always be grateful."

He laughed and gave her a friendly pat on the shoulder. "Well then, I'm happy to have provided your wheels." Kam opened the door for her. "Have a good day, Jess."

****

Everyone was excited to see their printed photos in Ronobe's class, but none more so than Jess. There were albums placed around the main table in the studio and Jess made a beeline for the one that had a tent card with her name sitting on top. Ronobe sidled up to her with a big grin on her face as soon as Jess opened her portfolio.

"You know, you've got a real eye for this kind of thing, Jess. I hope you pursue photography when you get home. Some of your perspective shots were quite powerful. That focused shot on the light pink blossom with the blurred image of the ocean in the background? Simply amazing! And the two you took of Lucia? Whew!" She fanned herself playfully.

Jess's cheeks grew warm at the praise, but she was secretly pleased that Ronobe liked her images so much. She also felt validated in what she told Kam, that she wanted to look into photography classes when she returned to St. Seren. Maybe one of her friends would be interested in taking it with her.

Ronobe spoke with all the guests in the class about their albums, giving constructive criticism and praise in turns. She covered cropping techniques and adjusting the focus of your photos to make them more visually appealing. They learned how to take a great shot and improve it with a simple trim job. Jess was giddy when she found out she'd be able to take her photo album with her at the end of her stay.

"Wow, Jess! I think you had the best pics of the entire group. Do you do photography or something back home?" Brittany had been wandering around the room, like most who were finished with their cropping and arranging.

Jess looked up from where she'd placed her last photo. "Not really. I've done casual photography over the years but never get out to take pictures anymore. It's such a pain to lug around a big camera when we've all got one on our cell phones, you know?"

"Yeah. I have a good webcam and microphone for my social media stuff but honestly, sometimes it's nice to just do stuff for myself and not worry about what everyone else likes."

Jess nodded, "I get that. I checked out one of the resort cameras and I've been taking so many pictures since I got here. Whether I'm on a bike ride or just walking the paths. There's a lot less pressure when I explore by myself. I can stop as often as I want to take photos, or I can just enjoy the view. I figure they don't need to be perfect. I just have to like them."

"That's pretty smart," Brittany said.

"What do you have scheduled today?" Jess didn't normally ask anyone else what they were doing but Brittany seemed particularly talkative, and Jess got the feeling that Brittany was feeling low. She figured it couldn't hurt to be friendly.

Brittany shrugged. "I have my therapy session with Doctor Berg after dinner. I was just going to go to one of the open yoga sessions as my third activity since I didn't sign up for anything else.

"Well," Jess offered. "If you like hiking, there is a session with Gus—uh, Gusion, immediately following the afternoon break. I'm taking the camera with me. You should come."

Brittany brightened. "Oh? I like hiking. You think there will be room for me?"

Jess nodded. "I just signed up this morning and was told it's another open activity like the gym and yoga. But you need to be there at three to hike with the group and have it counted for the day. Just show up and you should be fine."

"Badass, thanks Jess! I'll be there."

****

As promised, Brittany was waiting for her when Jess strolled up to the group standing outside the activity center door. Like Jess, she carried a sling bag with a water bottle.

But Jess also had the resort camera looped around her neck.

"Hey, where'd you get that?" Jess pointed toward the walking stick in Brittany's hand.

"Oh, there is a bucket full of them just inside the door. Gusion told everyone to grab one on their way out." Brittany glanced around. "Doesn't look like everyone is here yet. He said there would be seven total for the hike. You have time to grab one too."

"Cool, thanks!"

Jess got her own walking stick and came back outside as their seventh member arrived. Gus waved when he saw her. "Hey Jess. Glad to have you on the hike today."

"Thanks. Lucia told me about it."

He shook his head playfully. "She tells everyone else but never joins herself. I secretly think she doesn't like hiking up the hills."

"Who in the world does?" one of the other people in the group called out.

Jess remembered Tammy from the parasailing boat. She looked a lot happier. Jess also remembered another of their hiking group, Willy, from the same trip.

One guy that Jess only knew from a few classes together spoke up. "But think of what we'll see when we get to the top. I hiked Acadia National Park once." He shook his head. "Some views are worth it."

Gus laughed heartily. "Well, obviously I agree, or I wouldn't be leading you all today. So, let's get started." He took off at a moderate pace with the seven of them ranging behind. Jess fell toward the back just because she'd stop to take pictures every so often. She could hear Gus explaining the local flora and fauna but learning about the stuff wasn't really her jam. She just liked capturing beautiful moments, like the vivid blue butterfly sitting on a tropical blossom next to the path. Jess never did learn what that one was called.

Her hike involved a lot of falling behind, then hustling to catch up. Jess found herself pleasantly winded but able to stay with the group just fine. It was a nice feeling. Either she wasn't as out of shape as she thought, or all the fresh air on the island was doing her some good.

She stopped to get a shot of the ocean where it was perfectly framed through the trees. They were near the top but not above the thickest part of the forest yet.

"Oh, that's going to be so pretty. Now I wish I would have brought a resort camera, too." Brittany held up her cell phone. "I guess I'll have to make do with this."

Jess shrugged. "I mean, it looks pretty new, so I bet the images turn out amazing either way. Remember, it doesn't have to be perfect, you only need to like it."

Brittany laughed and sighed. "I remember. I'm still working on that bit of advice."

They fell into walking next to each other about ten feet behind the main group. "How's that going? I know you had concerns like I did about returning and falling back into old habits," Jess asked.

It took a few minutes for Brittany to answer. "I do." she admitted. "I guess I still feel guilty for how I've acted during the past few years. There's this huge part of me that is so ashamed." She looked at Jess with tears in her eyes. "If seeing myself is this bad, what do the people who know me think?"

"Your online friends?"

"No, my IRL friends and family. I've just always pushed them aside unless I needed something. I'm a bad sister and daughter, not to mention how I've used other people."

"People will learn to accept the new you back home. I realized that it's going to be a learning curve for me and my friends but if they're real friends, true ones, they'll support us on our journey."

"But what if they aren't real friends?"

"Then," Jess reached her arm out and gave Brittany a side hug. "You make new ones who appreciate how great you are. Think of this as your opportunity for a fresh start, to become a new person who wasn't built on the pain and misery of disappointment."

They walked along in silence for a few minutes before Brittany spoke again. "What if I don't deserve it? And why are you so nice to me? I was a royal bitch to you when we got to the island."

"Everyone deserves a second chance. And I'm not

being nice to you. I'm practicing engaging in the world, treating others as I'd like to be treated. And, well, a lot of the struggle you've told me about feels like my own. Brittany, this is our time to build bridges, not rivalries. Like this stupid hike."

Jess gestured up the hill where they could see the path curve around a bend out of sight. "It's hard but I think it will also be rewarding when we arrive."

Brittany rolled her eyes. "And where is that, exactly?"

Suddenly they broke free from the trees into the late afternoon sunshine. "Well, I'd say right here. Tired, sore, sweaty, but looking down at where we came from with a sense of accomplishment."

"I need more friends like you back in LA."

Jess smiled at her. "Who knows, maybe you already have them, but they've never met the real you. Only one way to find out."

"That's true." Brittany was quiet again, contemplative. Then she looked around and returned Jess's smile. "Thank you for being my first real friend. I couldn't begin to tell you what it means or repay your kindness."

"All I want is for you to find your joy. Do that and we'll call it good."

Brittany held out her hand. "It's a deal."

Jess laughed and shook it, then went off to explore the clearing with her trusty camera.

# Chapter Fourteen

The group spent hours hiking up and back down the small mountain, but the early afternoon departure meant that they arrived back at the resort just in time for dinner. Jess, Brittany, Tammy, and Willy had a great conversation about music throughout the decades that consumed the last hour of their trip. By mutual decision, they all walked into the main building to have dinner together.

Willy was first through the door of the dining room and pulled up short, causing a small backup behind him. "Sweet lordy, it's a taco bar!"

Jess tried to see around him. "Oh, I'm so down for that."

"Me too, as long as that bomb ass sangria is on the menu."

"Right?" Jess fist bumped Tammy. She turned to see Brittany hanging back a bit and made a point of tugging her shirt sleeve. "Come on, we earned these tacos. Besides, I want to hear about the community outreach project you started back home. It sounds cool."

Brittany's face brightened. "Really?"

The four hungry hikers made their way through the tables, heading for much deserved sustenance before Jess replied. "Yup. Do you work with local shelters or what?"

For the next hour, the quad of very different people from disparate walks of life carried on a conversation as though they'd known each other for years. Jess actually enjoyed their company and looked forward to doing more excursions since at least two of them were supposed to remain beyond the usual two weeks.

Willy was the first one to tap out a little after seven. He stood and gathered up his tray. "As much as I hate to call it a night, I've got an early session with Doctor Berg in the morning and I'm beat."

Jess looked around and noticed the resort dining staff were packing up the taco bar. She still had most of her drink so held it up in cheers toward Willy. "Have a good night, dude. It was great chatting about nineties grunge with you."

"Same." He gave the three of them a little wave and wandered off to drop his plate in the proper bin.

Tammy told them about her most recent disastrous blind date, and they were all laughing when she was done. Jess had finished her drink by that point and the other two were ready to go as well. Brittany put her dishes away then stood hesitantly in front of Jess and Tammy. "I think I'm going to head out, too."

"Fuck's sake, tell me your young body isn't tired already," Tammy said.

Brittany laughed. "No, I've still got my session with Dr. Berg tonight." She shook her head. "I have a feeling there will be a lot to discuss because today slapped harder than any others since I got here. I think I'm going to meditate a little before my time slot. Then maybe do some journaling about it and take a bath after. Have you used the soaker tubs yet? They're amazing!"

Jess nodded. "Yup. They make me want to put one into my own bathroom back home but frankly, I don't want to have to clean it."

"Oh god, tell me about it." Tammy agreed.

Brittany fidgeted a bit then gave Jess and Tammy a shy look. "I know I'm a lot younger than you all, but I appreciate being included today. I had a lot of fun."

Tammy patted her shoulder. "Girl, don't worry about it. We've got you and we'll definitely have to do something else together before you head back."

Jess winked at Brittany. "Real people aren't so bad, huh?"

Brittany sighed dramatically and smiled. "I suppose not."

The three walked down the hallway toward the main entrance of the resort together. As soon as they got to the large glass doors, Jess realized she'd forgotten something important. "Oh shit! I left the camera in the dining hall. You two go ahead."

"Are you sure? We can totally wait for you."

Jess waved off Brittany's suggestion. "No, it's fine.

The paths are safe and well-lit and I'm not in any danger with Donovan gone. Maybe I'll even wander through the garden on the way back to my cabin and see if I can get a few pictures of those night blooms that Gus was telling us about."

"Okay. See you tomorrow."

"Bye, Jess." Brittany waved as she followed Tammy through the doors.

It didn't take long for Jess to retrace her steps and retrieve the camera she'd placed on the chair next to where she'd sat through dinner. Everything was already cleared away and the room empty when she made her second trip toward the front of the building. Jess slowed when she noticed the light on in Lucia's office. Seeing nobody else around, she walked over and knocked on the open door.

Lucia was seated at her desk, head resting in her hands. Her head shot up at the sound and the look on her face was one Jess never expected to see. Anger, heartbreak, and hopelessness.

"Are you okay? Did something happen with your father?"

Lucia scrubbed at her face and abruptly stood. "Just business, you know? How was your day?"

"I had a blast. You were totally right. I convinced Brittany to join the hike and a few of us all went to dinner together. Some of the others aren't so bad once you get to know them."

"That's great. I'm happy for you." Lucia gave her a smile, but it was tight and didn't reach her eyes.

Jess moved closer. "Something *is* wrong." She got concerned when Lucia came around the desk and pulled her into a hug.

"Some days I love what I do here. We help people, give them a second chance at life more often than not. But other times..." She trailed off and Jess had no idea what Lucia was getting at.

"Other times people are like Stephen?"

Lucia pulled back and cupped Jess's cheeks. Jess never realized how expressive her dark eyes were. Soulful, bottomless, and filled with an emotion that Jess herself refused to even admit. "No. Sometimes I meet people like you, ones who leave a mark on what passes for my soul, and I know the loss will hurt."

Jess covered one of Lucia's hands with her own. "I don't understand. I've got weeks before I need to go home."

"No, sweetness, your time is up now."

"What?" Jess stepped back and wrapped her arms around herself, suddenly cold. She looked around, expecting to see security waiting. "Are you, uh, are you returning me? Like Stephen? I haven't done anything wrong. I swear!"

Lucia didn't try to pursue her as Jess put a little more distance between them. Instead, she sat back on her desk, hands resting on each side. "Never like Stephen. He failed the test and was sent on to the Ternary."

Jess's head started to throb along the left side and she winced. The weird headache coincided with phantom pain in her abdomen, just beneath her ribs on the left side. "You're not making any sense. What's the Ternary?"

Lucia sighed and looked up. "How can I explain this?" She met Jess's gaze. "The Ternary is the place for all mortal ends. For the big, irreversible deaths, you go to the Ternary where you are allowed a choice of three paths. Let's call one reincarnation, hoping to do better in the next life than in your previous. The second is to be reborn as a higher form, like a cat or dolphin. The third choice is to end the cycle by becoming one with the Ternary Machine."

Not even twelve hours ago Jess would have insisted that Lucia was the most sane and rational person she'd ever met. Now she sounded like a raving lunatic. "You know, there are easier ways to get out of whatever this thing is we've been doing."

"I don't want to get out of anything! On the contrary, I can't bear to let you go."

Jess sucked in a breath at Lucia's outburst and willed her heart to slow. She tried to match Lucia's desperation with logic. "Okay, so if Stephen went on to this Ternary, where are we?"

Lucia held up her hands. "Paradise Island Resort or the Ternary Trial, though we just call it the Trial around here. Others refer to this place as oblivion, limbo, or purgatory."

She wasn't particularly religious, but Jess didn't like the sound of that. "I'm in hell?"

"No. There is no heaven or hell. That is a…human construct. There are pocket dimensions, and there is the Ternary. The dimensions for testing can take on many forms. The resort is exactly as you expect because you thought you were going on vacation. But it's not necessarily what everyone sees when they come through for testing. More end up at the Ternary than on the brink."

It was so much to process. Jess had no idea what to believe any more, but Lucia wasn't someone who seemed likely to go off the deep end one day. Jess's gut was telling her that no matter how fantastical the words coming from Lucia's mouth sounded, they were real. "If I'm being tested, does that mean I'm dead?" Jess felt a tingle in her nose and the burn of tears in her eyes as she fought the urge to cry. She'd just discovered all these new things and made the decision to move on with her life, live, be happy, and take each day as an adventure. She wasn't ready for it to all be over. Her voice quavered as she spoke quietly. "I don't want to die, Luce."

That had Lucia up and moving toward her in two long strides. She wrapped Jess in an embrace, cupping the back of Jess's head. "No, no, no. That's not it at all. You're on the cusp of eternity. It means that your life hangs in the balance and there are only two paths forward. Either you pass the test to prove that your continued existence on your home plane brings value, and you return to your earthly body, or you fail the test and move on to the Ternary."

"Like Stephen?"

"Exactly. But you passed. It's time for you to go back."

Jess met Lucia's intense gaze. "I—how do I know you're telling the truth?"

"Can I kiss you?"

She thought it couldn't hurt and at least she'd get to taste Lucia's lips one last time. "Yes."

Jess wasn't sure what she was expecting but certainly not the explosion of light that happened. Suddenly, Jess was floating above an ER gurney. There was chaos all around as people in scrubs were in motion. Voices yelled as though they came from underwater, words forming intermittently as Jess's hearing faded in and out. It felt as though time itself were in flux.

"Ultrasound…possible rupture."

"Blood loss…massive transfusion—"

"Pressure's dropping."

"Page surgery!"

The telltale sound of a cardiac monitor, the same you hear in the hospital dramas on TV, began beeping faster and faster. Additional alarms sounded elsewhere in the room. Then someone yelled "Clear!" Space opened around the gurney with the exception of one person. The blurry figures in scrubs kept a distance from the body as a red-haired man pressed two paddles on opposite corners of the patient's chest. Jess felt a jolt and was abruptly pulled away from the scene, but not before seeing her own face covered in blood on the gurney below.

Her legs gave out and she would have fallen to the floor if Lucia hadn't caught her. "Easy, Tiger. I've got you." Lucia picked her up and carried her over to the couch on the other side of the room.

It was a lot to accept, and it took Jess more than a minute to recover. Once her breathing slowed again, she turned to Lucia. "What the fuck was that?"

"That was your life in as close to real speed as we can witness in this place. Time works differently here. Less than thirty minutes on your plane of existence. From the moment the car turned into your path on the way to the airport to the events you just saw."

"But it's been weeks," Jess protested.

"Different planes. Much like when I visit my father on the big island. It's in a different plane, or dimension you might call it, so a few hours here is actually days there."

Comments between Lucia and Amy from before suddenly made sense. Stephen wasn't returning, as in going back home. He was going back to the Ternary, to re-tern in the cycle of life. And Lucia mentioned a series of dinners with her father despite being gone less than twelve hours. But if all that was true, that meant- "None of this is real?"

"Jess… love, it's as real as you need it to be."

"What about you? I suppose the connection we've had, everything we've done together and said is just another part of the test."

Lucia squeezed her hands. "No. This was part of nothing but you and I, and I refuse to let anyone take it away from me."

"What about me? If everything you've said is true and I have to go back, will I remember you?"

"Truthfully? I don't know. I've never followed a soul once they pass the test and go back to the earthly plane. There is a reason this kind of interaction is frowned upon."

"You think? Jesus—fuck, Luce! I thought it was because you were a resort manager and I was a guest. I had no idea it was because I'm just a shitty human and you're what exactly? Angel, demon, or something in between maybe?" Jess laughed hysterically because it was either that or cry.

"Again, angels, demons, they're not necessarily different, and definitely not good or evil as humans write in their books. They're—*we're* creatures from different planes of existence, all tasked with helping to maintain the cycle structure."

Jess's hands began to shake, and her upper left abdomen ached fiercely. "I'm not sure what to think any more. How do I go back with all this in my head, or you in my heart?"

"I don't know. But regardless, you must go back." Lucia pulled Jess to her feet and cradled her face again. In that moment, Jess recognized the power of her lover's gaze.

"What am I supposed to do?"

"You'll do what you promised. Live each day better than the last and be happy."

Jess's bottom lip trembled. "Without you?"

"No, *with* yourself. You have much life to live yet, Jess. Make it count."

Tears slid down Jess's cheeks as Lucia leaned down and pressed a kiss to her forehead. There was a blinding flash of light and Jess cried out in pain, then nothing. Somewhere in her memory was the sound of gentle beeping.

# Chapter Fifteen

Beeping. That was the first thing Jess heard as she swam up from the depths of unconsciousness. The smell of antiseptic was pungent and her body ached all over. Something was missing. She was with…with…Lucia!

Jess opened her eyes. They felt heavy and stuck together. Someone in scrubs stood next to her bed checking one of the machines. She must have made a sound or something because the man turned to look at her.

"Oh, you're awake. Let me page the doctor. Do you need anything?"

Jess was groggy and disoriented. Her lips were parched, her tongue felt thick and too big for her mouth, but her throat was the worst. She shivered at the bone-deep chill. Her eyes grew heavy again and everything went dark before she could answer the nurse.

The next time Jess woke it was in a different room. Sunlight slanted through the blinds in a way that made her think it was late afternoon. She was still thirsty, but her throat felt better. Jess tried to sit forward but sharp pain put her back onto the bed. She looked around and unfortunately didn't see any nurses. Fumbling with the hand not sporting an IV, she found the white plastic call button and pressed it.

A different nurse pushed into her room a few minutes later. "Good afternoon, Miss Parker. My name is Tina and I'll be your nurse for the next few hours. It's good to see you awake."

It was strange how a simple name could open a pathway of memories that led straight to sorrow. Jess gasped. "I—I'm not supposed to be here. Where's Lucia? Where is the resort?"

"Resort? I'm sorry, Miss Parker, but there is nobody here but you. I could look at the visitor log for your room to see if anyone named Lucia has come in."

"No, I was at the resort with Lucia," Jess insisted.

The nurse frowned and picked up Jess's chart. "Do you know what day it is?" she asked after looking at it for a few seconds.

Jess thought back but couldn't remember the exact date when she arrived on the island, or when Lucia sent her back. It was all a blur. "I don't remember. But it was real."

"Miss Parker—"

"Please, call me Jess."

"Jess, do you remember what happened?"

She thought she did but now, after everything she'd learned from Lucia and what she saw while floating above the ER table, Jess wasn't sure. Other memories layered over some of the earlier ones from before the resort. She was trying to beat a yellow light, as was another car that was turning left from the opposite direction. The flash of light. Jess remembered that but thought she made it through the intersection.

Obviously, she didn't, and Jess found herself with two sets of memories. One where she totaled her car and the other...it grew hazier by the minute. "I, I was in an accident?"

"Yes, you were. A pretty bad one from what I understand."

While the overlapping memories were vague, that wasn't the case for her weeks spent at Paradise Island. She remembered Lucia, Brittany, Lahash and Ronobe. They were real. They had to be. "I know this is going to sound crazy, but I swear I spent the past few weeks at this place called Paradise Island Resort. It, uh, was a testing place. I thought I was on vacation but then I found out I didn't fully die, that I was just being tested and I passed. They sent me back here."

The nurse gave Jess a look and she knew there was no way anyone would believe her. Tina hung the chart back on the end of Jess's bed and pointed toward the door. "I'm just going to page the on-duty doctor. She can probably address any questions you have about the surgery and post op treatment."

"Wait," Jess held up her free hand but Tina was already out of the room. "Fuck." Her mind raced with memories that were real but also not real somehow. It wasn't long before a doctor pushed into the room ahead of her nurse.

The woman had a serious look about her but gave Jess an easy smile. She picked up Jess's chart from the end of the bed before coming to stand by her side. "Hi, Jess. I'm Doctor Sloan. Tina says you appear to be suffering from some confusion."

"I'm not confused. I know what I remember but even I'll admit it sounds pretty crazy."

The doctor was quiet for a few seconds before offering, "Would you like to tell me what you remember before I list what you were brought in for?"

Jess sighed because she knew that recounting her time on the island was probably pointless, but she humored Dr. Sloan anyway. "I woke late at home and had to rush out of the house. There was a bright light on the way to the airport, but I still made my flight. I spent a few weeks on this tropical island as part of a self-help getaway. I made friends, saw a therapist daily, and took art classes. It's very clear in my memory. I'm not making this up."

"And after? Did you leave the island, or…"

"I, uh, Lucia," She paused. "That's the resort manager. She told me that it wasn't real. She said there was no heaven or hell, that there was something called the Ternary. But for people like me, who were on the edge of life and death and couldn't be sorted one way or another, we were given a test to see if we could be better. I passed and Lucia said I had to go back."

Dr. Sloan nodded. "Then what?"

"Then there was a bright light and I came back!"

The doctor's lips thinned and she regarded Jess in silence. She could see the nurse out of the corner of her eye and Tina wore a look that said Jess was absolutely kitty bonkers. Dr. Sloan sighed. "Let me start by saying that perceiving bright lights or other intense hallucinations during a near-death experience are fairly common and normal. Are you a person of logic, or spiritual belief, Jess?"

She snorted. "Definitely logic."

"Okay, then I'll tell you that a woman named Jimo Borjigin found regions of the brain responsible for your internal visual experiences to be more active during a cardiac arrest. She postulated that the sudden surge in brain activity could be what causes people to perceive a bright white light at that time."

With details so specific, Jess got a feeling the doctor had given the speech before. It certainly made sense and her rational brain wanted to latch on to the explanation for something so fantastical. But her heart wouldn't let Lucia go. "I understand what you're saying, I really do. But I know what I saw, what I lived, for the past few weeks."

The doctor seemed at a loss. "Would it help if I listed what your injuries were at the time paramedics brought you in?"

"I saw some of it."

Dr. Sloan appeared startled. "Saw?"

Jess nodded. "Right before Lucia sent me back, she showed me what was happening here, in real time. It was…confusing, like having my head in a bucket of water. But I floated above the table watching my body below. I was in an ER bay surrounded by people. Someone said something about a rupture, uh, I think I got a massive transfusion. I guess that's probably blood. Oh, and obviously they sent me to surgery."

"Um, well that's pretty general stuff for what happened to you. It's possible you have aural recollection of the events even if you were unconscious—"

"The doctor that shocked me while I was on the table had short, dark red hair."

Dr. Sloan's eyes widened and she turned to the nurse. "Do you know who the on-duty doctor was in emergency at the time Jess was brought in?"

Tina said quietly, "Blake was the emergency physician that morning."

"Oh." The doctor appeared to collect herself before looking at Jess with a placating expression. "Many patients aren't fully unconscious during a medical emergency and have reported all sorts of strange sights and sounds. But even as a doctor, I've discovered some things that just can't be explained. Regarding the ones that can, let's discuss your current condition."

That was the point Jess knew she wouldn't get anywhere with the medical personnel. "Fine."

Dr. Sloan looked down at the chart. "You were brought in by paramedics. Multiple contusions from the seatbelt and airbag. Lacerations on your arm, cheek, and head from striking the driver's side window. That's also why you have a mild concussion. You will have a headache and maybe some nausea. Let us know if they become worse, or if you experience double vision."

Jess's head did hurt and listing her injuries suddenly brought every one of them to her attention. She could feel the pull of stitches on her cheek and somewhere near her temple. "I will."

"Are you okay to continue? Some people don't like to hear the details of their emergency."

She shrugged. "Like I said, I saw some of it. Go ahead."

The doctor didn't acknowledge Jess's insistence that she saw the events in the emergency room. "The collision was hard enough to rupture your spleen on impact. Internal bleeding was discovered by Doctor Blake after doing an ultrasound when you arrived pale and tachycardic with hypotension. The emergency team started a massive transfusion to combat blood loss and you coded shortly after. Once you were resuscitated, you were sent up to surgery."

Jess swallowed and rubbed the sheet under her hand. It sure sounded like a lot of damage.

"How are you doing, Jess?"

"I'm good. Go ahead."

"The rupture was discovered when they opened you up, and Doctor James performed a successful partial splenectomy at that time." She glanced down through the paperwork. "Surgery lasted a little more than two hours."

"This big transfusion, is that a lot?"

"Yes. You were given blood, platelets, and plasma for balanced replenishment to help with the circulating volume and help with clotting capabilities. But to continue, you've got bruising on the ninth and tenth ribs of your left side. That and the head wound are typical injuries in accidents like these where you're thrown into the driver's door."

The pain in her abdomen and everywhere else grew

steadily sharper the longer Jess listened. As if listing all her ailments brought them to the forefront of Jess's attention. She winced when she shifted in the bed. "Damn, that hurts."

Dr. Sloan motioned to the nurse. "If you're in pain, let us know. We can adjust the drip rate."

Jess nodded. "What happens now? When can I go home?"

"I'm afraid that given the blood loss, severity of your injuries, and surgery, you'll be our guest here for a few days. The open abdominal surgery leaves you with an incision wound and we want to make sure you don't have any secondary infections. I'd say that most people with injuries like yours, can recover in as little as four to eight weeks."

Jess groaned. That meant missing half the summer. She shifted again and winced, now aware of all her sore muscles and the pull of even more stitches on her stomach. "I'm guessing the accident itself is why my entire body hurts like I went four rounds against Tyson."

The doctor snickered at Jess's attempt at a joke. "Most likely, yes."

"So, what exactly does the spleen do? Partial isn't as bad as full removal, right?"

The doctor went on to explain what Jess could expect from her injuries, in both a short-term and long-term sense. By the time Jess ran out of questions, she'd long run out of steam. She was grateful when the pain medication kicked in again.

She asked if her sling bag was brought in with her and Tina said that it was in the closet. Lucky for Jess, she'd stuffed her cell phone in her bag instead of in the center console when she left the house. She didn't want to accidentally forget it in the car in her rush to make her flight.

Once the doctor and nurse left, promising to send a delicious meal of broth at dinner time, Jess was left to her thoughts. No matter what anyone told her, Jess knew what was missing from her life and grieved at her loss. Pain, disappointment, and heartache made her angry and sad. Jess was tempted to rage at everyone around her, but one thing kept her mouth shut. The promise she made before Lucia sent her back.

It didn't matter if Lucia, Doctor Kam, or the stupid island *were* real. One thing she knew beyond a shadow of a doubt was that she'd been given a second chance, and she wasn't going to waste it being sad and miserable anymore. Jess may have been sore and broken, but she certainly wasn't beaten. She had plans and they were going to start as soon as she got out of the hospital.

****

It was early enough that she knew most people would still be in the office at work. Jess had to call to make new arrangements for time off. She had short-term and long-term disability, as well as her savings, so wasn't worried too much about money. But there was no way she was going to burn her vacation time on something like a hospital stay unless she absolutely had to. Jess only had one concern about calling work. She'd have to talk to her own manager and the human resources manager. That meant calling Shell and she didn't want to worry her friend more than she had to. It couldn't be avoided though.

Sure enough, her senior manager was very understanding and wished her a speedy recovery. Once Jess hung up, she took a few steadying breaths before dialing Shell's cell phone. She hoped her friend wasn't on a call on the work phone, and also hoped she was.

"Hey, J! Shouldn't you be having dinner poolside with a drink in hand right now?"

"Shell..." Jess's throat closed up and she couldn't speak while fighting the imminent tears.

"Babe, what's wrong?"

"I, um, I was in an accident this morning. I'm at St. Seren General. I'll be here for a few days actually. I already called Martinez and let him know I'd be out for at least a month, maybe more."

There was a gasp on the other end of the line. "Holy shit, what happened?"

Jess swallowed a few times, then recounted what the doctor had told her. "Car turned right in front of me on the way to the airport. Lacerations, mild concussion, bruised ribs, and a ruptured spleen which required a partial splenectomy." Silence met her words. "You still there?"

"Fuck." Shell using an expletive was rare, let alone while she was still at work. "How is the other guy?"

"I don't know. I only just woke up a little while ago. Long enough to get the full explanation of events from the doc, then for her to check me over and I'm sure mark that I'm crazy on my chart."

"Uh, crazy?"

"Long story that I may or may not feel like recounting."

Shell sighed over the phone. "What do you need from me, J?"

"I guess nothing. I was told to inform HR of my absence—"

"No way, babe. What do you need from *me*? Your friend, not coworker. How long are you there, do you need stuff from home, what about long term care? Those kinds of things."

"Oh. I'm not sure. I've never had surgery or had to stay in a hospital before. I mean, I packed the communication and entertainment essentials in my sling bag, phone, charger, and kindle. The paramedics were nice enough to grab that and bring it in with me. I'd like to know what's going on with my car and get my luggage back home though."

"Leave it to me. I've got the spare key you gave me to water your plants. I'll make a few phone calls to learn where the car was towed and what you need to begin the insurance process. Probably an accident report. Even if they won't release anything to me, I can find out how you can get it released. We'll also get your short-term disability started. I've had some experience with that so don't worry. Unfortunately, you'll need to exhaust all your sick time first."

"But not my vacation, right?"

"Correct. Vacation and sick time are marked differently in our system. You have five days of sick time because I know you haven't taken any yet this year."

Jess snorted. "I never take my sick time."

"Leave it to me, sweetie. I'll wrap everything up early and start making calls. Then Tam and I will drop by to see you later. Okay?"

For once, Jess didn't protest the attention or help from others. She felt lost and alone and was still processing everything she thought had happened during the past few weeks. No, during the past few hours. It was all so confusing. "I would like that. Thanks." She bit her bottom lip. "I don't say it enough, but I love you guys. I appreciate all my friends and I know I haven't been very good about showing it. I was in a dark place for years and I'm going to do my best to pull myself out of it. I won't let the past drag me down anymore."

Her words must have shocked Shell based on the silence that followed. It took a good ten seconds for her friend to respond. "What brought all that on, the accident?"

"Weeks of therapy."

"You started therapy before you left? Why didn't you say anything?"

"No, while I was gone—uh, it's hard to explain. Forget I said anything. Let's just chalk up my new outlook on life to dying on the ER table and being brought back."

"Put a pin in that because I know you sweetie, and you're holding something in. Rest assured, I'll wait until you're on the mend again but then you and I are going to have a talk."

Jess smiled. She knew that no matter what she said or what the real truth was, Shell would always have her back. If Jess said something made her sad, whether it was real or not, Shell was there. "Thank you."

"Anytime, babe. Now, let me go and we'll see you later."

"Bye, Shell. And thanks again."

Shell hung up and Jess let the phone fall to the covers in her lap. She didn't have the energy to make any more calls and it was getting late enough in the day that some places might be closed anyway. Tomorrow would bring another day and more pain, of that she was sure. Jess winced as she tried to get comfortable enough to take a quick nap before dinner.

****

The meal tray had long been cleared away when shift change for the nurses occurred at seven. It was shortly after that when Jess heard someone call into her open door, "Hey, check out who I found loitering around the lobby."

Jess looked up from her cell phone to see a pack of her closest friends. Shell and Tam led the way into her room, with Jenn, Jamie, Kelsey, Caleb, and Richard crowding in behind them. Richard walked right up to the side of her bed opposite the IV and other wires. He rubbed her shoulder. "Oh, sweetie. Who do we need to beat up?" He clucked his tongue. "And stitches up in your cute new hairdo, too. Drastic."

She laughed at his dramatics, then groaned as the stitches in her abdomen pulled, and sore ribs made themselves known. "Don't make me laugh, it hurts. I've got bruised ribs, and I ruptured my spleen in the accident."

"Ouch." Kelsey made a face and Jamie patted Jess's leg.

Jenn walked right up to the foot of the bed and grabbed her chart because, of course, she would. "Well, doc? Am I going to make it?" Jess asked, joking.

"Dammit, Jess! Don't even joke about that." Shell came around the bed and Richard moved out of the way. She leaned over, despite her short stature, and gave Jess the gentlest hug possible. "You scared me when you called earlier."

Jess noticed for the first time that they were alone. "Hey, where's the squirt?"

"Rory's with his grandma," Tam said.

"Damn, girl. You sure did a number on yourself. You'll probably be here through Friday."

Jess sighed at Jenn's proclamation. "I just want to go home."

Jenn hung the chart back on the bed. "Just listen to your doctors, okay? Partial splenectomy is no joke. That's open surgery and you don't want any secondary infections.

Once you're cleared to go home, we'll take care of you."

She held up her hands, eyes wide. "Oh, you all don't have to do that. I'll be fine."

"Nope." Kelsey shook her head. "No way are we letting you do this on your own. We'll bring you meals, pick up your mail, do all the things you're not going to be able to do while you're healing."

Jamie snorted. "What meals? Are you going to cook?"

"Oh, hell no. You're going to cook, and I'll be the delivery service."

"Uh huh, that's what I thought."

Jess giggled then clenched her teeth. "You two are funny, and I told you not to make me laugh."

Jamie grimaced. "Sorry."

"You know, I can stay with you for a few days when you get home," Caleb offered. "I know I switched over to management at Sage Oaks, but I haven't let my RN certification lapse. You'll need someone to help with wound care for a little bit." He paused. "I mean, if you're comfortable with it."

"I'd be a hell of a lot more comfortable with you helping me than all these strangers. I'm not a fan of people I don't know touching me."

"Girl, I'd feel the same way. Ugh! Well," Richard said. "That and I only like my Caleb-bear's strong hands." Everyone chuckled except Caleb, who rolled his eyes with a smile.

She threw a salt packet that must have fallen off her meal tray at Richard and responded to Caleb. "I'd be happy for the assistance because I don't know what to expect here. I've only ever had a few staples above my eyebrow from catching a line drive to the head."

"Obviously, I'll help too. Malcom is plenty old enough to fend for himself a few nights a week. I've also got lots of vacation time I never take so I think between Caleb and I, we've got your home care covered. The peanut gallery can help with all the other stuff."

Shell flipped Jenn the bird. "Who are you calling peanut gallery, you glorified baby-puller!"

"I pulled your baby and don't you forget it."

Shell paused, then conceded. "Good point."

Their support, teasing, and overall laughter left Jess more hopeful than battered. Her nose stung first, followed quickly by the tears. Jess didn't like to cry, let alone in front of so many people, but she couldn't help it. She woke feeling hurt, alone, and confused. And now her heart had been filled in the most unexpected ways. Despite how prickly she was, sometimes being just a downright bitch, none of them would abandon her. Whether it was two weeks of imaginary therapy, or Jess's brush with death, something in her had definitively shifted and she wasn't going to throw away the opportunity to come out of this stronger than before.

Jess sniffled. "Thank you." She looked around the group of concerned faces. "All of you. I know I haven't been the easiest friend to have but you've all been there for me when it counts. I love you all so fucking much."

Tam stood next to Shell. "We love you too, and we're here for you."

"Not just for my Jello shots?"

Kelsey shrugged. "I mean, those are hella awesome." Jamie elbowed her and she added with a smile. "But definitely not what we like most. You do the healing and we'll do the helping."

She smiled back. "Sounds like a deal."

Caleb, Richard, Jamie, and Kelsey stayed for about an hour. Jenn a little longer than that. But Tam and Shell kept her company until visiting hours ended at nine. Shell promised to bring Jess a few toiletries the next day and make some calls for her. After that, Jess was left with her own thoughts again. All at once, the day came crashing down and her eyelids grew heavy. There would be time enough to think about the rest later.

# Chapter Sixteen

Jenn and Caleb took turns staying with her for the first two weeks after being released from the hospital. The pain and nature of Jess's injuries and incision meant she couldn't do anything but rest. No heavy lifting or strenuous exercise. Lucky for Jess, her friends took turns dropping off easy to heat meals or Fleet Eats gift cards.

By week three, Jess was going stir crazy. She'd read countless books, devoured gobs of fan fiction online, and blew through her entire saved watchlist on her streaming service.

Halfway through the week, Jess turned the TV off and threw the remote onto her side table. "Recovery sucks."

Jess received a nice check for her five-year-old Subaru from the insurance company but hadn't gotten around to looking for something else. Partly because she was more than a little put out that she'd only just gotten the car paid off the year before. The other reason was that she felt nervous to get behind the wheel again. As part of her recovery, Jess started walking around the neighborhood. While her house was situated nicely near one of the local metro parks, she was still within walking distance of at least one coffee shop.

She missed her friends and being social. Jess checked the time and picked up her cell and tapped the name at the top of her favorites list. It was picked up on the second ring.

"I just got Rory to bed. Don't tell me you're out of food already."

Jess groaned at Shell's demand. "I think I have enough food or gift cards to last me until Christmas. Especially since I haven't had much of an appetite during the past few weeks."

"You better—"

"I'm still eating, mama bear. Jeez."

Shell snickered on the other end of the line. "So, what

do you need? Or did you just call to experience my sparkling personality paired with a genial sense of humor?"

That made Jess laugh. "As if. No, I was calling to see if I could ride with you guys to the game tomorrow. I'm bored and want to get some fresh air."

Jess pulled the phone away from her ear when Shell yelled to someone else on her end. "Hey, you owe me ten dollars!" Obviously, Tam. Then in a quieter voice Shell spoke to her. "Thanks, J. You just scored me lunch from Mancino's tomorrow courtesy of the wife."

"Glad to be of service."

"So, you've got yourself a case of cabin fever, huh? Are you regretting that Jenn and Caleb are no longer staying over?"

"Nope. I've been cleared to do most things myself and I've got my wound care down pat. There was no real reason to have anyone stay. I'm fully capable of light housework and running the microwave."

"I would have totally milked that shit," Shell said.

That brought a smile to Jess's face. "Oh, I know. So, will you pick me up?"

"Sure. The game's at seven. If you don't feel like going to Cranker's after, we'll drop you back home before we head over for post-game beers."

"Damn. I probably shouldn't drink."

"Yeah, probably not. Sucks to be you. You could still come for appetizers and company though."

"True. And, you know what, I don't even care that I can't have alcohol. I'm just excited to see the first game of the season. I may not be able to play with you, but I can still cheer with the best of them." Jess wasn't going to wallow in what she couldn't change. At least that's what the new therapist she'd found online said. They had video sessions twice a week for the past few weeks. Could she have waited until farther into her physical recovery? Sure. But if Jess seriously wanted things to change, there was no point in waiting around. After all, it wasn't like she was busy.

"You know, I haven't said anything before now, but you've been acting different since the hospital. You said some strange stuff the day you called me after your accident and I'm still waiting for an explanation. But barring all that, I just wanted to say that I'm here when you want to talk."

The loss of something she wasn't sure ever existed still stung. Jess thought about Lucia and the resort every day, but she was smart enough not to bring it up to anyone, especially her therapist. She wasn't ready to revisit her vision yet, but she appreciated Shell's offer. "Thanks. You'll be the first to know when I'm ready to spill. Well, I mean outside my new therapy sessions."

"So, you are going to therapy now? How?"

"Remote meetings. It's great because I don't have to leave my house."

Shell snorted. "Now, if they could make remote grocery shopping a thing, that would be great."

"They have that, numpty. Even Meijer has home delivery now."

"Yeah, well, unfortunately for me, Tam is adamantly opposed to it."

"It's good for you."

"So says the woman that hasn't had to grocery shop in… how long now?"

Jess giggled. "At least a month and a half. Maybe I'll start using home delivery."

"Oh, look at me," Shell mocked. "Miss money bags with her fat insurance check. Say, when are you going to get another car? You're cleared to drive, right?"

"Yeah, just nervous still. And I don't want another car payment, which, unless I buy used, I'm going to be stuck with one."

"True dat."

They chatted for a little while longer until Shell had to go shower. Jess didn't necessarily miss work, but she definitely missed talking to other people. Well, maybe not that. She missed regular companionship. She'd have to see what the doctor said about her timeline for returning to work at her next appointment.

****

"Hey Jess, I completed the VixCom project earlier this week and I gathered the files for the next two on my list. But they're not due for months still. Plenty of time, even with my vacation. Speaking of which, do you mind if I cut out early today?"

She smiled at Jon. "I looked over the completed material already. Nicely done, Jon. As for leaving early," Jess paused to make him sweat. "Make sure your time sheet is filled out for the week then take off. I hope you and Sue have fun in Traverse."

He pumped his fist. "Awesome, and I will. Thanks, boss!" Jon left her office in a rush and Jess couldn't help but remember back to several months before when her engineer left in a much different manner. One of the things she was learning in her therapy sessions was that rules didn't always play well with empathy, and that she needed to learn to recognize when one should be prioritized over the other.

Jess had returned to work five weeks after leaving the hospital. Her doctor was impressed by her healing progress and cleared her for full activity after her most recent appointment. Shell had been a good sport by waiting patiently and driving her home after. Jess had yet to replace her car but with Shell giving her a ride to work each day, she hadn't been in a hurry. However, she found something online at lunch and called to put a hold down-payment on it. She planned to ride her bike there since the dealership was only a couple miles from her house.

That was the best news about being cleared by the doctor. Jess was excited to start riding her bike again. It was warm in the afternoons but she figured she would just bring a change of clothes in a backpack so she didn't stroke out on the way home.

Jess worked for another hour, mostly approving timesheets that had already cleared, but her thoughts kept wandering back to her dream vision from the hospital. She found it especially hard to stay focused on the days she was most introspective because those were the times she fell into her memories of Dr. Kam, the friends she'd made just before leaving, and most importantly, Lucia.

Knocking on her door startled Jess from her thoughts

before Shell pushed into her office, red hair looking a little wilder than normal. "Did I just see Jon skipping out of your office a while ago?"

Jess laughed. "Maybe. I told him he could go early since he's on vacation next week."

"You feeling okay, sweetie?"

Shell walked around the desk to press a palm to her forehead and Jess pushed her friend's hand away. "Haha, you're hilarious. He's all caught up on his work and did the prep needed for the projects he'll start when he returns. There was no reason to keep him cooling his heels here."

"What happened to," Shell held up her hand and mimed a puppet talking. "We have rules for a reason?"

Jess threw a paperclip at her. "Don't be an ass. I'm making a real effort here so cut me some slack."

Shell pulled one of the chairs closer to the desk and took a seat. "Oh, I'm well aware of all the work you've done. Some days," she shook her head, "I don't know. But whatever you're doing, the therapy, deep breathing, all that, keep it up. Because this is the happiest that I've seen you in a long time."

Jess sat back in her chair and leveled a serious look toward her best friend. "You know what? I am happy. That's one of the things I promised Lucia—" Jess cut off her sentence, but it was too late.

"Who's Lucia? Your therapist? I thought you said their name was Sam."

"Uh…" Jess glanced around her office, unwilling to bring up anything serious at work, let alone *that* particular subject. "It's nothing."

Shell pointed at her. "Nope. I know that expression on your face and I think you're long overdue for an explanation." She looked at her watch. "You know what? Let's get the hell out of here. It's Friday, I spent half my day dealing with the mad pooper and I'm just done."

"You caught the person leaving shitty underwear in the men's room on the third floor?"

Shell made a face. "All I can say is that it wasn't a man, and they've been reprimanded. But after that conversation, I'm ready to start my weekend."

Jess looked around and didn't see anything pressing

that couldn't wait until Monday. "You don't have to twist my arm. Timecards are done so let me log off and I'll meet you out front."

"Great. See you then." Shell left the office looking as spry as Jon had earlier. On one hand, Jess was happy to leave work forty minutes early on a Friday. On the other, she wasn't at all ready for the conversation that Shell would lock her into. Maybe it would be good for her to talk it out.

Despite being mentally prepared, Jess felt anxiety creep in as Shell shut the car off in her driveway. She tried to stall the conversation. "Don't you have to pick up Rory?"

"Nope. Tam's on for tonight. It's just you and me for however long it takes to tell me what's going on." Shell turned to face her. "I said you look happier than I've seen you in a long time but there's also something…something I can't put my finger on. Like you're a little bit sad, too. It's weird and I promised to be here for you. Are you ready to talk yet?"

Jess sighed. "You're not going to believe me. Nobody would believe it at the hospital so clearly, it's all in my head. But it's hard to forget, you know?"

"I don't actually. But maybe I will if you tell me."

"Fine. Come in then. I've got a pitcher of lemonade in the fridge."

A fine red eyebrow lifted. "With or without cherry vodka?"

Jess laughed at her friend. "Whichever way you'd like it. The mad pooper was really bad, huh?"

Shell groaned then sent a quick text message. "You have no idea. Come on, I'm thirsty."

"I bet." They got out of the car. "Are you sure you don't want any gas money? I mean, you've been driving me to doctor appointments on top of the daily work commute. I don't want you to think I'm taking advantage."

"It's like you don't even know me. I've told you before, you're my best friend and you're practically on my way to work. I don't want anything—" Shell stopped then grinned. "Actually, you can promise me that you won't buy anything that makes noise for Rory's next birthday. I can't even begin to tell you how many speakers we've covered with tape, or how many times we've used the excuse that the batteries must be broken. He's already starting to get wise to our tricks."

Jess snickered as she unlocked the side door into her house. "Silence is golden, huh?"

"And duct tape is silver but they frown on that when you are a parent."

That sent Jess into a fit of laughter as she dropped her keys into her sling bag and hung it on the coat hook by the door, then left her shoes on the mat. "Not like I'll ever need to know that."

"You don't want kids?" Shell asked as she kicked off her own shoes.

Jess shuddered, comically. "Not even a little bit. I'm fully content being Auntie Jess, even if I can't bring noisy toys as gifts."

Shell grabbed two glasses out of the cupboard while Jess fetched the pitcher from her fridge. Her friend used the icemaker on the door and Jess retrieved the cherry vodka from a cabinet on the adjacent wall. They were like a well-oiled machine. If said machine was like the robot bartender on the cruise ship Jess read about a few years ago.

Drinks in hand, they went through the living room out to Jess's back deck. Shell collapsed into the patio chair and took a healthy swig of her drink. "Damn. Today was a *day*."

Jess snickered. "Did the person at least give a reason?"

"It's... ugh. I'm not allowed to disclose that information. I just hope I never have to deal with it again, or the other person who is involved in the event."

"Two were doing it?" Jess's eyes widened.

"No, just one. But two people were tangled in the situation. Don't ask anymore. Legal was involved."

Jess winced and took her own swallow of lemonade, smacking her lips when she was done.

"You know, I forget how nice your back yard is. Why don't we ever have our summer barbeques here? Look, you even have a fence so Rory can't escape."

"Maybe because I'm an antisocial bitch nine days out of seven?"

"Not anymore."

Jess shrugged and grinned at her friend. "So, you admit that I was an antisocial bitch?"

Shell tapped a nail against her glass. "I'm not going to blow smoke up your ass, J. You're my bestest out the nestest—"

"That's not a thing."

"Whatever. My point is I know you better than anyone and I saw that you were struggling. But it wasn't a struggle I could win for you. All Tam and I could do was give you the space and support you needed to the best of our ability. The rest of our friends felt the same way. Jenn said the important steps had to come from you, and clearly, you're making them now."

Jess wasn't surprised she had come up in conversation. They were all friends because they could discuss anything and support each other, even when someone was being an asshole or ditched the group after starting a new relationship. Richard did it, but eventually came back around and Caleb was added to their circle of friends. "What do you mean by important steps?"

"Jess," Shell pursed her lips, then continued. "Are you telling me you would have taken any of us seriously if we'd suggested therapy to you?"

She thought back over the past few years. It seemed like a lot longer, not just because of the fantasy weeks she wasn't living on the island, but because of how much bigger she felt after all the progress she'd made since then. Jess snorted. "I'd have told you all to fuck off."

"Exactly. Your journey had to start with you."

"Have you been watching those BS affirmation videos on social media again?"

Shell grinned. "Maybe, but that doesn't mean I'm wrong."

"Fine. I'll concede your point."

"Good. Now you can tell me who Lucia is."

Jess was mid-swallow and abruptly sucked air at Shell's words, lemonade going down the wrong pipe. She coughed for a few minutes while Shell, unhelpfully, slapped her back. Jess got control of herself and waved her friend's hand away. "Jesus, a little warning next time."

"Maybe if you knew the difference between ingest and inhale, you wouldn't try to absorb your alcohol through your bronchial passageways."

She rolled her eyes. "You spend way too much time with Jenn."

"Oh no, that's from watching the new medical drama on StreamNet. It's really good, you should check it out. Jenn's cousin Mia told us about it when she invited us over for a barbeque at her place next month. Said it was way more realistic than most shows on TV."

"Cool. Though I think I'll pass on the drama. I've had enough medical shit to last me a lifetime now."

Shell winced. "Sorry. Yeah, good point." They sat in silence for a minute before Shell asked her question again. "And Lucia? Who is she?"

Jess sighed and put her drink on the patio table. She played with the pocket of her safari shorts while she tried to think of the best way to explain her near death experience, to tell her best friend something that was so unexplainable.

Shell stilled her nervous fingers by grabbing Jess's hand. "Hey, you can tell me anything. I hope you know that. This..." She gestured toward her own face. "This is a no judgement place."

"I know, I know. It's just...crazy. Like, I know the doctor and nurse that asked me questions when I came out of recovery probably wanted to admit me to the other side of the hospital."

"What did you tell them?"

Jess took a deep breath and forged ahead. "You know how the vacation I won was listed as a self-help retreat?"

Shell nodded.

"I woke up late for my flight. I was in a rush but had already packed and showered the night before. Let's see, I was mean to some kid collecting cans for soccer, then I bolted out of the house with my luggage. I barely made it through a yellow light on the way to the airport. There was a flash or something behind me, but I was late so didn't stop."

"Uh, you mean the very light where you totaled your car?"

"That comes later. Let me finish, okay?"

Shell mimed zipping her lips. "Yup, go ahead."

"Anyway, the trip was uneventful. I had the row to myself on the small jet that carried us on the last leg to the island. It was on the bus ride to the resort that I discovered everyone was just... shitty." She laughed and shook her head. "I mean, to be honest they probably weren't any shittier than me. So, we arrive at the resort, and we're greeted by the manager, Lucia Cruz."

"Ooh, Lucia Cruz." Shell rolled her *R* in a bad attempt to sound exotic.

Jess snorted and covered her eyes. "Please don't ever do that again."

Shell held up her hands. "Sorry. Continue."

"Anyway, Lucia's voice was like honey, she was hot as fuck, tall, personable, and smart. So, of course I hated her on instinct. Reject before you can be rejected, right?"

"You know, I could kick your fucking ex for the number she did on you."

She shrugged at Shell's angry statement. "Eh, that's one of the things I've been working on and I'm much better now. To continue, we learned during orientation that we all signed paperwork agreeing to attend one therapy session and two activities each day. If we didn't, we'd be kicked out of the resort."

"Harsh, but okay."

Jess paused. "I'm surprised you're not asking more questions right now."

Shell waved her on. "I'm digging it. I'll ask questions after."

"I was definitely not very nice, but something about the place really got to me. I don't know if it was the therapy sessions with Doctor Kam, the beautiful location, or just being away from everything back home that made me sad. But whatever it was, I started to open up. Lucia had been flirting with me from the beginning and let me tell you, the chemistry between us was off the chart."

Her friend's eyes practically sparkled as she leaned forward in the chair. "Tell me more about that. Did you have vacation boom-boom?"

"I'm getting there, jeez."

Shell groaned dramatically. "Fine. Carry on then."

"Yes. We did have sex and it was fantastic."

"Details, woman!

"Let's see, we hooked up in my cabin and at her house. First on the rooftop patio, then in her room. We knew it was only going to be a short thing. Lucia works, worked, for her father and I had to come home when my trip was up."

"Sweetie, you're not a casual kind of gal."

Jess shrugged. "Well, normally I'm not. But like I said, the chemistry was insane, and I decided that I needed to start experiencing life again and not let things slip by me."

Shell fished an ice cube out of her glass and started crunching it. "That sounds great and all but what happened?"

"It wasn't real." Duh was left unspoken but the expression on Shell's face said louder than words what she was thinking. Jess went on to explain those lasts few minutes with Lucia. About whatever Jess had come to understand was going on at Paradise Island Resort, which admittedly wasn't a whole lot of information. But she was able to convey the gist of it.

Shell sat forward and held up a hand. "Wait a minute. You're telling me that you spent more than two weeks on this tropical island, went on excursions, took classes, went to therapy, and had a freaking relationship... only to learn it wasn't real, that it was only a test—"

"Yes, but—"

"Not only that, but you wake up after surgery and are told *again* that none of it was real, but in a different kind of way. Because brains are weird and make you hallucinate and shit when you're having a cardiac event."

It sounded fucking insane to have it laid out for her like that. Jess groaned. "Yeah, basically."

"Did I ever tell you that I had an aunt who supposedly floated above her body during surgery and said she followed her daughter, my cousin, down the hospital hallway?"

"That's odd. And you're telling me this, why?"

"Because she accurately told my cousin what she was wearing that day, what kind of pop she got out of the machine in the vending room, and candy bar she ate later. My aunt apparently didn't wake for a few days and would have had no way of knowing all that."

That struck a note with Jess. "Oh. Actually, something funny about my story. When I tried telling the doctor that I remembered a little of what was happening to me in the ER, when I coded on the table, she told me that it was possible I had aural memories even though I was unconscious. But I accurately described the red-headed doctor that had shocked me. A guy that isn't particularly common looking. They just brushed it off."

Shell tilted her head and gave Jess a puzzled look. "So, what do you think it all means? Do you believe your memories, or the doctor's explanation? The second of which does make sense."

Jess was torn. She had always been an *I'll believe it when I see it* type of person and the events of her near-death experience were pretty out there. On the other hand…

"I don't know what to think most days. I have memories of doing shit I've never done before. Parasailing, painting, therapy, and—" Jess closed her eyes and Lucia's face filled the red darkness behind her lids. While other memories and images from her time at the resort had faded or fuzzed to her mind's eye, Lucia remained clear.

"Hon?"

Jess shook her head and looked back at Shell. "I don't know. But even if everything was nothing more than my brain playing tricks on me, or, if the afterlife is a strange and fantastical place, ghosts are real, and out of body experiences happen to folks on the regular, it doesn't stop the pain of loss." She looked out toward the trees at the back of her yard. "I miss her. How do I cope with pining for someone who never existed?"

Shell reached across the distance between their chairs and squeezed Jess's hand. "I know, sweetie. It sucks." She was quiet for a moment and Jess was grateful for the opportunity to collect her thoughts. "Do you think this could be your brain's way of telling you that you're ready to move on?"

"I—" The idea hit Jess like a gut punch, and she tensed in her chair. "Truthfully, I hadn't even thought of that. And you mean like when you dream about a bunch of stuff as a way for you to work through whatever thoughts are heavy in the waking hours?"

Shell nodded.

The more Jess turned it over in her mind, the more it made sense. Maybe that's why her white light hallucination, or whatever it was, made her romance at the resort a short-term only kind of thing. Despite the fact that Jess had never been interested in short-term relationships. She turned wide eyes toward her friend. "I can't believe I didn't even consider that. It seems way more legit than some of the other explanations I could come up with."

"Glad I could help."

Her suggestion was certainly worth thinking about more. "You know what? I'm going to ask my therapist about that in our next session."

Shell finished that last little bit of her lemonade and placed the sweating glass back on the table. "I'm here for you in whatever way you need. You want some good suggestions for dates? I'll put on my matchmaker pants. On the other hand, if you just need someone to vet some folks for you? Well, you've got a whole team of people that would jump at the chance."

Jess snickered.

"Oh, speaking of team. You said the doc cleared you for sports again. Are you ready to play the last couple games of the season?"

"Dude," Jess scoffed. "I haven't even practiced. I'd suck so hard right now."

"Then let's hit the batting cages this weekend. You can invite everyone over for a barbecue on Sunday and we'll throw the ball around."

"You just don't want to cook this weekend because it's your turn."

She got an unrepentant grin from Shell. "Maybe, but I still think you should have a cookout."

Jess gave in because she missed her friends and had

been looking forward to getting back to the things she used to love. She was definitely going to want a car if she were going to start playing sports again, or if she wanted to take any of the art classes that she'd looked up at the community center. "Fine, but I held a vehicle at Maxwell Motors today. Want to give me one last ride tomorrow morning?"

Shell made a face. "Exactly how early are we talking?"

"They're open until four so I figured I'd be there around noon. I was going to ride my bike, but I'd rather not do that until I see how much space I have to carry the bike around in."

"Oh, noon I can do. That means Tam has to take Rory to his swim lessons."

"Uh, I thought you loved taking him to all that stuff."

Shell shuddered. "The shrieks of children echo off the walls of the pool and it's enough to make your ears bleed. Besides, I took him the last few times. I'm happy to hand off the duty for a weekend."

Jess considered how young Rory was. "Can he even swim? Little squirt is barely walking."

"Believe it or not, he took to it like, well, like a fish to water."

They both laughed at that, and Jess flicked some of the water from the sweating glass at her. "You're such a dork."

"Maybe. But I'm the dork that's going to give you a ride tomorrow."

"Hmm, good point."

Shell nodded. "That's what I thought."

They talked for a little while longer. Mostly about drama happening between players on two of the other softball teams. Some sort of weird love triangle. Jess's subconscious mind may be ready for her to date again, but she definitely wasn't looking for drama. For now, she was going to focus on herself. Get all her ducks in a row and be happy before looking to add another person into the mix. She deserved to put her joy first.

# Chapter Seventeen

"This is what you held?" Shell tilted her head one way then the other. "What even *is it*?"

"It's a Hyundai."

Shell rolled her eyes. "No shit, Sherlock. I mean, is it a truck, an SUV, or some Frankenstein hybrid of the two?"

Jess snickered. "Both, I think. But more importantly to me, it's used. I'm guessing it was a lease so I have low mileage and a single owner vehicle, without paying the ridiculous markup of a new vehicle."

"I'm mean, that's fair." She made a face. "White is gonna show dirt like crazy."

"Whatever. They don't have many base colors available and with me wanting a used one, well, beggars couldn't be choosers. It was already like looking for a unicorn trying to find the right trim level. I've actually had my eye on this model for the past eight months, when it first caught my attention. I just never had a reason to upgrade to another vehicle that required payments when my Subaru was paid off."

Shell tugged her away from the weird SUV with a four-foot truck bed on the back. "Whatever you say, Captain Cheap Ass. Let's get through the paperwork so I can go."

Jess shook off her hand. "You're so weird. I only needed a ride here, not a chaperone. Go enjoy some quiet time while Tam and Rory are at the pool."

Shell's eyes lit up at that suggestion. "Ooh, good idea! Maybe I'll swing by the Bean Bag and get an iced caramel macchiato."

She shrugged. "You do you. Have fun and wish me luck on spending a big chunk of money. It's gonna give me hives."

"Live a little, babe. Will that trucklet make you happy?"

The comment made Jess smile and she nodded.

"Good. That's all that matters. Go spend the money, then get your own coffee, ride your bike, take a walk in the park, or pick up babes at Culture. I just want you to put yourself first for once."

Jess pulled her into a tight hug. "This is why I love you. And I plan to."

"Pick up babes?"

Jess rolled her eyes. "As if. I'm too fucking old for all that. I think I've always been. Now scram. Your free time is running out."

"Gotcha. See you tomorrow. I'll text in the morning with a time for the batting cages, and we'll determine the best time for all of us to come over after."

"Sounds good. Thanks again."

Two hours later, after a test drive and detailed explanation of all the vehicle's features, Jess walked out with a sleek black and silver fob in hand. She was the proud new owner of her truck thing. The insurance check for her other vehicle covered all but the last six thousand of the Hyundai so she made the difficult decision to take the money out of her hard fought for savings. Sure, it hurt, but it was better to avoid payments and the interest that came with a bank loan. She'd be able to build it back up in no time. Especially since she found out the Santa Cruz had a cheaper insurance cost, and she had plans to start riding her bike a lot more to work.

Jess sat in the driver's seat with both hands on the steering wheel. She didn't have any place she had to be for the day since she and Shell agreed that Sunday would be better for a trip to the batting cages because it wouldn't be as busy.

Jess thought about the other phone call she'd made at the beginning of the week. It was one of the wish list items that she spoke with her therapist about. One of the many things she remembered writing down in her hallucination dream at the hospital. After a quick search on her phone, Jess set the course on her nav screen and turned right out of the dealership.

Ten minutes later she turned onto a dirt lot and parked outside a concrete building. The sign on the side read Dragonfly Rescue Center. Jess took a deep breath and shut off the truck. She didn't get her hopes up that she'd find a new friend right away, but she'd never get a dog if she didn't take the first steps toward adoption.

Inside, she heard a cacophony of barking coming from somewhere on the other side of a heavy door at the opposite end of the room.

"Hi, can I help you?"

Someone young enough to be Jess's kid sat at a desk in the corner. The androgynous youth wore a T-shirt with the shelter's logo and a name tag that said their name was Max. Jess liked their friendly smile. An adorable white Pit Bull watched Jess from a dog bed against the wall behind Max. Every time Jess glanced at the pup, their whippy tail thumped against the bed. "Yeah. I've been wanting to adopt a dog for a while now and thought I'd come in and see who you've got available." She shuffled her feet and admitted that she had actually called and checked out their site at the beginning of the week to see what the requirements were. "I provided references at the time and brought a picture of my yard and house today."

Max grinned. "That's great. You're further ahead than most that come in. It's usually a very spur of the moment thing, which we don't actually encourage. Would you like to tour the kennel?"

"Yes, please." She nodded toward the dog. "Who is that happy baby?"

The dog came off the bed as if it knew Jess was talking about it, stretched, and then stood cautiously next to the desk with its tail whirling in circles. Max patted their back. "This sweet girl is Alice. She's been back at the shelter for about a month. She'd previously been with one of our foster families for a while, but they got another foster that required a lot more attention and money and had to return her. We don't have any other foster families available right now."

Jess held out her hand and Alice came up to give her a sniff, then a lick. "Can I pet her?"

"Oh sure. She's nothing but a big, affectionate, goober. Great personality and super friendly. Given her disposition and history, I couldn't bear to put her in the back with the others. I wish I could adopt her myself, but my mom put her foot down on bringing home any more dogs or cats."

Once Jess started petting Alice, the dog was completely won over. She wiggled her butt around in hopes of scratches. Jess laughed and humored her. She scratched behind Alice's ears, then moved up to pet her head. "Oh, her ears are so soft!"

Max nodded. "I love the floppy ears on pitties. I hate it when they come in cropped and we have so many that come in."

A thick, panting, tongue appeared, and Jess smiled at Alice's big doggy grin. "I have a hard time believing that nobody has adopted this one."

A shrug met her declaration. "Eh, sadly it's all too common. Between bullshit breed legislation laws, ignorance about dogs in general, and specific misconceptions about Pit Bulls, most are afraid to adopt."

Jess's knees hurt from squatting, so she sank down to the floor as Alice begged for even more attention. She ignored Max's sly look. Jess laughed and cooed at Alice. "You are just the biggest, sweetest, baby girl, aren't you?" She looked up to where Max had come around the desk and perched on the edge. "Do you know how old she is?"

"Alice first showed up a year ago. The staff veterinarian thought she was maybe a year old at the time, if that. Clearly a stray on the streets and she'd recently had pups but we never found those. After a month, she got paired with a foster family and has done well there the past ten or so months."

"Is she good with other pets, little kids, strangers?" Jess was thinking about her friends, and specifically Rory.

"The foster family had three kids, a one-year-old, four, and ten. They also had two other rescue dogs and three cats. A full house. I don't blame them for making the hard call when another, harder, to adopt rescue came in needing a home. We figured Alice would go fast because she's so sweet, but like I said, she's been here a month."

Jess stopped petting and stared into Alice's deep brown eyes. "Hi Alice. I've had a rough past couple of years and could use the company. Would you like to come home with me?"

Alice lunged forward and licked her face.

Max laughed. "That sounds like her answer. You said you brought pictures of your yard?"

"I did." Jess took a few seconds to get to her feet again then pulled out her cell phone. She showed Max the yard and pics she snapped of the inside of her house. Satisfied, Max got out the paperwork for adoption and set Jess up at a nearby table with a pen.

Never in a million years would Jess have predicted where the afternoon had taken her. Sure, she'd been planning to get a vehicle, and had been leaning hard into the idea of getting a dog. But the spontaneous stop at the animal shelter that day? Especially since Alice may not have been there if she'd waited a few more days, or worse, another week. She was a gorgeous girl.

As if sensing Jess was going to be her new person, Alice sat to Jess's left so Jess could pet her while filling out the paperwork with her right hand. It was tricky but worth it when Alice leaned over and rested her big blocky head on Jess's thigh and sighed. Jess was already in love. Who needed a girlfriend anyway?

Jess's first stop after the shelter was to Pet Palace. She was told that Alice was kennel trained so she wanted to pick up all the supplies she'd need before taking her home and introducing her sweet girl to the house and yard. What was even more money spent when her happiness was on the line?

Everyone ooh'd and aww'd over Alice in the store. In the end, Jess walked out with a large crate and crate pad, a dog bed, harness, heavy duty leash, seatbelt, food and water bowls, dog food, tons of treats, and a multitude of Tuffy and Kong dog toys. She was told that Pit Bulls were strong chewers and cautioned away from playing games like tug because Alice could accidentally hurt her if she lost her grip on the rope.

Jess may or may not have also purchased an adorable MSU bandanna and jersey. It was too warm for the second one, but the harness and bandanna went on before leaving the store. Jess couldn't be sure but Alice looked like a state fan. Besides, the green and white colors of the bandanna looked good with her white coat.

After PetSmart, Jess sat in her new truck with her new dog. "Are you ready to go home, Alice?" Alice woofed and that was all the answer she needed.

****

Jess drove up to the batting cages the next day with Alice in the back seat. She knew they wouldn't be there long and it was a beautiful sixty-six degrees outside. She backed her little truck up so the bed was in the shade of the tree next to the group of cages that Shell, Tam, Jamie, and Kelsey stood near. Then she got out and moved to the back door. Alice learned quickly to wait for Jess to unhook the seatbelt from her harness before trying to exit the back seat. Leash in hand, she moved so Alice could jump out then took her new pupper to meet her friends.

"Oh, my freaking God! I only left you alone for a few hours, woman. When did you get this sweetheart?" Shell said.

Alice did the wiggle butt over to the group of waiting people and everyone gave her the expected level of attention her cuteness deserved.

Jess laughed. "I'd been thinking about adopting for a while. I just happened to head over to the shelter after signing the paperwork on my truck."

"Man, I was looking at those a while back. That's one sick ride. Who knows? If I ever decide to get rid of my Olivia, I may consider the Santa Cruz."

Kelsey snickered. "Babe, she's five years old now. It's totally time for a change."

Jamie glanced over her shoulder toward the pretty blue Veloster. "Not so loud, you'll hurt my girl's feelings."

Kelsey scowled. "I'm your girl and you're a weirdo."

Tam rolled her eyes and squatted down to love on Alice alongside her wife. "Do you think Jess would notice if I stole Alice and took her home with us?"

"Pretty sure Jess would know," Jess said dryly. "Anyway, if you all give me a minute to get her situated, I'm ready to hit some balls, or not hit some as will probably be the case. If only to prove how much I shouldn't be playing after so long out of the game."

Shell gave Alice a few more scratches under the chin. "Don't you worry. Auntie Shell will give you more love later."

A few minutes later, Jess had an old blanket laid out in the bed of her truck with Alice's leash clipped to the tie-down inside. There was a little dish of water in the bed with her as well. She seemed content laying there in the shade, watching the group take turns in the batting cages.

Jamie and Kelsey bickered in one cage while Tam, Shell, and Jess shared the other. The bickering stopped and Jess looked over to see Jamie standing behind Kelsey. At first glance she thought the taller woman was helping Kelsey with her batting stance. Then she noticed the wandering hands and snickered.

Tam batted first in their cage. Her hits were solid, as always. Tam wasn't a power hitter, but she was a dependable player who usually hit singles or doubles. Shell batted next. Her bats weren't as strong as Tam's, but she was quicker so usually got on first.

Jess pulled on her gloves and grabbed one of her junk bats when Shell was finished. She didn't want to wreck her favorite on the hard rubber balls. Shell slapped her ass on the way into the cage. "You've got this, J. It's like riding a bike."

"And I haven't done that in probably just as long."

"You'll be fine," Tam called.

Embarrassingly, Jess missed the first three pitches. She caught the next on the edge and sent it behind her in the box. The fifth pitch bounced and skittered forward, a sure easy pick for any pitcher. "Goddamn it. This is stupid."

Jamie yelled from the other cage. "You've got this, Jess! I heard about those bats and I want to see the magic."

Jess fouled another then caught the seventh for what would have been a decent line drive. She hit the last three then propped her bat between her knees and shook out her hands. "I'm not sure I've got it in me anymore. I'm so far out of practice I'm practically a softball virgin again."

Tam laughed and Shell elbowed her. "I have full faith

in you. How do you feel? Any pain?"

"No, Mom," Jess said back to Shell.

"Good. I think you should move up a little in the box. It looks like your style has changed and you're swinging slower than you used to. You need to adjust and get to it faster, so you stop sending it into the right foul line. Just be careful you don't pull it hard in the other direction and foul down the opposite line. Heads up, I'm putting more quarters in."

Jess did as she was instructed and right away, she had solid hits as soon as the balls started coming. On the fourth, she sent it deep into the back of the overhead net. She grunted, "About time."

"Holy shit, that's the ticket!"

The rest of the round was full of deep, power hits. Jess came out of the cage and was mobbed by her friends. Kelsey slapped her ass. "I want to be you when I grow up." Then she turned to Jamie. "How do I learn to bat like Jess?"

Poor Jamie looked like a deer in the headlights and Jess snickered. "Uh, well, maybe more practice, and um, natural talent?"

Kelsey got a look in her eye and Jamie took off running.

Jess's attention was diverted from the playful couple when Alice let out an excited woo-woo from the truck, clearly wanting in on the action. "Sorry, sweetheart. I'll give you love when we're done." She jogged over and gave Alice a dog treat from inside the truck then went back to watch Tam take her second turn in the cage.

They practiced for a few more rounds before calling it a day. "Who's ready for barbecue?" Jess asked.

"Can we play euchre?"

"I don't like euchre," Jamie whined.

Jess scoffed. "Who doesn't like euchre? Are you even from Michigan?"

"Have you played with her?" Jamie pointed toward a suspiciously innocent-looking Kelsey.

Jess shrugged. "I know she's competitive but you're on the same team when you play euchre."

The unfairly attractive woman with the shock of dark

hair shuddered. "It's even worse." She leaned closer. "She's so mean if we don't take the tricks."

Kelsey swatted her arm. "I'm right here, you ass." Then she grinned at Jess. "But she's right, I will call her on her shitty plays."

"See?"

Shell laughed. "We've got four if Jamie doesn't play. So, it's no big deal. Let's go, I need drinks and dinner. Mom practically demanded Rory for an overnight and I wasn't going to argue with her after the week I've had."

After collecting personal bats, they started walking toward the vehicles. Shell suddenly stopped and turned, calling out to Jamie, "Hey!" Jamie and Kelsey looked in her direction. "Did you only say you didn't want to play euchre so you could play with the dog?"

"Who, me?" Jamie said. "See you at Jess's house!" Then she started walking backward to her pretty blue car and saluted Shell on the way.

"Your girlfriend is a sneaky asshole, Kelsey!" Shell yelled.

"Why do you think I love her so much?"

Jess laughed at the motley crew and went to get Alice from the bed of her truck. She had known they wouldn't be able to resist such a sweet puppy face. "Come on little girl. Let's go home and pick up your poops before anyone sees them."

She had a few minutes to mentally prepare for company because Shell had to run home for her potato salad while Jamie and Kelsey wanted to stop at the party store for drinks. Jess had time to pick up a few groceries that morning so she was supplying brats, buns, and corn on the cob. The menu was easy once she knew the lone vegan of their close friend group wouldn't be there.

Jenn and Malcom had previous plans with Jenn's mom. Richard and Caleb were in Grand Rapids for the weekend. Jess loved GR but it was stupid to drive nearly two hours only to hang out by herself.

It was too early for dinner still, so Jess and Kelsey partnered against Tam and Shell for euchre on the patio table while Jamie threw the frisbee for Alice. Jess had picked a pair of them up the day before with all the other toys but hadn't gotten the opportunity to throw it for her yet. She was happy to see that Alice loved it as much as she did the rest.

"Will she be okay by herself tomorrow when you're at work?" Shell asked.

Jess followed her king with an ace of the same suit. "They said she was good to spend up to twelve hours alone so I'm not worried about her bladder. My main concern is that she's still unfamiliar with the house and will get anxious with me gone so long."

Tam grumbled and thew off. "This is bullshit. You two have never even played together and you're kicking our asses."

Kelsey grinned and went low, letting Jess scoop the last trick of the deal. She moved their score up to eight. Poor Tam and Shell were still sitting on three. "I know. Isn't it great? And don't you guys have personal days or something?"

"We do, but I had to take all my personal and sick days when I was off work. I can call in up to three vacation days without prior notice if I need to, but I hate to take even more time off for something so trivial."

Shell shuffled and started dealing out the cards. "You could argue that Alice is part of your healing journey so taking a day off would be essential self-care."

"Get a load of this one! Must be nice having HR in your back pocket, J," Kelsey said.

"Babe, your boss loves you like a daughter. Don't act like you've got it so hard."

Kelsey leaned over the railing and blew her girlfriend a kiss. "It's true, though. I get away with murder."

Jess shuddered. "Shell has told me some of the spider stories. I'm glad I don't work with you."

Shell scooped a trick then threw down both bowers. "Cough them up, people. And Jess, just take the day."

"Damn it. Is that where they were? I was hoping Kelsey had one or both."

"Nope and you've been euched."

Shell moved her score up two points and Jess shifted uncomfortably beneath Kelsey's glare. "Sorry, Kelse. I was counting on you for at least one."

"Yeah, well, my hand was total shit."

Tam laughed and did a dance in her chair. "Woo, yeah. We're coming back."

Jess finished shuffling and tapped the top of the deck. She shot a cocky grin at Shell. "If I deal myself a loner right now, I'll take the day off. Otherwise, I'll work it and hope for the best."

"You know what, Tam will give you ten dollars if you deal yourself a loner, but if you don't you owe us ten."

"Hey, why me?"

Shell gave her wife a sweet smile. "Because I forgot my purse." Tam sighed.

"You're on." Jess swiftly dealt out the cards by twos and threes.

She flipped up a ten of spades and Shell crowed. "Not looking good for you, babe!"

Jess picked up her hand and looked at the cards. Jack of spades, ace of spades, king of spades, queen of spades, and an ace of diamonds. She kept her face neutral and waited while the call went around the table.

"Pass."

"Fucking pass!" Kelsey met her gaze. "I will murder you if you pick that shit up."

Shell snickered. "Table talk. Pass. And I dare you."

Jess reached for the card slowly, then met Kelsey's gaze and gave her a wink. She picked up the card and both Tam and Shell groaned. Jess put the Ace of diamonds face down on top of the stack leaving all trump cards in her hand. "I'm going alone."

"You bitch. You never go alone which means your hand must be fucking good."

Jess shrugged at Shell then looked at Tam. "Your lead."

Kelsey made a face and set her cards aside since she wouldn't be playing. Tam threw down an ace of hearts.

"I don't have any hearts and I don't trust you," Shell said. She threw down the left bower, the jack of clubs, on top of the pile. "Go big or go home, J."

She laughed. "Sorry Shell, but you've just lost." She threw the Jack of spades on top and scooped the whole pile. Then she put her entire hand down. There was nothing either of them could do when she had all the remaining high trump cards in her hand.

"Hell, yes! Up here." Kelsey stood and held both hands up for double high fives.

Jess slapped her hands then gathered all the cards. "Who's ready for me to start the grill?"

"I'm so ready," Jamie called from below the deck. "Who knew playing frisbee was such hard work?"

Jess looked over the railing at them. Alice was lying on the grass, panting. She looked worn out and happy. "Thanks for keeping her company." Then she turned to Tam. "Oh, and apparently you owe me a ten."

"Dammit, Jess. I rescind your approval for a vacation call-in."

She snorted at Shell. "Uh huh, try again. You don't have any say over that."

"Fine. Come on then. I'll help you get the stuff ready for the grill." Shell bumped Jess's hip then led the way into the house. It had turned into a pretty good day. Jess felt lighter in spirit than she had in a very long time. Maybe she'd look at available community center classes tomorrow while she was hanging out with Alice. Life was short and she wanted to make the most of her new beginning.

# Chapter Eighteen

"I see everyone has their drawing tablet and recommended pencil pack so let's get started. As you all know, my name is Delilah Darren and I'll be your instructor for the next three Intro to Drawing sessions."

It was August before Jess made the decision to look up art classes at the local community center. She couldn't convince any of her friends to take these ones with her, but Richard said to let him know if she decided on cooking classes next.

Jess's one-game return to softball the previous month had gone okay, about as could be expected after years away from the sport. Surprisingly, her knees didn't ache terribly after. At least nothing a little ice therapy couldn't take care of. She assumed it had to do with the twenty pounds she'd dropped since her accident. Between riding her bike to work every day and hiking all over the park behind her house with Alice, her activity level had gone through the roof. Jess felt good and was getting around better than she had since before her ex.

Her friends were a little surprised by all the changes. Jenn even pulled her aside and asked if she was going through a midlife crisis. Jess explained that nearly dying put her entire existence into perspective and made her realize how much she was throwing away by refusing to live life to its fullest.

Now here she was, embarking on yet another new thing. The reason Jess waited so long after adopting Alice to look into expanding her hobbies was so she could get enough bonding time in with the pup.

"We're going to start this session learning basic drawing skills. Just a few introductory, fun exercises. How many of you regularly draw?" Everyone in the room except Jess raised their hand. "What prompted you to take this class, Ms. Parker?"

She shrugged. "It's Jess, please. And I'm not really

artistic. I've just always enjoyed making little sketches and stuff. I doodle a lot but don't know anything about actual drawing."

Delilah smiled at her. "I'm going to let you in on a secret. Doodling *is* drawing. If you're putting pencil to paper and creating art, you're drawing. That includes cartoons, doodles, figures, and freehand…it's all drawing. What I'm going to teach you in these two-hour sessions is how to hone and expand your skills."

Jess spent the next two hours soaking up everything Delilah had to offer and found she enjoyed the peaceful scratching of pencil against the surface of her drawing pad. They practiced a series of shape studies before progressing to drawing a carefully constructed pile of items on the table in the center of the room. Jess thought it was cool that each artist had a slightly different perspective on what they were drawing. Besides individual artistic styles, it made each piece created unique.

She jumped when Delilah said from behind her, "And you say you're not very artistic. I like your use of shading with this piece. You've truly captured the lights reflecting off the objects below. Nicely done."

Jess's cheeks warmed. "Thanks."

"Have you ever done any painting?"

She thought back to Ronobe's classes, the ones that were nothing more than a figment of her imagination. "Not really. I tried once but my style is more…abstract. I don't know that I could sit down and paint something intentionally. You know?"

Delilah chuckled. "I get it. Painting isn't for everyone. Even if that's not interesting to you, we do have an intermediate drawing class beginning the first week of December. Keep it in mind if you enjoy this one."

Jess brightened. "Oh, I for sure will. I think I'm going to try cooking classes next, but I wanted to start with Intro to Drawing because I figured I could always draw anywhere on my own time once I have the basics down."

"Very true. You'll never lack for anything to do as long as you have a piece of paper and pencil. Either way, I look forward to seeing what else you create in these sessions."

"Thanks. Me, too."

****

Jess's class ended by seven but since it was Sunday night, she decided she'd stop by the Bean Bag for a sandwich and muffin to go rather than cook at home. She'd fed Alice before she left the house. It wasn't like her pup would let her leave otherwise. Jess learned within the first few weeks that Alice's dinner bell went off any time after four and she had no problems sitting in your lap and yodeling until you fed her.

There was a crowd inside, mostly gathered at the far end of the coffee shop next to the small stage along the street side picture window. Jess came in the back entrance nearest the counter to avoid attracting everyone's attention. She'd seen flyers for the poetry open mic but never gave it much thought. However, standing there waiting for her food, Jess found that she enjoyed the people reading. They weren't just reciting a bunch of words on a page. The poets were full of emotion and energy, and they were performers as much as anything else.

What did surprise her was seeing Jamie get up on the stage. Her piece was about surviving the darkness of toxic love and finding redemption later in life. It was powerful and Jess had no idea her friend was that talented. Of course, Kelsey sat at their table listening and snapped with both hands when Jamie was done.

There was a break right after Jamie read, so many people stood to go refill drinks or hit the bathroom. Jamie and Kelsey spied her as they were coming up to make their own orders.

"Hey, how's it going?" Kelsey gave Jess a hug, with Jamie following right after. "Are you here for the reading?"

Jess shook her head. "I just finished my first drawing class down the street so thought I'd be lazy and pick up dinner on the way home. I love their sandwiches."

"They're good, but the Scalded Crow makes the best

in the city. One thing the Bean Bag does better though is their hot chai latte, despite being a national chain."

Kelsey laughed. "Don't let James get started on the Crow's sandwiches. We'll be here all night."

Jess snorted. "Message received. Anyway, I didn't know you wrote poetry, Jamie."

She blushed and shrugged. "Eh, I've always done it but I wasn't comfortable sharing until after Kelsey and I had been dating for a while. Now it's kind of fun to perform it for others. It's cathartic writing and listening to other people recite their thoughts, fears, and loves. I figured maybe someone would get something out of my words as well."

Jess nodded. "Well, I don't know anything about poetry but what I just heard was good. I think you made the right call to share."

"You could always join our poetry group every Tuesday at Scalded Crow."

"Yeah, I think I'll skip that. Not my thing but good on you."

Kelsey burst into laughter. "That's what I told her."

She shrugged. "I've only just started my drawing sessions. I like it so far and can't wait to look into cooking classes when this is done. Richard promised he'd sign up with me."

Jamie jogged Kelsey with her elbow. "Babe, you should totally take cooking classes with them. Maybe you'll expand your knowledge base beyond tuna sandwiches and frozen burritos."

As if Jess were in a dramedy, she watched Kelsey turn her head slowly to the left to level a glare at Jamie. The taller woman visibly shrank back then held up her hands and gave Kelsey a weak smile. "Or, uh, not? Your tuna fish sandwiches are the bomb." Then, as if to seal the declaration, she gave a double thumbs up.

Jess snickered. "You two are funny. I'll let everyone know the dates and times for any cooking classes I find. That way if anyone else is interested, they can sign up with me and Richard. The more the merrier, right?"

Kelsey gave Jamie a quick kiss to show she was teasing then looked at Jess. "That sounds good. Who knows, maybe I'll finally do something about my inability to cook."

"Jess!"

She glanced toward the counter to see a bag with her name on it. "Whoop, looks like my dinner is ready. I'll catch you two later."

"Are you going to Caleb's birthday dinner Saturday, and Culture after?"

Jess snapped her fingers. "Oh yeah, that's right. I almost forgot. Thanks for reminding me. Yeah, I guess I'll see you all there." She gave a little salute. "Okay, I'm off for real now. I don't want to leave Alice home alone any longer. It's close to poopie time."

Kelsey snickered.

"Give that sweet baby angel lots of smooches from her auntie James," Jamie said.

"Will do. Bye ladies!"

If the interaction taught Jess anything, it was that she couldn't make assumptions about people. Who knew Jamie was a poet, or that Kelsey didn't know how to cook? She wondered how many assumptions people made about her.

****

Richard had made reservations at a popular tapas restaurant for Saturday night. Jess only knew half the people in attendance, but she had fun nonetheless. Richard even arranged to have an adorable little cake brought out for Caleb to make a wish. Jess was jealous of how young Caleb was. Richard was near Shell's age, but Caleb was only twenty-eight.

Culture wasn't far from the restaurant so most parked where they'd be able to walk to both. Tam and Shell came up to flank Jess on either side as they walked the two blocks to the club after dinner.

"Are you ready to let your freak flag fly?" Tam said.

Jess snorted and jogged Shell with her elbow. "Get your wife under control. One, nobody says that anymore and two, I've never had a freak flag to fly."

Shell hip-checked her back. "Maybe that's part of your problem, J," She pointed back and forth between Tam and herself. "We will be on the lookout for a good lady love tonight."

"Why? Are you two planning a threesome?"

She got a swat to the backside for her smartass comment. "For you, numpty!"

Jess shook her head and held up her hands. "No way! I've heard all about your terrible matchmaking. I remember the story Kelsey told us where you tried to set her up with Jenn. Hello? That couldn't have been a worse idea."

"It wasn't that bad," Shell huffed.

"Oh, please. Let me prove it." Jess called out to the big group walking ten feet ahead of them. "Hey, Kelsey and Jenn, is Shell a good matchmaker?"

"Hell, no."

"Fuck, no."

The two women in question looked at each other then started laughing.

Shell rolled her eyes. "Juveniles. And you know what? I clearly did a good job setting them up as besties...so there's that."

"Well, you're my bestie so I don't need any help there either."

Richard dropped back and shooed Shell away from Jess. "Girl, don't let Shell get her claws in you. Stick with me and just be chill with the gay boys tonight if you don't want to fend off the ladies."

Jess made a face. "As if I'd be fending off anyone. Literally nobody my age still goes to the bar."

"And no parents go to the bar anymore either, yet here I am."

Jenn raised a hand in solidarity with Shell. "Girl, same. Live a little, J. As long as you have fun, we don't care how you do it."

"Fine," Jess conceded. "But my knees prefer to play pool over dancing so someone better keep me company upstairs."

"Ooh, I'll play," Kelsey said. They were all bunched together at the door to Culture while everyone showed

ID's and paid the cover charge.

Jenn leaned close and whispered a warning. "Don't play against her. She's a shark."

She snickered. "Noted. Thanks for the heads up."

After drinks were procured by everyone, Jess and a few others wandered upstairs to shoot pool. The center of the upstairs was open to show the dance floor below, surrounded only by a drink railing. It wasn't any quieter but less space meant there were less people. Unfortunately, after a few games, most people wandered back downstairs to dance. Jess watched her friends get their groove on and laughed at Shell's antics. Her best friend did tend to strip down when cutting loose. Jess's attention was diverted by a conversation at the pool table right behind her.

"Seriously? I hate the club and only came here because you insisted you were lonely and needed to get out. I'd rather be home hanging out with George."

"You mean your freaking turtle? Give me a break! Lanie."

There was a pause where Jess didn't know if the pushy friend was going to start speaking again. The music was loud, so she relied on the skills of her eavesdropping alone to keep up with the conversation. Luckily, she didn't have to wait long. "Laney, this is why you never meet anyone. You just hole up in your apartment and don't put yourself out there."

"People suck and my turtle doesn't."

Jess snickered. The mystery woman wasn't that far off. In an effort to assuage her burning curiosity, Jess casually turned and leaned back against the railing to look toward the pool tables. She picked out the pushy woman and her turtle lady friend immediately. Laney was hella tall, sporting short dark hair and stylish glasses. She looked like a cute, lanky, librarian. Neither butch nor femme, just kind of sporty. Even more interesting was that, with the gray hair near her temples, she appeared closer to Jess's age than anyone else in the club that night. A little tendril of interest sat up at attention and Jess found herself drawn into the conversation.

"Come on, Vic. Can't we just play pool?"

Vic gestured toward the dance floor. "Hannah just got

here and you know I've been talking to her for a while. Maybe this is what I need to get over Taylor."

Laney threw up her hands. "Fine, go dance then. But I'm definitely not coming down there to be a third wheel while you grind on your newest flirt."

"Whatever." Vic stalked off toward the stairs leading down to the first level. Laney's expressions ran the gamut of emotions. Irritation, frustration, and sadness.

Jess felt bad for her. After all, she herself was in a similar situation. But at least her friends weren't assholes. She called out to Laney. "That was a dick move. I'd be more than happy to play pool with you. All my friends wanted to dance so I told them to go ahead."

Laney tilted her head as Jess walked closer. "Did they ditch you, too?"

"No. We're all here for another friend's birthday. I couldn't let Caleb down even though the club scene isn't really my thing."

"Ugh," Laney frowned. "Exactly."

"Would you like a drink?"

"I'm good right now, thanks."

"Okay. So…pool?" That got Laney to smile, and Jess was startled to see how it transformed her face. She was quite pretty. Jess felt a little twinge when she realized how much Laney's smile reminded her of Lucia's.

"Absolutely. I like pool a lot, I just don't like coming to the bars to play."

Jess paused. "I'm not very good." She said it at the same time that Laney said the same thing. They burst into laughter and Jess walked over to the stick rack to choose the least warped one. When she came back to the table, she held out her hand. "I'm Jess."

"Laney. But you probably already heard Vic say my name.

Jess shrugged. "You want to break?"

"Why not. I can pretend like it's my cousin's head."

Jess laughed. "Eh, whatever works to get the balls in, right?"

"Exactly."

They played and kept up friendly chatter throughout the game.

"So how long have you lived in St. Seren?" Jess asked.

"Only a few months. I moved here after a bad breakup to be closer to my cousin. Vic is the only family member I've got that doesn't treat me like the black sheep. Probably because she's a blacker sheep than I am. Kind of an asshole if I'm being honest."

Jess laughed.

"What about you?" Laney asked.

"Oh, I've lived here my whole life. I love this city and couldn't picture myself anywhere else."

"I'll admit that it does have its charm. I fell in love with the river running through downtown, and all the parks they've got around the city. I've been looking for good places to ride my bike since moving here from Plymouth. I'm not all hardcore like some people but I still enjoy it."

Jess lit up at that. "Oh, there's a great park behind my house. It has easy to moderate trails for biking and great walking paths. They're separate so nobody gets hurt. I ride my bike there all the time when I'm not walking my dog, Alice."

"Where do you live?"

"Over on the northeast side. Next to Cedar Ridge Metro Park."

"I've heard of that but haven't had the chance to check it out yet."

Jess thought for a second then went out on a limb. What's the point of a second chance at life if you don't live it? Worst case scenario, Laney would say no. But if she said yes, Jess may get a new friend out of it and Laney would have another person in St. Seren she could hang out with. Someone beside her asshole cousin, Vic. "If you want a riding buddy, I can give you my number. I'm usually free on the weekends. Nobody else in my friend group rides."

Laney looked hesitant. "I'm not very fast."

That made Jess laugh. "No worries. I only started riding again after stopping for five years. So, I'm just getting back into the swing of things."

Laney brightened. "You know what? That sounds great." She pulled out her phone and she and Jess exchanged numbers. They made plans to meet up the next afternoon for a short ride. After that, they played one more game before Jess decided she was going to call it a night.

She looked down at her watch then finished off her drink and smiled at Laney. "I think I'm going to head out before I turn into a pumpkin."

"Yeah, same. Clubbing loses its interest once you realize there are people drinking at the bar young enough to be your kid."

"Right?" Jess held up her hand. "Forty-six."

Laney grinned and answered back, "Forty-five."

"Ooh, look at us old ladies out on the town." They burst into laughter. "I'll walk out with you if you'd like. I just need to let my friends know I'm leaving."

"I'm parked on the street two blocks over."

"Yup, me too."

Once downstairs, Laney stood off to the side while Jess braved the throngs of people on the dance floor to find her friends. She said goodbye to Caleb and Richard first, wishing Caleb a happy birthday. Then she moved along the outer edge of the crowd until she found the rest. Shell was down to a tank top and looking a little less than sober. Jess shook her head, waded in, and pulled Shell off to the side where she could be heard over the music.

"What's up, buttercup? You coming down to join us heathens?"

"I'm actually leaving and wanted to say goodbye."

Shell pouted. "No, you can't leave! You're supposed to stay until you pick up some ladies."

"You're ridiculous. And I may not be picking up any ladies, but I did make a new friend. We're going to go bike riding tomorrow at Cedar Ridge."

Shell craned her neck around. "Where is she?" Then she caught sight of Laney off behind Jess. "Ooh, is that her? She's cute!"

Jess's cheeks grew warm. "Knock it off before I tit punch you."

In her inebriation, Shell swayed. "You wouldn't dare."

Jess barked out a laugh. "I may not be tall but I've still got a few inches on you."

"Oh, yeah? I'll tell Jamie."

"Try again, she wouldn't hurt a fly," Jess said,

confidently.

"I'll tell Kelsey then. She'll go all Krav Maga on your ass." Then Shell crossed her arms, looking a little too smug while people gyrated behind her.

At those words, Jess held up her hands and admitted defeat. She moved close enough for Shell to hear without having to yell. "You win. Let's call a truce. And Laney seems like good people. She doesn't know anyone in St. Seren. I think she could use some friends and I know I certainly can."

"Fine, call me tomorrow and let me know how it goes."

"Dude, it's just a bike ride."

Jess was rescued when Tam and Kelsey came up behind Shell and began pulling her away, but not before Shell gave Jess finger guns and an exaggerated wink. "Go get em, Tiger!"

Jess was startled at the nickname, her mind conjuring up the memory of someone very different saying it. After the two new friends successfully escaped the steamy club, Jess let out an exaggerated sigh. "Sorry that took so long. I didn't think I was ever going to get away."

"Not a big deal. Your friend was definitely having fun."

"That's Shell. She's been my bff for a long time. The short butch that pulled her away is her wife, Tam. Their nights out have been few and far between during the past few years. Pretty much since Shell got pregnant with their son Rory. He's at grandma's tonight so Shell is living it up."

Laney gave her a concerned look. "You didn't have to leave just because I was."

"Oh, I was always going to leave. That's why the rest of them only waved. They know I don't like the club or staying out so late. They're pretty cool."

"I think that's what I was hoping to find when I moved here for a fresh start. A good group of friends. But how do you make friends when you're in your forties and don't frequent the bars? For that matter, how do you meet anyone at all?"

"That's a question I've been asking for years. I think

all of us just get lucky at some point. You meet people to meet even more people. Take my friend Kelsey. She was the other one pulling Shell away before I left. Kelsey was good friends with Tam, they went to school together. Kels had a bad breakup and moved to St. Seren for a fresh start. They introduced her to Jenn, who was good friends with Jamie. But in a strange coincidence, Jamie and Kelsey had already become friends over some navigation app."

"Was it Drīv? I use that all the time. It's crazy how much better my commute is now."

"Yup, that's the one. Anyway, now Kelsey and Jamie are together, and we've all found ourselves in the same core friend group."

"Wow. That's kind of cool."

"Yeah." They approached Jess's truck. "This is me."

"I'd ask what the hell you're driving but I'm too tired tonight."

Jess laughed. "Ask me tomorrow while we're riding."

Laney shook her head and grinned ruefully. "You're assuming I'll have breath enough to carry on a conversation while I ride."

"You'll be fine." She held out her arms. "Are you a hugger? Because all my friends are."

"Absolutely." They gave each other a brief hug before Jess unlocked her truck and Laney stepped back.

She had one foot in the vehicle when Laney called to her.

"Hey Jess."

"Yeah?"

"Thanks. You were a life saver tonight. I appreciated hanging out with you."

Jess snickered. "I could say the same to you. I think we saved each other. See ya tomorrow!"

Laney gave a little wave then walked across the street to a small SUV. Jess hesitated to pull away until she knew Laney was safe inside her own vehicle. Jess couldn't wait to hit the trail with someone else for once. She also looked forward to getting to know Laney better.

****

They arranged to meet each other at the first trail head located not far inside the park. Jess usually rode her bike through the woods from the house to connect with the trail a little way in. But she thought Laney may want to know how to get to the trail parking in case she wanted to go for a ride by herself sometime.

Despite Laney's fears, they were able to carry on a conversation on the mild trails. The harder ones were a lot farther into the park. Much like Kelsey, Laney moved to St. Seren after a bad breakup eight months before. She got tired of seeing her ex everywhere in the small sapphic community so decided it was time for a change. Jess didn't blame her. If she had to see Beth everywhere after their terrible divorce, she'd have moved too, no matter how much she loved St. Seren.

Jess found the ride invigorating and felt pretty good about her returned stamina over the summer. She'd been pretty focused on giving Alice a lot of attention with walks so hadn't done much riding outside going back and forth to work during the week. It was nice to get off the pavement and onto some dirt.

A while later, the pair found themselves back in the parking lot, sweaty and sucking down water. Jess took off her helmet and hung it from the handlebars then wiped her forehead. "You did all that talking down about yourself before we started but kept up just fine."

Laney gave her a shy smile. "You think so? I've never ridden with anyone else. I've only gotten into it over the past couple years. More of a casual rider."

"Yeah, I'd say I'm pretty casual, too. I don't have fancy shoes, or a four-thousand-dollar bike and I'll never tackle the hard trails. But I do ride to work most days, at least for the past month or so."

"Probably saves on gas. Maybe even time, depending on where you work. Unfortunately, I work in Livingston so that's not an option for me."

"Hey, Jamie and Kelsey work in Livingston, too."

Laney laughed. "Nexus of the universe, am I right?" She made a face. "Ugh, I have to pee like crazy." Laney looked around, presumably for a nearby park bathroom.

Jess tucked her water bottle into the holder on her bike. "There is a bathroom on the far side of the lot but I noticed it was out of order when I pulled in. I literally live four minutes from here. You can use my bathroom if you like. I've also got a pitcher of lemonade in the fridge to share if you hang around for a bit."

Laney appeared hesitant. "I don't want to impose."

"Trust me, you're fine. Oh wait, how do you feel about dogs?"

"I love them, why?"

Jess grinned. "Because I adopted one a few months ago and she thinks that everyone who comes over is clearly there to see her. I do have more than lemonade, that was just what I was thinking about."

Laney gave Jess another one of those familiar smiles. "That sounds good. My bladder is telling me to say yes."

"Well, then, the sooner we get the bikes loaded up, the sooner you and your bladder can follow me." Laney had a rack that inserted into the small hitch on the back of her SUV. While Jess's bike would fit crossways in the tiny bed of her truck, she preferred to use a tailgate bike pad.

The drive only took a few minutes. Laney followed Jess as she turned left out of the park entrance then continued down the road for about a half mile. Her house was as close as promised. After introducing Laney to Alice, Jess showed her new friend to the bathroom and went off to see what she had in the way of snacks.

"Are you hungry?" Jess called out when Laney came out of the bathroom.

Laney shrugged. "I'm fine. I have a pretty restrictive diet."

Jess made a face. "What are you, a vegan or something?"

"Actually, I am."

That cut off Jess's laughter before it could begin. "Oh no, not another one," she joked. At Laney's curious look, she elaborated. "My friend Jenn that I was telling you about? She's a vegan, too. It keeps our cookouts interesting, that's for sure. Though I'll admit that new Impossible Burger tastes pretty close to a fast-food burger."

She gestured toward the lemonade she'd gotten out of the fridge. "Did you want some?"

Laney laughed. "Sure. And I've been a vegan for so long I couldn't tell you what tastes like real meat and what doesn't."

After pouring the drinks, Jess led the way through the house to the back deck with Alice following close behind them. Jess immediately removed an outdoor cushion from one of the chairs at the table and dropped it on the deck for Alice to lay on. She and Laney took two of the other chairs at the table.

"Yeah, she's a little spoiled," Jess said, at Laney's look,

"She's a sweet baby and probably deserves the pampering. I like your place here. It's peaceful so close to the park."

"It's one of my favorite things about the house. The fenced back yard turned out to be a real boon when I adopted Alice a few months ago."

"Is she your first dog?"

"Yeah. I've always wanted one but my ex-wife was allergic. Then after the divorce...well," Jess paused before shyly admitting, "I was in a pretty bad place and could barely take care of myself for a long time." She looked up to see Laney nodding.

"I wasn't married but my ex and I were together for six years." She frowned. "That was about six years too long."

"Oh. That bad, huh?" Laney got quiet and looked down into her glass. "Oh, sorry. You don't have to talk about it."

Dark eyes met Jess's gaze. "No, it's okay. Eight months of therapy and I'm finally at the place where I can face what she did, and what I allowed her to do. She was abusive, verbally, and physically. I thought for the longest time that it was my fault, but it turns out she was just an awful person."

Sadness washed through Jess to hear what Laney had experienced. It was no wonder she was on the timid side. "That sucks. I'm sorry you had to deal with that. Mine wasn't so traumatic. I hit menopause, got depressed, then my ex had an affair and ran off with her professor. Oh, and cleaned out my savings after I paid for three-quarters of her education while we were married."

Laney winced. "Ouch. That's a dick move worthy of my cousin. Are you sure you weren't married to Vic?"

Jess snickered. "Pretty sure. What a pair we are, huh?"

"Right?" Laney laughed with her.

Then Jess thought about where she'd been not even six months before. Unhealthy, depressed, lonely, and bitter. She looked across the table at Laney and held up her glass for a salute. "But look at us now. We're survivors."

Laney held up her glass as well and gave Jess a smile that said befriending her was a good call. "Survivors. I like that."

Life was a journey of individual moments and maybe they all deserved to be happy. Jess certainly wasn't going to waste any more time on bitterness and resentment over her ex. It was time to move forward and that's exactly what she'd been doing since dying on that ER table. Yup. Survivor.

# Chapter Nineteen

Jess was standing on the rooftop patio of Lucia's house. Lucia stood at the wall looking out over the ocean. It was odd because there were clouds in the sky. Suddenly, Lucia turned around to face her. Jess smiled and quickly made her way across the ten feet that separated them and threw her arms around Lucia.

"I've missed you!"

"Yeah, I've missed you too. Things haven't been the same here since you left."

Jess stepped back and looked around. "Is this even real?"

Lucia smiled at her. "It's as real as you want it to be, Tiger."

She shook her head. "No, I was in an accident. So many things in my life have changed since that moment. I—" Jess looked away then met Lucia's dark gaze. "I know none of it happened, but I kept my promise. I've taken my life back and I'm happier than I've been in years." She laughed. "I even adopted a dog. Her name is Alice and she's the sweetest, most gentle girl ever."

Lucia's smile crinkled the corners of her eyes. "She sounds adorable."

Jess glanced out toward the ocean and remembered what Shell suggested when Jess told her about the resort. Looking around now, it didn't seem real. "My friend Shell says that the vision I had when I nearly died in the hospital was just my brain's way of telling me that it was okay to move on and start dating again."

"Are you asking me? Because this is your dream, *cariño*. What do you think?"

"I think…" Jess sighed. "I think that you remind me of a lot of people I've met over the years. All wrapped up into a very attractive package."

"And?" Lucia prompted.

"And it sucks missing something that was never real.

But if this is my dream, then I should at least get to say goodbye properly."

Lucia got a twinkle in her eyes as she pulled Jess closer. "Oh, really?"

"Yup. Also, if this is my dream, I should be able to snap my fingers and we would be in your bedroom." She snapped her fingers then laughed to find them suddenly standing next to Lucia's large bed. Jess wasted no time pushing Lucia down to the bed and crawling onto her lap.

"You've gotten very demanding over the years."

She snorted and cradled Lucia's face between her hands. "It's only been a few months and I'm getting better at going after what I want."

"What is that?"

"You." Jess found a willing partner when she leaned closer and kissed Lucia. Her lips were exactly as soft as she remembered. It didn't take long before they were undressed and writhing on the bed. Jess had never had such an erotic dream, before or after menopause. She couldn't even remember being as turned on during her near-death hallucination.

Lucia grasped at her like she was possessed or seeking to possess. She left no part of Jess's skin untouched by fingers or mouth. Pressure built in Jess's head as her body tightened with the impending explosion of pleasure.

She yelled and sat up when the orgasm hit. Jess rode the waves for a long time, her voice hoarse from the guttural sounds that came out of her mouth. Then she fell back onto the bed and caught her breath. Jess removed her hand from between her legs and wiped her fingers on the sheet next to her. The sky was still dark around her blinds so she looked over at her clock.

It was too early to get up for work but she wasn't sure she wanted to go back to sleep. The dream felt like a message of sorts. As if it were the confirmation Jess needed to finally put the events of Paradise Island behind her. The vision of Lucia was familiar because clearly that's what brains did. They took every one of your experiences and put them in a blender, then spit out entire new scenarios, scenes, and situations to help you work through whatever is most important.

Even knowing all that, Jess was still glad she got to see her one more time. She hated the thought that something so meaningful, a connection that touched her so deeply was nothing more than her own mind. Neither truth nor the passage of time completely took away the ache of missing Lucia. But maybe her entire experience was one grand message telling Jess to love herself first before she could love others.

Jess found all the introspection tiring and she was lethargic from her orgasm. She yawned then closed her eyes again. She could analyze her erotic dreams in the morning after she had more sleep.

****

Jess glanced across the room and smiled. Laney stood there in an animated conversation with Jenn. Suddenly Laney burst into laughter, covering her mouth as a snort came out.

"Have you asked her out yet?"

She jumped at Shell's voice so close to her ear. "Shit! Don't scare me like that."

Shell snickered. "You would have seen me coming if you weren't staring so hard at your crush."

"It's not like that at all. I'm just…she looks a lot happier than when I first met her."

"Hmm, she does appear a lot more relaxed since you first introduced her to the group."

It was the end of October and everyone was at Kelsey and Jamie's annual Halloween get together. There was quite a crowd in attendance, despite the moderate size of their apartment. Even folks that weren't part of Jess's core group, or just didn't come to St. Seren very often, had shown up. Ash and Mia made the hour-long drive from Detroit, and Jamie's friend Burke had driven across the state from his new place in Grand Rapids. Even Gonzo, the other two Sarahs, and Heather were in attendance and clamoring to play a game called ass quarters.

It had become a tradition during the past few years for

everyone to dress up and bring a dish to pass for the party. Most just wore onesies, a habit started by Shell when she was pregnant. Now that Jess knew more about Kelsey, she figured the potluck style gathering was probably so the hostess didn't have to cook. Jess giggled and took a swallow of her beer.

"What are you laughing at?"

"I just remembered that Kelsey doesn't cook and that's probably why this party is always a potluck."

"She literally made the cake pops. Which are fucking delicious, by the way. Easily on par with your rainbow shots, if not as boozy."

Jess shrugged. "I can't explain it. I only know what they told me. Apparently, Jamie does most of the cooking. If it were me, I'd just order pizza and make everyone chip in."

Shell tilted her head. "Huh. Come to think of it, I remember Tam saying something about Kelsey's lack of culinary skills. But back to the question at hand, are you going to ask her out?"

Jess moved her gaze from Laney and smiled at Shell. "Nope."

"Why the hell not?" A few people nearby turned to stare at Shell after her outburst.

"Jesus, could you be any louder? To answer your question, I'm happy. I've clawed my way back to where I'm at now. I'm riding my bike again, I've got a dog I love more than anything in this world, new hobbies, and friends who I know will stick by me through thick and thin. I finally get it."

Shell gave her a curious look. "Get what, J?"

"I don't need anyone else to be happy." She shook her head and smiled at her long-time friend. "I feel whole, like I'm present in my own life for the first time in years. If someone comes along that knocks me off kilter, well, I'll see what happens. Until then, I plan to just enjoy my life."

"I mean, if you're sure?" Shell sighed and rolled her eyes. "Of course, you're sure. I've known you a long damn time. This is the most…full I've ever seen you. I just want my friend to be as happy as possible."

Jess pulled her into a one-armed hug. "I am, promise.

Besides," She lifted her chin in Laney and Jenn's direction. "Look."

It was easy enough to read Jenn's interest. The casual touches to Laney's arm, the way Jenn leaned closer while they spoke. She was clearly smitten. Jess knew that Jenn liked the more androgynous, sometimes butch, aesthetic, but Laney still fit. Tall and slender with short hair, they were things everyone in their friends group knew would draw Jenn in. Throw in the fact that Laney was also a vegan and bam, perfect combo.

Shell chuckled. "You are so damned sneaky. Did you plan this from the beginning?"

"No. I really like Laney. She's smart, attractive, and a real sweetheart. But the more I got to know her, the more I realized what a good fit she was for Jenn."

"You just didn't want to have to have two sets of pans in the house in the event that you settled down and married a vegan."

Jess cracked a smile. "That, too." They looked at each other for a few seconds then burst into laughter.

A huge cheer went up on the other side of the room where space had been cleared for a series of plastic cups. Kelsey strutted around with her hands in the air.

"Ass quarters champion!"

Jess and Shell applauded with everyone else. Jamie's best friend Robbie Burke threw a wadded-up napkin at her. "You cheated, Ramirez! Your onesie is baggy and doesn't even have a tail like the rest of ours."

Kelsey flipped him off and collected the pile of dollar bills from the coffee table. "I didn't tell you to wear an otter this year."

"Really, that's all you have to say for yourself?" Burke gave Kelsey a little shove and a ripple went through the crowd of onlookers. Jess glanced over at Jamie and saw the tall woman's eyes go wide. She looked on the verge of panic. Kelsey paused, then squared her shoulders and stepped in close to Burke.

Everyone knew about her temper, though Jess didn't think she'd ever picked a fight with anyone. She whispered to Shell, "What the hell is going on?"

"No freaking clue, dude. But those two are tight. This

can't be real."

Jamie tried to intervene. "Uh, guys? It's just a game. Maybe we can move on and play Left Right Center."

Kelsey was stubborn. She shook her head. "No. I won fair and square. And now that Burke is being a poor sport, I demand extra payment from him for my win."

He rolled his eyes. "Really?"

"Yes, really. Give me whatever is in your pocket right now."

Burke reached into his right pocket and flipped it inside out. "Whoops, looks like lint. Sorry about your luck, Kels."

She growled. "The other pocket then."

He dug deep into the other pocket and Jess felt a surge of jealousy for his guy pockets. Whatever Burke pulled out couldn't have been very big because he kept it closed within his fist. He held it out to Kelsey, then she took it in a weirdly secretive way. It looked like some kind of comical drug deal between two people who had never seen drugs, let alone done them.

"I'm so lost right now," Jess whispered.

Tam had joined the two of them from wherever she'd been standing. "Same."

Burke grinned and poked Kelsey in the chest after the exchange. "You got what you want, Kels. Time to chick-up."

Someone had turned off the music and the party had gone silent while everyone waited for something, anything, to happen. Multiple people stepped back when Kelsey abruptly spun in place to face Jamie. Then she dropped to one knee. The lack of music and conversation in general meant that Jenn's exclamation of *holy shit* came out as nearly a yell.

"Jamie Alexa Schultz—"

For her part, Jamie already had tears running down her face. She held up her hands toward Kelsey. "Okay, I'm gonna stop you right there because I'm already crying. Can I just say yes and you give me the ring?"

Kelsey snickered, then stood up and swatted Burke. "I told you it was a stupid idea!" Then she turned back to Jamie. "Are you sure, babe? I had this whole speech planned out involving Nigel, potholes, and me becoming your butch queen for life." Then she flexed and laughter went around the room.

"Consider the speech given. And if you hadn't asked me, I was going to ask you before the year was out." Jamie grinned stupidly at Kelsey then pulled her into a kiss. The music suddenly came back on and everyone crowded around them to offer up congratulations. The mass of furries in the middle of the room wearing onesies made for a very weird scene, but Jess was so happy for them.

They stepped back after doling out hugs to let the happy couple cuddle on the loveseat. Jenn and Laney joined Tam, Shell, and Jess a minute later.

Tam shook her head. "Well, that was unexpected. I thought those two were just going to date forever."

They all looked over to see Burke laughing and throwing popcorn at Jamie and Kelsey. They kept kissing. Jenn had a soft smile on her face. "No way. They were so gone on each other. I know for a fact James wanted to ask last year. But she's got her own past trauma that she's still working through and wasn't confident that Kels would say yes."

"Really?" Shell moved her gaze back to the couple in question.

Jess wasn't that shocked. Between the short conversation with them in the coffee shop on poetry night and a few other comments she'd heard over the years, she assumed Jamie's previous serious relationship was horribly damaging. Besides, if anyone was going to do the asking, it would definitely be the bolder of the two.

"In the end, it doesn't matter who asks, right?" Everyone looked at Jess. "Because those two weirdos were made for each other."

"What?" Everyone turned back toward the happy couple to see Jamie staring at Kelsey in horror. "What do you mean we need to go to Texas to announce it to your family?"

Kelsey sighed. "I promised my *abuela*."

Jamie threw herself back on the arm of the couch. "Oh God, oh God, oh God," It sent the room into laughter yet again.

Jess hung out for another hour playing Left Right Center with a big crowd of people. She didn't win but had a great time pounding the table and catcalling with everyone else. She helped clean up some of the stuff in their small kitchen, ate another cake pop, then looked at her watch. It was closing in onto midnight and just seeing the time made her realize how tired she was. She stifled a yawn but knew she'd probably sit up for a little bit reading when she got home, just to spend time with Alice before putting her in the kennel for the night.

She found Laney talking to Jenn again by the patio door. "Hey, I'm getting ready to head out. Are you riding with me still, or staying a while longer?" Jess did her best to keep a straight face.

Laney gave Jenn a shy look, which Jenn returned. Then, exactly as Jess expected, Jenn spoke up. "I can give you a ride home if you want to stay longer."

"Really?" Laney looked over at Jess. "Normally I'm tired by now and ready to go home, but I'm pretty energized tonight."

Jess snorted. "It was probably the punch. I think someone spiked it with an energy drink."

"You're kidding!" Laney's mouth dropped open at the news and Jenn started laughing.

"Middle age sure changes a crowd, doesn't it?"

"Right?" Then Jess shrugged at Laney. "It's fine. Jenn will make sure you're taken care of. Have fun, this party only happens once a year and it's always a riot." Behind Laney, Jenn's eyes widened at the *take care of* comment.

"Cool. Thanks, J. See you Wednesday for our weekly ride?"

"At least until the weather turns and we get snow. I don't do snow."

"And yet she lives in Michigan," Jenn said.

Jess defended herself. "We live here because we love it, but we're still allowed to complain about snow and road construction."

Laney laughed and raised her drink. "Here's to the two official seasons in the mitten, snow removal, and road construction."

Jenn and Jess followed suit then Jess drained the last

partial swallow from her beer. She'd purposely stretched it out and stayed away from the punch knowing she was driving home. Especially after she saw some of the ingredients being poured into the igloo cooler holding the drink earlier. No thank you.

"Okay, give me hugs because I'm off. I need some bonding time with Alice before I hit the sack. Hopefully I won't fall asleep on the couch."

Laney laughed and gave her a hug. "I bet she doesn't care."

"You're probably right."

When Laney pulled away, she held up her empty glass. "I'm going for a refill, you want a water, Jenn?"

"Yes, thanks."

Jenn pulled Jess into a hug when Laney left. She lowered her voice. "You cool with this?"

Jess tsk'd. "Who do you think has been pushing you together again and again the past few months?"

"What?"

"Hello, how many game nights did I suggest you two should be partners?"

Jenn blinked. "Oh." Suddenly her face lit up and she pulled Jess into another hug. "I thought you were interested in her so had been keeping my distance."

"Well, I personally think you should make a move. Just be good, yeah? She had a really abusive ex."

Jenn nodded. "She told me some of it. Why are people so shitty?"

"Maybe because they don't know any better yet? They haven't been shown what a lifetime of pain and misery can do to the people all around them." She joked, "Not everyone can nearly die and get a second chance at life."

Jenn grabbed her hand and gave it a gentle squeeze. "You were never like that, J. And on that topic, I want to say that the changes you've made in your life, this new love you have for living..." She shook her head. "It's something special and I'm glad to see you happy. You're good people, Jess. And no matter what, you also deserve the best when it comes along."

"I understand that now. But you, get over there and make your move already because if you don't, Gonzo looks like she's gonna make it for you."

Jenn spun her head to look toward the kitchen. "Oh, hell no!"

Jess snickered as she stalked off looking like a woman on a mission. Jess made the rounds saying goodbye and giving hugs to all the people she knew best. She was never one to just slip out like some of her friends were notorious for doing.

When she got to Jamie and Kelsey, she pulled them close. "I've got a single piece of advice for you regarding marriage."

They looked at one another, then back to Jess.

"I've been to one bachelorette party for a same sex couple. It was in a strip club. One bride was pregnant, and the other bride got a lap dance up on the stage, paid for by the best friend. There were tears, lots of yelling, and a very hungover wedding party the next day. Zero out of ten stars, do not recommend."

Jamie nodded. "Gotcha, no strip clubs" at the same time Kelsey agreed to no joint bachelorette parties.

Then they looked at one another in shock and Jess gave a little wave. "Goodnight, ladies, and congrats again!"

She laughed all the way down to her truck because she knew neither of them would have something like that. If anything, they'd organize an entire drag show as part of the pre-wedding experience. On second thought, that wasn't a bad idea. Maybe she'd suggest it to them at their next gathering. For now, Alice, a book, and her couch were calling, and Jess wasn't going to miss out on any snuggle time with her sweet, soft-eared, baby. Just like the corny bumper sticker she had on the old Subaru, life *was* good. She'd come out of her experience with the sweet end of the stick for once.

****

Jess woke to the sound of the trash truck making its rounds on Saturday morning. She picked up her cell phone and panicked. It was only the second weekend in November but supposed to be the last of their decent weather. Sunny and strangely warm in the fifties and she and Laney had agreed on one more ride before putting their bikes up for the winter.

She rolled out of bed, cell in hand. Jess was annoyed that she forgot to set her alarm the night before. She'd stayed up late reading the newest book by one of her favorite authors and clearly forgot about her nine o'clock bike ride.

Lucky for her, the park was so close because she'd just be able to make it on time if she skipped breakfast and ate a granola bar on the way. Jess quickly dressed in layers in deference to the weather and likelihood that she'd still end up sweating, before rushing into the bathroom to pee and wash up.

Her doorbell rang while she was brushing her teeth. Jess had seen the flyers up around the neighborhood and she thought it was sweet that some of the local kids were having a bottle and can drive. Especially as it was to help fund a Thanksgiving dinner at the nearby community center for folks in need or without any family to celebrate with. She quickly rinsed and spit, then rushed through the house to answer. Jess glanced to the left at her overflowing returnable bin and moved to grab a trash bag from beneath the sink.

"Just a minute," she called as she stuffed her returnables into the sack.

Out of breath and with a giant bag full of empty pop cans in one hand, she threw open her door.

# Chapter Twenty

A tall woman with short dark hair pushed into the ornate office. It smelled of ancient tomes, aged leather, and wood polish. Dust motes floated in the air where the desk lamp shone onto the wooden top. The shelves were full of collectibles and curiosities, trivial things in the lives of the owner, but well-loved just the same.

A massive raven perched on the back of the chair. Large talons came close to puncturing the leather but not quite. Still, they dimpled the surface in a precarious way. Its thick neck and shaggy throat feathers lent an air of nobility to the bird. He tilted his head left, then right, while watching the woman in front of him.

She sighed. "You knew I was coming to visit."

The long bill parted and an odd mimicry of human voice emerged. "Of course, I did."

"And you know I hate it when you're in this form. I find the beady stare unnerving."

He cackled back at her. "I'm aware."

"Please?"

The raven abruptly flapped up into the air, kicking the chair backward away from the desk. Then his form shimmered in the space between the two pieces of furniture until he stood wearing another body. "Have a seat, Luce." His voice had gone deep, sounding like the offspring of a bass drum and a gravel truck. He didn't know why his daughter preferred this form, most didn't like the stone texture of his skin, or the blackness of his eyes. Personally, they were his favorite feature which was why he liked the raven so much.

"I'd rather stand for what I need to say."

He casually waved a hand through the air and the chair against one wall moved until it gently bumped against the back of Lucia's legs. "Sitting won't stay your words. You may as well be comfortable." He smiled as she gave in and sat down. Headstrong she was, but definitely his favorite of all the children. Maybe it was because Lucia was his firstborn.

It didn't take long in the silence of the room for Lucia to blurt out what she had come to say. "I need a break."

"And, just like all the other times you've asked, the answer is still no."

Lucia frowned. "I'm not asking anymore."

"The answer is still no."

"I've been doing this job for longer than anyone before me and—"

"It's because you're the best. I'm afraid you're not going anywhere, Lucia. My word is law." He counted the seconds in his head. One, two…

She jumped to her feet again and stalked toward the desk. She placed both hands flat on the surface, leaning as close as possible to him without going over the blotter. "I *will* leave, whether you want me to or not. I'd rather have your permission, but I certainly don't need it. Free will and all that, am I right?" Then she gave him that infuriating smirk he'd both loathed and loved for centuries.

"You know I can't have just anyone running the Trial, love. And if I let you go, then everyone will want to leave."

Lucia straightened and threw her arms out to the sides. "Who? Everyone assigned to the Trial wanted to be there. Nobody is going to leave."

"You will. You said it yourself."

"That's different. I—" She ran a hand through her hair. "There is something I need to do."

He cocked his head and gave her a smile. "That's not it at all. It's about Miss Parker, isn't it?"

She sagged and looked away. "Yes."

"What exactly do you want from me?"

Lucia met his gaze, unflinching. "I want one hundred years."

"Impossible. Not to mention, it's significantly more time than you'd need in that dimension." Her eyes grew watery. He'd never once seen his daughter shed a tear, but she was near enough over a mere mortal. A reformed one at that.

"Father…please. I need this. I need her."

"What's it worth to you?"

Lucia clenched her fists. "Anything."

"Fine." It was true that Lucia had been asking to leave for a long time. However, he never got the sense she truly wanted it, until now. He stood and held out a giant hand, fingers ending in sharp black nails. "A fifty-year full package for one soul." His intent was obvious as was the solution. He watched Lucia's eyes light up as she shook on it.

"Deal."

# Epilogue

Jess dropped the bag of cans and even the loud clatter on her kitchen tiles didn't break her from shock. She blinked, then blinked again. "You're real."

Someone who looked a whole fucking lot like Lucia stood on her doorstep, appearing for all the world like she belonged there. "I am."

"You're here."

"Um, yes? I just moved into the neighborhood, and I know this is a stupid cliché but wondered if you had some sugar I could borrow."

Poor Jess's brain was still registering an error. "Sugar?"

"Yes. Is that not something people do? Borrow sugar?"

Jess rubbed her eyes, but the vision stayed the same. Then she remembered hearing the name Luce months before while waiting for her coffee at the Bean Bag. Was this a cruel twist of fate or just a beneficial coincidence? Based on the way the other woman was eyeing Jess up and down, maybe both. Her brain unstuck enough to answer, "I've, uh, never had anyone borrow baking supplies from me at," she looked at her watch, "nine-oh-one in the morning."

"Hmm, interesting." The woman said. Then she broke into a broad smile, one that Jess had been missing for months. "I suppose you've never had anyone fight like hell to find you because they were missing a little sweetness in their life either."

Time stopped. The sound of cars in the distance grew muffled as she tried to process the new information. Jess's phone suddenly rang while she stood in her doorway staring at Lucia. She answered it, knowing who was on the other end. "Hey, Laney. Sorry but something came up and I can't make it today. You should ask Jenn if she wants to go for a hike. I bet she says yes. Nope, I'm good. Just, uh, dealing with unexpected company. Okay, bye." Then she hung up and dropped the phone back into her pocket.

"Well?"

Jess swallowed. "You're Lucia. Luce."

"Yes."

"My Lucia."

The tall woman suddenly looked shy. "I hope so."

That broke the dam of Jess's emotions. "Jesus! I thought I was crazy, that I'd imagined it all in that ER as part of some near-death experience."

"I'm definitely not him, and you imagined nothing. The Ternary Trial, Paradise Island, it's all real. As was your time there. And Jess—"

"Yes?"

"Everything we had was real as well." Lucia snapped her fingers and Jess's portfolio from Ronobe's class appeared in her hands. It smelled like sun, salt, and tropical blossoms.

Jess's heart hammered in her chest, and she grinned like an idiot. "How long?"

"For the rest of our lives and beyond."

# Acknowledgments

Big thanks to Lori for giving me the 'winner winner chicken dinner' answer of spleen, Chris Zett for giving me that authentic medical scene perspective, Catherine and Alex for helping to clarify other injuries and recovery time. Another round of thanks goes out to my extremely talented beta readers, Anne Pace (the person who keeps my stories up to snuff), and Lyss Wolf, (the one who holds this book's secrets). Lastly, thank you to Patty and Natty, my editors extraordinaire. My books wouldn't be the same without you.

# About the Author

Award winning author and Michigan native, Kelly Aten brings heroines to life in a variety of blended sapphic fiction genres. She specializes in speculative fiction romance, focusing on extra-ordinary women who are as flawed as they are compelling.

Email: killerwit68@gmail.com
Website: http://www.katenauthor.com

# Books by K. Aten

### Arrow of Artemis Series

*The Fletcher*
*The Archer*
*The Sagittarius*

### Mystery of the Makers Series

*Sovereign of Psiere*
*The Lost Temple of Psiere*
*The Rebels of Psiere*

### Blood Resonance Series

*Running From Forever*
*Embracing Forever*

### Other Titles

*Rules of the Road*
*Waking the Dreamer*
*Burn it Down*
*Children of the Stars*
*Remember Me, Synthetica*
*Elemental Attraction*
*The Last Scion of Ra*

Bringing rainbow stories to life.

Flashpoint Publications welcomes submissions from writers of every color and books featuring characters of every color. In addition, Flashpoint Publications encourages job applicants of every color whenever a staff position becomes available. We believe that EVERYONE is entitled to a seat at our table.

www.flashpointpublications.com

9 781619 295506